A FLIGHT OF BIRDS

ROBERTS

Flight of birds

823 STACK

ROBERTS

Flight of birds

823 STACK

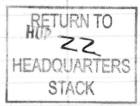

7 0 0 0 0 0 0 0 0 7 2 4 6 6

A FLIGHT OF BIRDS

By
CECIL ROBERTS

HODDER AND STOUGHTON

PRINTED IN GREAT BRITAIN FOR HODDER
AND STOUGHTON LIMITED, ST. PAUL'S HOUSE,
WARWICK LANE, LONDON, E.C.4 BY C. TINLING
AND CO. LIMITED, LIVERPOOL, LONDON AND
PRESCOT

To

ALIDA BOCK

CONTENTS

CONTENTS

BOOK 1

The Green Budgerigar

CHAPTER 1

IT WAS IN Florence that Henry Newsome first met them. He had noticed them in the lounge of the Excelsior Hotel. Obviously they were Americans. For a time he thought they were mother and son. The old lady called him Bobo, which Newsome assumed was an endearing substitute for Robin. He was a thin, fair-haired fellow of about forty, perfectly dressed except for a curious tendency to wear bright coloured clothes, a tendency to which many Americans are prone. His manner was quiet, his voice pleasant, but he had moments of flamboyancy, a Latin freedom with his hands. His hair was too perfectly set and he had a nervous habit of producing a gold-mounted tortoiseshell comb out of a leather case and running it over his temples, to assure himself that he was not unkempt. Newsome felt that his ring, gold-crested, was a little too large, but Englishmen are over-sensitive to any kind of Latin ebullience. With them a diamond ring on a male finger is damning. Bobo had no diamond ring. He had no jewellery to speak of, except a pearl pin in a white tie. He favoured white ties which emphasized his fresh complexion.

He was very intelligent and easy in conversation. Newsome liked the fellow but with a reservation. He could never quite define why, fighting a distrust backed by no real evidence. He had been introduced to them by a tall English widow, Mrs. Pippitt, who had smiled at his wife and begun a conversation. They had been astonished to learn that Bobo was not the old lady's son but her husband and that the wife was eighty-four. They had been married ten years. He called her "Marie darling". Her name and her expensive Paris clothes gave her a slightly French air. She was always cleverly made-up. A French maid was in attendance. Newsome had surmised that she was about sixty-five years old. She walked easily but she was small and stout and rather breathless. The French illusion was dispelled by her voice. Alas, it had the "barbaric yawp", with a

11

Middle West cutting-edge. She could have passed for a retired musical-comedy actress. She had a glint in her rheumy dark eyes. Her hands were singularly veinless, her feet quite exquisite. At a third her present age she must have been an alluring woman.

It was some time before Newsome learned their history. He owed it to Mrs. Pippitt who knew everybody, and everything about everybody. No lawyer could have surpassed her in cross-examination. There was something almost surgical in her relentless method. It was as if she anaesthetized her victims with a hypodermic syringe and, in an unconscious state, they surrendered all the details of their lives; where they came from, whether single or married, the number of their children, their tastes, fortune, history, future plans. It was so skilful, so professional, that the victim was never conscious of the process, just as a flower never realizes the probing of the bee. Then off Mrs. Pippitt flew with all the facts, to trade with them in her general inquisition. Newsome, too, had suffered the process, unaware until he had witnessed her tireless pursuit around the hotel lounge.

The facts Mrs. Pippitt dispensed were these. They were Mr. and Mrs. Robinson Gehr, of Baltimore. She was eighty-four, he was forty-two. They had been married ten years. No one had thought it would work, but everyone had been wrong. A widow twice, with three sons and five grandchildren, she had a large house in Baltimore, Maryland, and a beautiful winter home in Coconut Grove, Florida, the legacy of her first husband, Mr. Fuller, who had left a large fortune after a life passed in the canning business. A Georgian, Mr. Fuller had been self-slaughtered by drink, but it had been a happy marriage. There were no children of a second marriage. Mr. Fuller had left a fortune of six million dollars.

"There is no money, of course, from her present husband, Mr. Gehr—he has nothing at all," said Mrs. Pippitt. "Their marriage created quite a sensation, as you can imagine—he was only thirty-two, she seventy-four. There was no sex in it, I'm told."

"How do you know that?" asked Newsome, rather annoyed at having his curiosity stimulated.

"Mrs. Crosby, the lady with the white lock over there, told me. She's a lifelong friend of Mrs. Gehr. It's just companionship. She can't bear to be alone. He'd been called in to decorate her house in Baltimore—he's an interior decorator but doesn't work any more. She took a fancy to him—he's quite charming, isn't he? She proposed to him, so he gave up his business and they married. Of course there was a settlement. I don't suppose he ever thought that she'd last so long."

"Didn't her family object—all that money imperilled?"

"Not at all. A great part of it is in a trust and goes to the sons and grandchildren, though she's plenty of her own—property and jewellery and some shares in the pecan business."

"Pecan?"

"Mr. Fuller canned pecan nuts grown in Georgia. No, her sons didn't make a fuss. As a matter of fact their mother—she's a sweet old thing, isn't she?—had become a bit of a nuisance so they were quite agreeable when Bobo Gehr came along. It leaves them free. Of course he's terribly tied—but so patient with her, and he never plays around with other women. She says she feels quite safe about that. You'll excuse me," said Mrs. Pippitt, having glanced across the lounge, "There's pretty Mrs. Lehigh—she's on her honeymoon. Such a dear young woman!"

Mrs. Pippitt went off in the direction of Mrs. Lehigh. Newsome almost saw the invisible hypodermic syringe being drawn for action.

Yes, there was something odd about the Gehrs, particularly now that he knew their relationship. He felt contempt for any man who sold himself to a dominant old woman. For she was dominant. "Take it away!" she cried one morning when her husband came into the lounge with a small radio. "When I want it I'll tell you!" He picked it up and departed as bidden. "It's no use to me," she complained to Newsome, with whom she had been talking. "The programme's Italian. Of course it's all right for Bobo—he's fluent in Italian. He's fluent in every language—Italian, Spanish, French, German—it's all the same to him. Bobo's very gifted but it annoys me sometimes—he understands everything, and I nothing!"

There were other incidents that jarred. She had turned her Bobo into a poodle dog. He was at her beck and call. He fetched and carried, he adjusted her cushions, moved her chair, picked up her shawl, carried her mink coat, said "Yes, Marie darling", "No, Marie darling", "Do you feel a draught, Marie darling?" Sometimes in company Bobo would talk. He talked very well. He could tell a story with an actor's sense of timing. He was full of all kinds of information. He astonished Newsome one evening, at cocktails in the lounge, with an impromptu dissertation on the Cosmati School of mosaic workers, and on the indigenous Florentine industry of *pietra dura*. But Newsome noticed that after a time, when he was in full flight, Mrs. Gehr would stop him with "Bobo dear—there's a draught", or, "Bobo dear, I'd like another cocktail, and I'm sure the company would." So Bobo came off the hobby horse he was riding so well and searched for the draught or ordered another round of cocktails.

Disgusted, Newsome tried to avoid Bobo and Marie darling but it became difficult. Mrs. Gehr called him "That dear man!" Unhappily, he and his wife had to pass them in the dining-room. They had themselves moved to the other end but it proved useless. As soon as they came out of the room Bobo was sent over to ask them to join them at coffee. Bobo, too, seemed especially attracted to Newsome. In the first place it was a man to talk to; in the second, he was always seeking information, very humbly, very politely and appreciatively. Then one day there was an astonishing revelation. When Gehr learned that Newsome was a portrait painter of distinction, who had just finished a commission in Rome, he asked him if he knew B.B.

Of course he knew Bernard Berenson. It had become the essential fashion if you were visiting Florence, and at all "arty", to arrive with a letter of introduction to B.B. and call at *I Tatti*, the sage's home-art gallery at Settignano.

"Yes," replied Newsome, adding in an unguarded moment, spurred by a little snobbery designed to put Bobo in his place, "As a matter of fact I'm lunching there tomorrow." He could have bitten off his hand at what followed.

"You are? Why, so am I! You must let me drive you there!" exclaimed Bobo, elated to be of service.

In vain Newsome demurred. Of course he must come, it was folly to think of hiring a car. There followed a request that was a revelation.

"Marie darling doesn't know—I've told her I'm meeting an old schoolfellow who has a villa at Settignano. I'm not taking the chauffeur. Please don't say anything to her, will you? She might feel upset."

So Newsome was involved in a conspiracy. He began to be alarmed by Bobo. How well did he know B.B.? How had he got invited to lunch? B.B. was exclusive in the matter of his guests. They had to be somebodies.

It was obvious the next day that Gehr knew B.B. very well. His welcome was warm. And after lunch in that choice villa, with its art treasures, rich library, magnificent *objets d'art* and lovely gardens, there was another surprise for Newsome. Bobo was able to keep himself in the full stream of the conversation and was never out of his depth. A new Bobo emerged and left Newsome stunned.

"Wonderful old boy, isn't he?" asked Gehr as they drove away.

"Yes, quite wonderful at his great age. Have you known him long?"

"Oh, quite some time. I once put a nice bit of business his way—through Duveens, you know."

An interior decorator would naturally have some opportunities of business in the art line. But the most astonishing thing was the fellow's intellectual grasp. Gehr had easily held his own where he, a professional artist, had faltered.

"He seemed quite surprised by what I told him about Magnasco—of course Magnasco is not really his field," said Gehr.

"He's yours?" asked Newsome.

"Oh no, I wouldn't say that, but I have a fairly wide knowledge in the art field, you know," said Bobo with a smile.

"And you gave it all up?"

Gehr's reply was startling. He raised his hands off the wheel. "Yes, like a bloody fool!" he said, with emphasis.

Newsome looked at him but said nothing. They read each other's mind in silence. Then, after a long pause, as if talking to himself—"I hope Marie doesn't find out I've been playing hookey," said Gehr, changing down. "Don't say a word."

"I won't. Doesn't Mrs. Gehr give you any freedom?"

"She can't bear me out of her sight. Do you know, she can't go to sleep unless I hold her hand. So there I sit. If only she'd go to sleep early, but it's never before eleven. I have to sleep in her room—says it makes her feel safe. I don't want to give you a false picture. She's a kind woman and I'm very fond of her. The trouble is I should have had a working arrangement from the beginning, but I hadn't the sense, and little by little I've been possessed. She doesn't realize how very exacting she is—old people get like that, selfish and dominant."

"With some women if you don't put your foot down you find yourself converted into a poodle," said Newsome. "I once had a wife like that."

"Had?"

"This is my second wife."

"And what did you do about your first wife?"

"I finally got a divorce."

"Ah," said Gehr, reflectively. "She hadn't the money?"

"No. I'd never dream of putting myself in that position."

"And so you married again?"

"Yes, very happily. My wife is a perfect companion. We respect each other's freedom," said Newsome. "My work takes me away a good deal. I've just been in India a year painting portraits of half a dozen rajahs. My wife doesn't fret. But then we are both at a sensible age."

"The first fine rapture over?" asked Gehr, smiling. He switched the wheel to avoid a hen. He was a fierce but capable driver.

"Yes, happily," said Newsome.

"Rapture—I've never known it," observed Gehr. "Not in the sense that you've known it."

"Then in what sense?"

Gehr made no reply, concentrating on his driving as he threaded a narrow village full of women, babies and animals. When at last he spoke, continuing the subject, his voice was very quiet.

"It would be difficult to tell you, you must have guessed. I married for money, for security, as I thought."

"May I ask—do you regret it? I find it incomprehensible," said Newsome. "I'm afraid I'm being rather personal—but you started the subject."

"I did. What I like about you is you're so damned balanced and honest. I've never talked to anyone as I've talked to you. It's a great relief—though I feel a little disloyal to Marie—she means well."

"Hell is often created by people who mean well."

"How brutally right you are!"

"I'm sorry."

They drove on in silence, the scenery was beautiful. All Florence lay out on her hills, flowery in the spring sunshine.

The great dome of the Duomo was glowing apricot in the slanting sun, its white ribs shining. The grim tower of the Palazzo Vecchio cut the cool blue sky like a blade.

"I was very impressed with your knowledge of art. You quite held your own with old B.B.," observed Newsome, wishing to change the subject.

"You know, she can be good to me. She gave me this Rolls," said Gehr, pursuing his own thoughts, and speaking as if to counterbalance the guilt of disloyalty. "My art knowledge—it's not very deep, really! An art dealer in Baltimore took me up when I was a boy. I learnt everything from him—he specialized in the French Impressionists. That's my field, really. You know, I started life as an errand boy, I was an orphan. When my mother died I went to live with him, a queer fish, but I owed him everything—he was a French Jew. He left me his business. I was very young and lost my head and my business. Then I went into interior decorating with another young man, but he drank terribly and we had frightful rows. So I was glad to get out. Marie, a customer, came along and made me a proposal.

B

Now you know the whole story—well, not all of it," he added with a laugh.

"I suppose at the time you didn't think the old lady would last so long?" asked Newsome.

"My God, you're terribly frank, aren't you? If I told you that never entered my head you wouldn't believe me?"

"I wouldn't."

"You'd be right! I thought four or five years at the most—and yet in a way I'm very fond of the old girl. If only I had a little more freedom!"

"I believe you, but you sold yourself without conditions. That was idiotic."

There was a long silence, only the purr of the tyres on the tarmac. They were coming into Florence.

"I've never let anybody talk to me as you've talked," said Gehr quietly, breaking the silence. "It's odd, but from you I can take it. From the first moment I saw you I felt confidence in you. If ever I was in a bad jam I'd feel I could trust you."

"That might be a mistake," replied Newsome. "We've not known each other a week."

"You feel contempt for me, don't you?"

"Frankly, yes."

"That's what I like about you—you're so bloody honest. There's no dollar crap about you," said Gehr vehemently. The thickening traffic took his attention.

Two days later Newsome and his wife left for London. He said goodbye to the Robinson Gehrs who were going to Rome. And then he forgot all about them.

CHAPTER 2

I

THE FOLLOWING two years were not kind to Henry Newsome. He had an avalanche of troubles. His wife had an illness terminating in a costly operation. He too had been ill subsequently, unable to work. A sitter for a portrait died suddenly when the painting was only half-finished. The lawyers told him that he had no claim for the agreed fee of one thousand pounds. The heir didn't want the portrait of his father, with whom he had not been on speaking terms. Then an irascible new income-tax inspector harassed Newsome with back claims, disputing expenses. The fellow was imbued with the hostility that seems to invest all Englishmen confronted with the arts. He appeared to regard it as outrageous for Newsome to be able to earn his living in pleasant places merely by daubing paint on a canvas. A settlement, after a protracted argument, covering six years of returns, cost him five hundred pounds. Clients being scarce owing to a Stock Exchange scare, and the Bank of England playing with the bank rate again, he let his country retreat in Sussex and raised a mortgage on his London studio.

Then the tide turned. An American woman who had been visiting the Maharani of Jaipur was greatly impressed by a portrait Newsome had painted during his Indian tour. He met Mrs. Fay Dugdale in Paris. She commissioned him to paint her portrait and that of her son, a youth at Harvard. A Texan oil heiress, Mrs. Dugdale, four times married, now a divorcée, demanded and always got what she wanted. The fee asked was agreed to without cavil. Newsome had made it a figure that amazed himself but not Mrs. Dugdale. The conditions were imperative. She was spending the winter at Coconut Grove, Florida, just south of Miami. She would go there from New York in December, and her son Jerry would come for the Christmas vacation. "He's good to look at so you'll be under no strain," said Mrs. Dugdale, smiling.

As for Mrs. Dugdale herself, she was more than good to look at. At fifty-four she was still a very beautiful woman. Tall, slender, she had a gift for dressing. She commanded all that Paris, Rome and New York could give her. A French maid, Adèle, of fathomless devotion, struggled with an immense caravan of dresses, hats, shoes, furs and various impedimenta, including Inky, a poodle to which her heart was wholly given.

Mrs. Dugdale had run through four husbands and two fortunes. She would have been destitute but for a large trust she could not break despite the efforts of Messrs. Fishbein, Cohen and Guggenheim, renowned trust breakers. Mrs. Dugdale's grandfather, Roddy Frazer, had foreseen the money-scattering propensities of heirs and had secured his fortune for three generations to follow him. Even so, now trust-bound, Mrs. Dugdale lived on a scale of uninhibited extravagance. A house in Paris, an apartment in New York, a winter home in Florida, a yacht at Cannes, a fleet of automobiles, a handsome and transferable French butler, a harassed secretary, a chauffeur, a handyman, numerous servants at various establishments, a habit of dropping in at Harry Winston's New York office for a diamond trifle to hang on her ears or bosom, sometimes on deferred payment, contrived to keep the large Frazer Trust under severe strain.

"I shall want you to be in Coconut Grove by the tenth of December and stay until the end of January. You'll like *El Mirador*. You can be on your own and work in the tower suite. There's a swimming-pool, and, of course, a car at your disposal. You play bridge and tennis, I suppose?" asked Mrs. Dugdale, offering him a cocktail in her favourite corner of the Hotel Georges Cinq. He played both, he said, and asked about sittings.

"Oh, a bit on and off—I don't suppose you'll mind that, as there's plenty of time, and you'll have Jerry to work on. I think you'll be quite a success," said Mrs. Dugdale, smiling archly. She had very pretty bright blue eyes to set off her Elizabeth Arden complexion. She liked good-looking men around her. "Are you married?"

"Very happily."

"That's nice to know! Well, my secretary will arrange your transport. Miss Fawthorpe is very capable. As it's now October you'll have plenty of time to prepare."

It would not give him too much time. There was a portrait of Lord Hinchlow to be finished for a directors' presentation to their chairman. Hinchlow was peremptory, headstrong, and remorseless in breaking sittings. Unlike Mrs. Dugdale, he was not pleasant to the eye. Newsome deemed it wise to say nothing to Mrs. Dugdale. With such a fee he could afford to drop Lord Hinchlow, if necessary. The very idea gave him pleasure.

II

Newsome arrived at Coconut Grove on time. Mrs. Dugdale did not. She had been delayed in Rome, said the butler. She would arrive on the twelfth. He was conducted to his suite in the tower. As soon as the young butler had gone Newsome looked around. He was still dazed by it all. It was his first time in Florida. An automobile, a large Cadillac with a coloured chauffeur, had met him at Miami station when he descended from the New York night train. It was four hours late owing to an accident on the line. For the next half-hour he had been rushed through a maelstrom of thronged streets and bright towering hotels. The car traversed long palm-tree-bordered avenues, gardens, and chalets ablaze with bougainvillaea, hibiscus, poinsettia, firegold bignonia, and white-belled datura plants. The houses seemed to have been transported from Spain, Italy, Portugal and Provence. They had verandahs, screened loggias, patios, coloured pantile roofs and medieval portcullis gateways. It was as if all the architects of Europe had tossed their models into a bag, shaken it, and poured them out on to the vivid spongy buffalo grass. It was a man-made paradise in a sub-tropical setting.

Newsome's suite consisted of a very large sitting-room and bedroom, with a wide canopied bed such as Marie Antoinette might have slept in. The suite was lavishly carpeted and furnished. A Beauvais tapestry, a hunting scene, covered one wall. There was a chandelier and a mirror of Murano glass. A corner of the room was filled with something swathed in a white sheet, its shape familiar. It was an easel, newly imported, as a label told him, from New York.

The butler returned with a tea tray. "Dinner is at eight o'clock, sir. Can I unpack?"

Newsome declined the offer. He drank the tea. Later, a glow through the windows at one side made him walk over and look out. An astonishing sight met his eyes. The heavens, rising to a strip of lemon-coloured sky, were blood-red. The sunset burned fiercely behind the black palm-trees on the horizon. A small lake, luminous from the upper sky, reflected the glory of the heavens, ranging from vermilion through mauve to diamond-white at the edge of the lawn sloping down from the house. Some wild-fowl flitted over the water, silhouetted against the afterglow. The sunset burned more fiercely, then, its summit of splendour reached, rapidly faded. The intense black night spread over the land in an obliterating tide.

From the opposite side of the room Newsome looked down on floodlights throwing their beams on the slim grey trunks of palms, lighting the underleaves of the tufty fronds. The lights were reflected in a long swimming-pool. The stars were coldly bright above. Newsome began to unpack—a large Breton armoire held his suits. Warmth came from the radiators under the windows, to take off the chill following sundown.

The bathroom was a small marble palace. He examined the books in the recessed shelves of the sitting-room. Books were often indicative of the owner's taste, but these were too various to offer any clue. He was interested in a small morocco-bound two-volumed French edition of Brillat-Savarin's *Physiologie du Goût*. Perhaps they were indicative of the delights to follow downstairs at eight o'clock.

He hesitated about changing for dinner. It seemed likely he would be dining alone, but he put on a white dinner-jacket. For a moment he felt he was back in Jaipur, but there were no slim soft-footed dark servants when he went downstairs.

The young butler gave him a cocktail in the long salon. It was brightly furnished. Eight French windows opened on to a flagged terrace, with the lawn and a rectangular swimming-pool beyond. A large painting of Mrs. Dugdale dominated one end of the salon. It revealed her in a long black gown. Diamonds sparkled on her beautiful throat, a spray of orchids shone in her corsage, her full dark hair was caught in a *diamanté* bandeau. The artist had exaggerated her height and slimness and all the flowing lines seemed to converge on two flower-like hands displayed over a blue purse. They were hands of incredible beauty. The portrait was a triumphant achievement. Newsome wondered why she wanted another painted. It could not be more than ten years old.

He crossed the room to look closer at the painting and to search for the artist's name. Of course a Frenchman, André Marin, school of Boldini. He looked round the salon and was surprised to find most of the pictures were of hunters, by Herring, Sartorius, Ferneley, Stubbs. One would never have expected to find Leicestershire studies in Florida. Squire Hartopp of the Quorn, mounted, in white kid breeches and topboots, with the family mansion in the background, presided over the fireplace. The pictures were probably a legacy of Mrs. Dugdale's English husband.

"Dinner is served, sir," said the young butler. He was alone, but the dinner and the service in no way suffered. It went sumptuously through five courses. The linen, silverware, glassware, the Vienna Royal Porcelain Lippizan horses as centrepiece, the Sèvres china, were worthy of an Empress, and the cuisine of Lucullus himself. What a prodigal waste on a single person, thought Newsome, but what taste directing it all, and how enjoyable!

He discovered that the butler was Puerto Rican, a slim youth whose clothes seemed to have been poured over him. He was delighted when Newsome spoke Spanish to him. He learned that his mother was the cook. They lived all the time, caretakers, in *El Mirador*. The staff would come down from the New York apartment.

Newsome spent the next day setting up his easel, canvas and painting-table. He then wandered around Coconut Grove. It was a select suburb that prided itself on being aloof from the vulgarity of Miami. A number of splendid villas fronted the Biscayne Bay opening on to the blue Atlantic. Pelicans haunted the shore. The wild terrain of the Spanish conquistadores seemed not far off, though it was being rapidly engulfed by the tide of a bungalow civilization. Automobiles on the highroad behind raced down the long flat swampy peninsula to Key West, the southernmost point of the United States.

Newsome spent two idle happy days, reading, swimming in the pool whose water, from reflecting tiles on the bottom, was a pellucid green. He dozed, read and enjoyed being pampered by the assiduous butler, Juan. Then on the third day Mrs. Dugdale arrived. Pandemonium broke forth. There was a whirring of automobiles in the courtyard, and the noise of baggage transported to the bedrooms. Mrs. Dugdale emerged, all smiles, with her son Jerry, picked up in New York. He was a handsome lad of about eighteen, dark like his mother, in the loose bright clothes affected by young Americans.

Another butler, François, young, sleek as a well-fed cat, another chauffeur, and an assistant chauffeur in a station-wagon crammed with more baggage, appeared with Adèle the French maid. Then came Miss Fawthorpe, the English secretary, large, cheery, highly capable and quite imperturbable, *confidante* of mother, son, butler and staff. Then the poodle, Inky, almost master of the household, certainly of the boudoir, where he sat on guard day and night, Adèle his slave. There was also Mr. Grant of the Frazer family's law firm, brought down to deal with some temporary financial difficulty. Mr. Grant was a brief visitor. He patiently proved to Mrs. Dugdale that another hundred thousand dollars could not be squeezed out of the funds. He sweated round the eyes under his rimless glasses, the only sign of strain. They all dined together quietly that evening. Four guests were to arrive on the morrow.

The more Newsome saw of Mrs. Dugdale the more he liked her. She was sweet-tempered, quiet, a lady in every respect, beautifully gowned, easy to talk with. She had been "finished" in Paris and Florence and was fluent in French and Italian. She insisted on inspecting his rooms, mounting the back stairs to the tower, despite a disability from a slight stroke that affected her walking. It was arranged for her to give him a sitting each morning for one hour between eleven and twelve, the "light"

hour he preferred. He could not foresee what a futile arrangement it would prove to be. Only the stroke betrayed the storms
through which Mrs. Dugdale had passed. Death, divorce, and
intermittent obsessions had made her life erratic. The husband
she adored, an Englishman of good family, had been killed in
the Second World War. His successor, a rake, she had divorced.
Later he was drowned by the capsizing of his yacht. "The
trouble with Mrs. Dugdale is that she can't tell a serpent from
a swan," said Miss Fawthorpe, one day. "At heart she's a kind,
sweet person who gets exploited."

The first morning Mrs. Dugdale was prompt. Newsome was
to remember it as an exception. She sat patiently for an hour
while he roughed-in with charcoal. The more he observed her
the more lovely she proved. Her dark eyes, liquid and beautiful,
were shaded by long thick lashes. Her complexion was exquisite,
and her black hair fell abundant and glossy in its waves. He
wondered sometimes what those long sessions with beauty
specialists could do for her, Nature had been so lavish. Like his
predecessor, he saw that her hands could be the dominant
feature. Long, perfect in form, they made every movement a
lyric. He felt he would have to keep their quality subdued in
order not to detract from the portrait, André Marin's one
failure. Newsome's pencil ran down the lovely long line of her
throat in one rhythmic sweep.

They talked as he worked. The more they talked the more he
liked her. Her voice was low and easy to the ear. He noticed
that in her gossip she never said an unkind thing. She had no
resentment against people or life. She had lived in many places,
known every kind of society. She had been *en poste* with her
English husband, a diplomat, in various appointments. She
had owned splendid houses, entertained lavishly. He alluded
to the paintings of hunters. She had hunted in Leicestershire.
"But I haven't a good seat. I was rather an ordeal for my
poor husband—quite horse-mad—he expected every moment
that I should break my neck!" She was grateful Jerry had
been too young to be engulfed in the war. He was the treasure
of her life.

Jerry, Newsome discovered, was shy and reserved in the

presence of his mother. He seemed repelled by her affectionate exuberance and watched her with meditative eyes, the ghosts of her husbands troubling him. At eighteen he was not yet engulfed in the usual pursuit of girls, the American boy's frenzied round of "dates". His mother's enthusiasms often bewildered him. He detested the smart social people who were drawn to the honeypot of her wealth, the parasites, adventurers, unaccountable counts, foreign princes, and well-dressed down-and-outs who were always trying to sell "darling Fay" something, from a ten-thousand-pound masterpiece to an emerald ring that belonged to an archduchess who "must raise some money". He hated social life and was somewhat surly on being exhibited. He clung to a child's memory of his father. He recoiled from the attentions of his mother's set who found him attractive in his maleness. His fur rose in the presence of pussy-cat men who slid through the open doors of the rich. He was an excellent swimmer, a daring young skin-diver, a skilled motorist, but in all these pastimes he walked alone. He was handsome and in maturity would certainly create currents in feminine society.

It was only after Jerry had sat several times to Newsome that the artist penetrated the surface of this reticent youth. One afternoon in an interval of the sitting he surprised Newsome by asking, "Do you like Prokofiev?"

"I'm afraid I know very little about him—he's a Russian composer, isn't he?" asked Newsome.

"A very great Russian composer—greater than Stravinsky, Mitropoulos told me."

"Mitropoulos?"

"The conductor, he came to conduct the Second Beethoven Symphony at Boston. I had lunch with him the next day. He told me that of all the moderns Prokofiev is the greatest."

"You are fond of music?"

"Yes. Do you know what I would really like to be—a conductor, a Bernstein, a Menotti or a Schippers."

Bernstein, Menotti, Schippers. Newsome was wholly out of his depth with these names pronounced by the young Dugdale as if they were gods. "You'll have to educate me. I know something of Rubinstein, Stokowski and Beecham—I've painted Beecham."

"They're great!" exclaimed Jerry with a fire now lighting his eyes. "But Bernstein, Menotti and Schippers are young geniuses—they're America's greatest! I've got all their recordings. You should hear them!"

"I would like to. Now let's go back to work. Go on talking, tell me about them, about the music you like," said Newsome, picking up his palette. The quiet youth had been suddenly transformed by his enthusiasm. This was something that he must catch in the portrait.

"Mr. Newsome, won't you come to my den? I'll put on some records."

"I would like to. Do you play any instrument?" asked Newsome, painting rapidly. It was like catching a sunset. And this youth had given no clue of any passion! The lines of the young dark face had suddenly taken on vitality.

"A little, the piano—not too well. I've got a Steinway in my den, mother's birthday present, but this climate plays hell with it."

"You must play to me. Is your mother fond of music?"

"No, she doesn't like it. It bores her. Do you know, someone brought Menotti to lunch, and she asked him what he did! I hauled her to Salzburg last August. Poor Mom, she couldn't take it. She thought me nuts. But she gave a wonderful party for Mitropoulos, and, would you believe it, she got Flagstad! In fact everybody was there and she made a terrific hit with dear old Rubinstein!"

Later that evening Newsome was taken to the boy's room. There was a great stack of gramophone records. There were signed portraits of musicians. "I get them when they come to Boston," he explained. There were porcelain busts of Beethoven, Wagner and Verdi. A grand piano occupied one side of the room. There was a violin case on a table.

"You play the violin also?" asked Newsome.

"Like hell!" replied Jerry. "But do you know who came up here, and played that violin—Yehudi Menuhin! He gave a concert in Miami last year and Mom put him up for two nights.

He's a wizard. He played for me, on that violin, in this room!"

It was a bright-eyed boy talking. He went over to a shelf, took down a long thin leather box and opened it. The inside lid was lined with crimson silk and had a silver inscription. In it was a baton.

"I got it in Paris this summer—Rossini's baton!"

He took it out and waved it solemnly. "I'm going to give it to Menotti when he comes to our music club next term."

He replaced the baton reverently.

"I'd like you to play something for me on the piano," said Newsome.

"Would you? I'm rather awful! Sit there, sir."

He turned out two of the lights, lowered the shade of another. "A little atmosphere!" he said, with a shy laugh, seating himself at the keyboard.

The boy played well, softly, with expression.

"What was that?" asked Newsome, when he finished.

"It's from the First Piano Concerto, written by Prokofiev when he was nineteen. He won the Rubinstein prize with it. Have you been to Russia?"

"No."

"I'd like to go. I've been introduced to Stravinsky. The Russians are very interesting, aren't they?"

"Very. I've been to only one music shrine—to the monastery of Valldemosa in Majorca, where Chopin wrote some of his *Preludes*."

"Chopin—so have I, and to George Sand's château at Nohant!" cried Jerry, exuberantly. "Every summer I make a pilgrimage. Next summer I'm going to Torre del Lago and Roncole—you know, Puccini and Verdi places."

He shut down the piano lid and stood up. The heaviness had gone out of his face and he looked an eager boy of fifteen.

"If you really like the piano, sir, we've got a neighbour who's a wizard player. You should hear him. People sneer at him but I take no notice of that—he's really a wonderful pianist."

"Why do they sneer at him?"

"Well, it's social—you know what snobs people are. He was an interior decorator who married an old girl who could be his grandmother, for her money of course. Funny how folks don't mind female gold-diggers, they're thick around here, and laugh when they get away with it, but they just hate male gold-diggers. I'll ask Bobo to play for us."

"Bobo?"

"Robinson Gehr, everyone calls him Bobo. They've got a house here," said Jerry. Then, seeing the expression on Newsome's face, "You've heard of him? Has Mom told you?"

"No, but I met him and his wife in Florence two years ago. He lives here?"

"Not half a mile away. I'll ask him in and make him play to you. He's a great guy at the keyboard."

III

Mr. and Mrs. Robinson Gehr came to lunch three days later.

"She's a nice old lady and he's very pleasant," said Mrs. Dugdale before they arrived. "Their marriage created a lot of talk, of course, but I can't see why two persons shouldn't be allowed to order their own lives together if it suits them that way. He looks after her wonderfully."

Gehr was effusive in his greeting of Newsome. "This is the nicest thing that has happened to us this year, isn't it, Marie darling?"

Mrs. Gehr agreed. "Fay must bring you along to dine with us now we're neighbours. We are all anxious to see your painting of dear Fay."

"I think it will be a great success. I'll give a party when it's finished. Of course it'll flatter me! But all the best artists flatter their subjects. Look at Lazló, Lavery and Sargent!" said Mrs. Dugdale.

"What about Modigliani?" asked Jerry.

"Those squint-eyed horrors! I'm sure Mr. Newsome won't see your mother like that!" cried Gehr.

"It's strange how some artists do see things," added his wife. "Now I know I'm out of fashion when I tell you I can't stand Botticelli. In Florence I had quite a dose of him. I thought his

Venus on the half-shell insipid—and as for that pot-bellied heroine of 'Primavera'!"

"You're forgetting, Mrs. Gehr, it was springtime and she was 'expecting'," said Jerry. The table was convulsed.

"Jerry!" said Mrs. Dugdale, reproachfully.

"Well, I must say I like his Venus," said a guest, Mr. Hutton, who had a pointed beard that gave him a Vandyck look. "Yes, I like her!"

"We must remember that beauty is a contemporary fashion. The face, like the female figure, changes," said Newsome. "Botticelli's model for his 'Venus' and 'Primavera' was Simonetta. Medicean Florence thought her the most beautiful woman in Italy. When she died at twenty-three they gave her a public funeral, and carried her *bara aperta*, in full view on her bier. All Florence walked behind—Lorenzo dei Medici and his brother Giuliano—whose mistress she had been—Leonardo da Vinci and Botticelli. They had all been hypnotized by her beauty."

"I find the feet of Venus very ugly, something very odd about her toenails," remarked Bobo. "But toenails are very odd!"

"My! You men! What we girls have to go through!" said Mrs. Dugdale, laughing.

"Oh, I don't think there'll be any doubt about you, Fay!" cried Bobo. "And I'm sure Mr. Newsome knows what a find you are!"

After lunch the party went to have coffee in the summer-house by the pool. Bobo drew Newsome aside.

"This is a pleasure! Fancy finding you here! My God, we need some fresh faces! All these old women and gouty bores! For God's sake don't finish your portrait in a hurry. Stay around!"

"I hear from Jerry, who's also sitting to me, that you're a wonderful pianist," said Newsome. "I want to hear you."

"I'm not wonderful but I'm pretty good. For a time I thought of taking it up professionally, but pianists are ten-a-dollar these days. Besides," added Bobo, "I lack the nose."

"The nose?"

"You can't beat the Jew-boys—Horowitz, Rubinstein—it's

shelling peas to them. And my hands aren't very good these days. See, all nervy!" He held up his coffee cup. The hand trembled. He had a tired look round his eyes.

"Aren't you well?"

"I'm getting worn down, old boy," replied Bobo. "It's Marie —she gets more and more exacting. I'm never off the leash, not even at night. I get no proper sleep. I don't have to go into details—with old men it's the prostate gland, with old women the fallen womb. It gets her up."

"But don't you have separate rooms?"

"No, she won't have that. Says she feels nervous. We have separate beds but I have to hold her hand until she goes to sleep—I told you last time we met, I think. If I say I want to go to bed she says I don't love her! Last night we had quite a scene. She told me to clear out."

"Why don't you?" asked Newsome.

"Oh, I can't! In a way I'm very fond of her," said Bobo. "Doesn't she look pretty today? No one would believe she's eighty-six, she's so tough! And actually she's fond of me, I'm sure of that. It's only when she's her old trouble and her nerves are frayed that she's testy and unkind . . . I suppose we should join the others."

They moved towards the coffee-table. Mrs. Gehr plainly wanted to leave. The party broke up.

"Sorry," said Bobo. "You know, Marie must have her nap after lunch. I must take her home."

"When are you going to play to us? Jerry said you would play."

Bobo looked round, then whispered—"Tomorrow afternoon about two-thirty? It's the only time I can get round, when Marie's having her nap. All right tomorrow?"

Newsome nodded. Bobo went across to shake Mrs. Dugdale's hand. "A lovely lunch," he said. "Thanks a lot."

"Delightful! Goodbye!" said Mrs. Gehr, taking Bobo's arm. "You must bring Mr. Newsome over. Do you like birds, Mr. Newsome?"

"Oh yes," replied Newsome, surprised.

"Bobo's got a wonderful aviary," said Jerry.

"Young birds, middle-aged birds, and old birds," cried Bobo, winking. "Every kind!"

Mrs. Gehr pulled his arm. "I'm not sure just what you mean by that remark!" she said.

"I'm certain Bobo doesn't mean it unkindly," said Mrs. Dugdale, kissing the old lady.

IV

True to his promise, Bobo Gehr came to *El Mirador* about half-past two the next day. They went at once to Jerry's room. The boy raised the lid of the piano, having given Bobo a liqueur.

"What do you want me to play?"

"Whatever you like," replied Jerry.

"Well, here goes," he said, finishing the liqueur and seating himself at the keyboard. He made a few [preliminary runs, paused, and began to play.

Newsome sat back in an easy chair. Jerry squatted on the floor, legs crossed.

There was no question that Bobo was a master pianist. Newsome listened with growing amazement. It was something he had never expected of this odd creature who had sold himself for an easy life.

The pianist stopped.

"What was that? I don't know it," asked Jerry.

"My own transcription from Borodin," said Bobo. He began to play again.

"Scriabin!" exclaimed Jerry.

Bobo smiled, then, caught up by his playing, seemed oblivious of them and played piece after piece, Debussy, Schumann, Brahms, Chopin. He stopped after the third *Étude*.

"And that's that!" exclaimed Bobo, getting up from the keyboard and mopping his brow. "Cortot, lost in Florida, and bird-keeping!" he added, a little bitterly.

"You're just as good!" affirmed Jerry. "It's a scandal you ever gave up!"

"My dear boy, I never really began! I've been a stop-short beginner at everything."

"You really astonish me. Delightful! Delightful!" said New-some. "I hope you will come and play again."

"If you do, perhaps Mr. Newsome will paint you instead of wasting time on me."

"I'm more pleased with you than with your mother," said Newsome.

"She doesn't keep to her schedule? I knew that would happen! My lovely and irresponsible mother ignores calendars and clocks!" said Jerry.

It was only too true. Newsome was in a state of nervous prostration. The first morning all had been well. Mrs. Dugdale was on time, charming, looking lovely. The third morning she was half an hour late. "You know, the telephoning here is dreadful," she said with a sweet smile, seating herself on the dais.

Within half an hour François, the butler, came in. A call from New York. Would Madam take it? Mrs. Dugdale rose and went over to the table with the telephone. There was an interminable discussion with a dressmaker. "It must be here for the New Year," said Mrs. Dugdale, and put down the receiver.

"How tiresome!" she said. "I am so sorry, I am quite worn out! Let's have a cocktail, Mr. Newsome. I'm sure you can't feel like work after this!" She ordered cocktails over the house telephone. "I know that I'll be in trouble—the servants hate climbing the stairs. But I like this room, don't you? You do feel you can work here?" she asked earnestly.

"The room is splendid," he replied, putting away his palette.

"Is Jerry a good sitter?" she asked.

"Very, he comes promptly every afternoon."

"Now, you're not scolding me, dear Mr. Newsome?" she cried.

He could not help but smile, his annoyance melting before this woman who was like an impulsive child. God help the husbands one, two, three, four, he thought.

"Can I have a peek at Jerry's portrait?" she asked.

"There's very little to see, I've put in very little colour."

"Oh, but can I see?"

C

"No. I must tell you frankly that I never let my sitters see a portrait until it is finished."

"Mr. Newsome, you're a tyrant!"

"No, I am an autocrat, and wise. You would not let me into your boudoir to see you half-way made-up?"

She regarded him with wide-open eyes.

"How does your wife put up with you?" she asked.

"Being a very sensible woman she never comes into my studio."

"Did you ever paint her?"

"Yes."

"And she didn't see it until it was finished? Did she like it?"

"No," he said, and they laughed together.

"What did you do, did you destroy it?"

"No, I sent it to the Royal Academy where, forgive my saying so, it was one of the successes of the year!"

CHAPTER 3

I

A FEW DAYS later they were the luncheon guests of Mr. and Mrs. Robinson Gehr at *Sunrise*. It was a large low white house built of coralstone around a patio. The open side, with a fountain and lawn, faced the Biscayne Bay with its long lido dividing the lagoon and the Atlantic Ocean beyond. Spanish architecture, a pattern set for all Florida by an architectural genius, Addison Mizner, at the beginning of the century, had been the keynote of *Sunrise*, well-named, for it faced the sun rising out of the ocean. The patio had ten palm-trees, bodily imported. An arcaded loggia ran round the open rectangle. Lunch for twelve was set in the loggia. On the right, near the corner, there was a tremendous twittering of birds. It came from a large aviary.

"Marie's mad about birds. We've got two hundred here—parrots, parakeets, orioles, mynas, cardinals, buntings, gold-finches, bobolinks, myrtle-warblers, and dozens and dozens of budgerigars—a whole rainbow of them, as you see!" said Bobo. "Somehow, I think she'd like to put me in with them! Noisy little bastards!"

"That reminds me—didn't I see you in the lounge of the Excelsior Hotel with a bird-cage?" asked Newsome, inspecting the large flashing aviary.

"Sure, with a green budgerigar. That was Timmy, god of this house. Marie won't travel anywhere without him. That bird's been all over Europe. She says he's her familiar spirit. It goes up into our bedroom at night. You'd imagine it was a piece of Cartier jewellery. If Timmy died, we'd be in black for a year. There he is, behind Marie."

Newsome looked across the patio. Mrs. Gehr appeared quite young in a flowered gown, waving a white Spanish fan as she sat by the cocktail table. She was very animated. Impossible to believe that she was eighty-six. Timmy was in a cage behind her, on a side table.

35

"Budgerigars generally go in pairs—hasn't he a partner?" asked Newsome.

"We got him one, it wasn't a success. The moment it came he never spoke a word. They sat all day kissing each other. That made Marie mad, she likes him to talk. So out went the partner. Come into the hall, I'll show you something," said Bobo.

Newsome followed his host through the long drawing-room into the glass-ceilinged hall. Its walls were lined with cases full of stuffed birds. They stood about two feet from the walls. Bobo turned one of them round. All the cases were on swivels.

"Now this is what I'm crazy about—humming-birds! Unhappily you can't keep them in captivity, I've tried and failed—but with luck we'll see them in the garden. You see all these cases, all on turntables? Perhaps you don't know, but their colours are structural, not pigmentary, they—"

"That's a bit beyond me, though I'm used to pigments."

"Well," said Bobo eagerly, "take for instance a rainbow, a flash of a diamond, the blue sky, or a spot of oil on a wet tarmac —their colours are structural, whereas your reds and blues on a palette are pigmentary colours in themselves. The humming-bird takes its brilliant colours from movement and light. If it turns a few degrees the iridescence is lost. The birds must face the light and you must have a quick eye. Look!"

He revolved a case. Endless changes of colours flashed from their plumage. They were mostly small birds, about three inches in size. There was a group with long, curved, yellow beaks tipped black, and green throat feathers. *Trochilus polytmus*, read Newsome on an ivory plaque.

"Humming-birds are the *Trochilidae* species. The name is from the Greek. No one knows now what the actual Greek bird was. According to Herodotus it was famous for picking the leeches out of the throats of crocodiles! But I'm told Herodotus was a bit of a liar!" laughed Bobo. "These birds are Ruby-throats. They go to breed in the north—we get them around Baltimore—but they migrate here and in the Caribbean and Mexico in winter. They visit our garden. You won't believe it, but they've a reverse gear. They can fly backwards as well as forwards! When they hover their bodies are motionless. You can't see their wings—they have a twenty-five-per-second wing-beat. Most small birds have half that. I often watch them over the hibiscus—they love red—you'll see that I've got red feeding-tubes of glass holding sugared water in the garden for them. They've an extensible tongue that reaches right down into the flowers for nectar—it's tubular and looks like a suction pump. In a sense they've got a fuel tank—they can take on fifty per cent extra fat for long migratory flights. I weigh one hundred and seventy pounds, so it means I'd have to be two hundred and fifty-five pounds if I wanted to migrate!"

He moved to the next case and swung it round. The birds flashed in their iridescent beauty.

"I had this hall ceiling removed and a glass one put in to give us the light. Look at this beauty. *Topaz palla*, the king of the lot. There are three hundred varieties of humming-birds, but only twelve indigenous to the U.S.A. This beauty comes from British Guiana and Venezuela. Look at him!"

The bird was gorgeous, a black head, bright yellow underbill, light brown wings, mauve claws, long black crossed tail feathers, and a brilliant ruby-red breast.

"Watch!" Bobo cried, swinging the case. "See, the colours have disappeared with turning from the light? Wonderful birds, humming-birds! And these tiny fellows are as brave as bulls. They'll take on a hawk a hundred times their size—there's some Irish in 'em, one would think. They love a fight. And yet they've got no gall-bladder. Tell me, why is the Holy Ghost portrayed as a dove? A colourless, senseless sort of bird, for ever cooing. Why didn't He come down as a humming-bird?"

They moved from case to case, Bobo delightedly riding his hobby. He quoted some verses softly.

> *"What heavenly tints in mingling radiance fly!*
> *Each rapid movement gives a different dye;*
> *Like scales of burnished gold they dazzling show—*
> *Now sink to shade, now like a furnace glow!*

"An ornithologist named Alexander Wilson wrote that."

Bobo passed on. "*Salasphorus platycereus*—the Flame-bearer! He whistles as he flies. Humming-birds have no voices, they can only chatter. This fellow whistles with the wind passing through his wing tips—like boys playing on a comb."

"Wherever did you find all these birds?" asked Newsome, passing case after case of glittering beauty.

"I've been almost eight years at it. Marie thinks me nuts—perhaps I am. We went down to Brazil for some. To Mexico and Venezuela for others. I've people all over the place collecting for me. There's a wonderful man in Delaware, Crawford H. Greenewalt, he's made a life study of them. He's photographed hundreds all over the world, and published a marvellous book about them. Fabulous colour plates. He had a special camera and waited weeks for some shots. There's a professor at the University of California also, who's studied their flight aerodynamics. They migrate as much as two thousand miles. They've a special metabolism, a sort of kilowatt rating. I say! I'll be in trouble with Marie—we must go!"

He hurried through to the patio. He was in trouble. Mrs. Gehr looked at him with angry eyes.

"What do you mean by keeping us all waiting! What manners!" she cried.

"I'm sorry, Marie darling, I've been showing my birds."

"Your birds! They are as much my birds as yours but I don't bore people with them!" she cried.

"It's a most wonderful collection—I've greatly enjoyed seeing them," said Newsome.

Mrs. Gehr rose, gave him a faint smile, and led the way to the lunch table. He was seated on her left. "You don't know what I have to put up with. Bobo has no sense of time," she said to him.

Newsome could have added that there were others, but refrained. A British peer with handlebar whiskers and a Guard's tie sat on his hostess's right. He was charming Mrs. Dugdale, who had missed the morning sitting altogether. She had sent up word that she had to go into Miami to see the dentist.

II

In six days Newsome had had only two full sittings. The portrait had not progressed at all. Now Christmas was on top of them, and he feared the worst. The house had filled up with guests. Mrs. Dugdale was not only late for sittings. She was late for the car waiting at the door, sometimes an hour late, and quarrels broke out between Henry, the English chauffeur, and Adèle her maid, whom he blamed for not getting her ready in time. Last night she had come down for dinner an hour and a quarter late. She swept into the drawing-room with a smile, looking very lovely but seeming unaware that she had kept eleven persons waiting. "My God, I'm rumbling!" whispered one of them to Newsome, taking his third whisky.

The scene each morning in the long corridor outside Mrs. Dugdale's bedroom recalled the court of Marie Antoinette. On chairs, patiently awaiting admittance, sat a hairdresser, brought in by car from Miami, together with a manicurist, a dressmaker, the typist who asisted Miss Fawthorpe—she carried fifty envelopes with Christmas cheques for the staff at *El Mirador*, in Paris, in New York, and for the skipper and hands of *Lucciola* in harbour at Cannes—the cook with the day's menu, and the handyman, in trouble because there were too many leaves in the swimming-pool. As they waited, Adèle went in and out, followed by Inky the poodle. If the doctor came—he always seemed in attendance—he took precedence. Miss Fawthorpe tried to remain in the office downstairs but was often commanded to attend. The sessions sometimes lasted beyond noon. Then Juan or François would appear in Newsome's room, with the apologetic air they assumed so well, to say Mrs. Dugdale was very sorry, she had had such a heavy morning that she felt she must have a swim and a cocktail, would Mr. Newsome join her?

Then there were the outdoor excursions and crises. A parlour-maid had been stunned by a falling coconut and had to be rushed to the doctor. Inky got tar on his paws and played havoc with the white drawing-room carpet just before guests arrived for lunch. One day the whole house-party left in three cars to lunch at the Bath and Tennis Club in Palm Beach, and to see an afternoon dress parade at the Everglades Club. Newsome found himself in a bright yellow brougham-de-ville with brass sidelamps. It was a vintage Rolls-Royce kept in store at *El Mirador*. It smelt so strongly of camphor, used to preserve its light suede upholstery, that they emerged smelling like mothballs. Mrs. Dugdale was leading in the long Cadillac. Jerry brought up the rear in the station-wagon, equally long.

Newsome was glad to see Palm Beach, the fashionable winter nest of millionaires. He found it wholly charming with its emerald lawns, tall royal palms, spacious boulevards bordered with shining villas set between the long Ocean Drive and Lake Worth, with its yachts at anchor. Not a blade of grass was out of order. The whole place was a verdant drawing-room with a kind of Dresden-china ornamentation.

Newsome found himself lunching in a patio of royal palm-trees amid a crowd of animated women who looked, despite the name of the club, as if they neither swam nor played tennis, and a number of well-groomed elderly men in summer clothes. The women were singularly uniform in appearance. Expensively dressed, carefully made-up, they almost all had frizzled grey hair and spectacles. They talked vivaciously about meetings in Paris, Vichy, Le Touquet, Venice, Rome or Athens. The men appeared subdued. Some of them had just come from an hour's session at the stockbrokers, where they had followed the rise and fall of their stocks on the tele-priceboard, a service from Wall Street to Palm Beach.

A fleet of very large cars filled the club's parking-block. Lines of well-equipped capannas faced the blue Atlantic. There was an inner swimming-pool, tennis courts, and a thronged bar. There was also a prodigious *smörgasbord* table at which the members and guests helped themselves. Under a blazing sun it was a well-equipped paradise.

At the Everglades Club Newsome, with Jerry, slipped away from the mannequin parade. They wandered down Worth Avenue with its *de luxe* shops. Had the Via Condotti, the Rue de la Paix, Bond Street and Kärntnerstrasse combined to put on window shows of *objets d'art* and the contrived luxuries of the moneyed world, they could not have equalled this long Aladdin's Cave. Cucci of Rome, Saks of New York, Cartier, Van Cleef and Arpel, and Elizabeth Arden of Paris had displays in great taste. Their bait was artfully cast. There were side-alleys bright with vines, clematis, bougainvillaea. There were boutiques and restaurants with Regency bow windows, plashing fountains and tiled patios. The alleys had names reminiscent of Europe—Via Parigi, Au Bon Gout, Salon Français. They entered Ta-boo, a dark bar, drank, and came out into the dazzling day. Jerry paused in front of a florist's that looked like a window in Eden. He went in and came out with some orchids in a cellophane box.

Newsome smiled at the lad. "You're meeting her tonight?" he asked. He had wondered about his girl friends.

"Oh, no! They're for Mom. She's just like a 'deb'—she loves to be given flowers!"

"What if I do?"

"She'd love it!" cried Jerry.

He went into the shop and bought a bouquet of roses. It was difficult to know what one could give a woman who had millions.

Back at the Everglades Club they found Henry, the chauffeur, just returned with Inky who had been to the "Poodles' Parlour" and had a ten-dollar shampoo and clip.

III

The next morning Newsome made a protest. Mrs. Dugdale was an hour late.

"I feel I must tell you that if I can't get the sittings I'll not be able to finish the portrait in time," he said.

"But surely you'll stay till you've finished it?" protested his model, looking at him with her candid dark eyes, aggrieved. "If it's taking too much valuable time I'll increase the fee."

"Thank you, it isn't that—it's my wife. I promised that I would be back at the end of January."

"Let's send for her, she's never been to Florida? I'm sure she'd love it!"

"But Mrs. Dugdale—" he began. She cut across his words.

"Why, it's a wonderful idea, you won't have to hurry and she'll have a holiday and you can go home together! You don't have to do anything about it. Miss Fawthorpe will take care of transport."

He thought of Lord Hinchlow's half-finished portrait on the easel at home. He thought of his wife's surprise. He thought—

"Now that we don't have to hurry, we'll enjoy Christmas!"

She turned to the right for him. "And I've a plan. You remember Mr. Hutton and his wife, they dined here last Tuesday? She seemed very interested in you—thought you were a most charming man. I'm going to suggest to Mr. Hutton that he has his wife's portrait done. He can pay anything, and will. He adores Susan. They're going to England in the Spring. If you can get her portrait in the Royal Academy they'd be in heaven!"

"I thought of sending your portrait to the R.A." said Newsome.

"You did? Well, send hers instead," said Mrs. Dugdale.

He looked at her, moved by her enthusiasm and unselfishness.

"Perhaps I could send both. As a Royal Academician I'm entitled to hang six pictures—however bad," he added with a twinkle.

Downstairs when he talked to Miss Fawthorpe in her office she seemed not at all surprised. She looked at a folder. "Mrs. Newsome could come on the *Queen Elizabeth* sailing from Southampton on the second of January. Will you draft a cable to her? I'll call the Cunard office in New York."

He drafted a cable. As he finished it she put down the telephone. "That's all right," she said, smiling and taking the cable. "I've booked a stateroom on the *Q.E.* for the second. Will you add that?"

Somewhat stunned, he added it.

IV

Almost every day around three o'clock when Jerry was sitting for his portrait, Bobo came in. He was free for an hour while Marie was having her siesta. He was in a nervous state. Domestic tension underlay his daily life. He often talked gaily, with an irresponsibility that showed he lacked a philosophic attitude to life. It became plain that he had no moral strength, and without that ballast to a gifted temperament the ship was storm-tossed on its mundane voyage.

There were some afternoons when Jerry was absent and Newsome worked without his sitter. He was not perturbed by Bobo's gossip, he attributed no importance to it. Bobo's facts were somewhat illusory. He suggested that he had sacrificed a business bringing him in twenty thousand dollars a year, but another version of his life in Baltimore revealed him as harassed by debts and unable to keep the business going. "So when Marie made me a proposition I took it. She was terrified of being alone. Her second husband had been dead two years, and she had dismissed three companions, women, in succession. If I married her she would have companionship. The family would raise no objections. They liked to see her happy. Anyhow, she was independent of them, having an income from the family trust."

"And what were you to get?" asked Newsome, working on his canvas while Bobo nervously walked up and down.

"Well, of course there was to be no sex in it, we had that very clear—no active sex."

"Any inactive—or was it to be mother and son?"

"Well, sort of. The old girl likes men. She must have been a tease when she was young. She'll flirt now! She likes to see me well-dressed. She likes to see me walk around the room undressed. She's had a glass door put in the shower so that she can watch me—says I've the body of a Greek god!"

"Have you?" asked Newsome, mischievously.

"Well, I'd heard that before—I'm not bad for forty-four. I keep pretty fit. She's a strange woman. Sometimes she's very kind, sometimes she's very mean. She hates me to play my piano. 'You don't love me,' she says, if I go to the keyboard. I have to read to her in bed every night. She falls asleep and I stop. Do you know, the moment I stop she wakes up and says 'Why've you stopped? Go on!' I don't know why I tell you all this—you must think I'm dreadfully disloyal, but I get so worked up I must talk to someone. Somehow I find you very sympathetic. I felt that the first time I met you in Florence. I always hoped we'd meet again."

Newsome put down his palette and rubbed his fingers with a turpentine rag.

"Won't you play me something," he asked, somewhat embarrassed by the conversation. "Let's go to Jerry's room."

"Well, for a few minutes, then I'll have to go. The moment Marie wakes up she calls 'Bobo!' "

They went to Jerry's room, where he began to play. Newsome sat down and watched his face. It was handsome, masculine, sensitive, but the mouth was weak, feminine, with a kind of baby's petulance. There was no doubt he was a superb artist. If he had decorated as well as he played it was strange he had not made a success. He played for some time, quite lost in the music. When he stopped Newsome asked him what it was.

"Beethoven—the *Appassionata*. Isn't it divine?" Then, glancing at his wrist-watch, he jumped up. "My God! I'll be in trouble! Goodbye!" he cried, and rushed to the door.

Newsome sat quietly in the chair, contemplative. The illimitable facets of life fascinated him. In the course of his career he had met some strange characters. This was one of the strangest. Bobo occasioned him no surprise. Long ago he had ceased to wonder at the human animal. The case here was clear, nor was it original. When a good-looking man of thirty-two marries a woman of seventy-four the reason is money, unless he is a psychological freak. There were young girls who fell in love with old men with beards, and refined white girls who married coal-black negroes. His friend Lowell had been shattered by his lovely young daughter, an heiress, who had insisted on marrying a dirty, pot-bellied, penniless, middle-aged farmer, a widower with two children. It was not always the handsome young chauffeur who stole the prize. Only Greek goddesses insisted on Adonises. Endymion would have had no luck with bandy legs, and Helen would not have dropped Menelaus for a bottle-nosed Paris. The Olympian Age had passed. The gods had never asked about the dowry. Stranger tastes prevailed today than any of those on Mount Olympus.

He wondered about Bobo Gehr's dowry. He had divulged

that he had an allowance of a thousand dollars a month and his keep, but on his wife's death his position was conjectural. Her money was in a trust whose income reverted to the children and grandchildren. "I've no idea where I'll be, possibly I'll get her personal belongings—but she's always making a new will," he said.

"You've not been very businesslike, have you?" asked Newsome.

"No. I've never been good at business."

"There's one possibility. She may outlive you."

"My God, you scare me! She may!" cried Bobo.

A mercenary marriage and yet not so mercenary. Well, there was give and take on both sides. Nor was the situation singular. Many marriages were an arrangement. That was a business of long standing. Where did one begin to criticize? Love, as the Western world knew it, was a comparatively modern convention, embroidered by the poets and novelists. There was no proof that Adam's was a love match. There had been no choice in the garden of Eden. He took what was offered, gratefully. Like Mrs. Gehr, Adam had not liked loneliness. There was no real Eden without a partner, but there had been little equality in the partnership. The marriage of old men to young girls throughout history had established a one-way pattern which had made the woman a chattel. No one had cavilled at the elderly Joseph's marriage to the young Virgin Mary. And no theologian had ever suggested it was a love match. Newsome recalled that some years back when he had painted the Maharani of Salagori she had told him that her marriage had been arranged when she was seven, and the Tika Raja, her husband, was nine. Her own mother had married at eleven and given birth to her at twelve; and orthodox Hinduism forbade the husband to see his wife's face before the wedding day. The Elizabethan aristocracy had set a pattern of marketing its daughters, with dowries, that had endured to modern times. It was not the unique privilege of royalty to buy kingdoms with flesh and blood. Now, in the New World the process had been reversed. The divorcée trod the path to affluence. Once upon a time statesmen had traded Bombay and Tangiers at the royal altar. The modern Catherines of Braganza accepted a block of shares to give their spouses freedom, and the Bobos traded themselves to rich old women.

By moral standards it was a shocking thing. It would seem that only the poor had the privilege of a love match; they had no crowns, lands or shares to bargain with. If one censured Bobo Gehr—and he did censure him—where and with whom did one stop? At a price Bobo was giving a lonely old woman some happiness. But the price! Ay, there was the rub! It was so easy to sit in moral judgement on others. The Great Moralist had been the most forbearing.

CHAPTER 4

I

WITH CHRISTMAS OVER at *El Mirador* a calm settled over the scene. Newsome had almost finished the portrait of Jerry. The boy had been very conscientious about his sittings, despite an influx of pretty girls over the holidays. They thronged the swimming-pool with their beaux and filled the air with their cries and laughter under the orange trees heavy with golden fruit. Cars roared in and out of the courtyard. There were dinner-dances with lanterns hung under the coconut trees and around the pool, which reflected the coloured lights. A negro jazz-band played at one end of the terrace on which they danced in the warm starlit night. The scent of the tuberoses became so powerful from the garden under Newsome's window that he had to close it, the room heavy with the sickly odour. The nights were glorious, with a young moon in a sky brilliant with stars. The countryside lay black and flat as seen from his tower. There was a sense of the jungle on the fringe of visibility.

One morning, by a hedge of scarlet-belled hibiscus, as he lay reading in a cane chair—Mrs. Dugdale had failed him again—he saw a humming-bird. He was alert at once, filled with Bobo's lore, and watched the tiny creature. Its beauty was incredible. He was proud to identify it as a Rubythroat. It hovered over the flowers, wings invisible, body motionless, and inserted its beak with flawless precision in the scented blossoms, the extensible tongue at its suction work. The task completed, the bird lifted itself, hovered again, reversed a little and flew off with a flash of iridescent colour. It was an enchantment of nature too brief in revelation. He understood Bobo's hobby, and for himself felt what good fortune was his to be following his profession in such lovely circumstances.

In one respect his hostess had not failed him. She had worked her will on Mr. Hutton. The portrait of his wife was commissioned. "I haven't asked you your fee, Mr. Newsome," he said, "My father told me that if you ask the price of anything you're poor. Well, I can't claim to be poor, and I'm always told you must be delicate with artistic people!" He laughed heavily and seemed shy.

"Mrs. Dugdale is paying five thousand dollars."

"Then that's all right by me. We're here until the end of January," said Hutton. "Can you do it in that time?"

"Yes, if Mrs. Hutton's regular with her sittings."

"My Susie's the most regular woman in America."

The statement was not belied. Mrs. Hutton gave him an hour at nine o'clock each morning without fail. She came on the second, and left on the second. She talked very little but to the point. Her features were regular, her profile excellent. He made a three-quarter face study. The sweep of her brown hair was luxuriant, remarkable for a woman who was a grandmother seven times.

"I suppose I'm not allowed to see?" asked Hutton.

"No."

"That's what Mrs. Dugdale told me," he said, as they sat smoking by the pool at sundown.

"If you will be good enough to go into the garden house—the inner room which I'm using as an extra studio for your wife—and get me the copy of *Time* I left on the table—" He took the key out of his pocket and gave it to Hutton.

"Thanks—that's very kind of you!" said Hutton.

"But say nothing," added Newsome.

"That's understood!"

After a few minutes Hutton returned with *Time*, and gave back the key. "I feel it's worth every dollar I'm paying. You've got Susie to a T," he said.

II

Mrs. Dugdale was more difficult than Mrs. Hutton. A human humming-bird, she flashed, she dashed, but could not hover. He had reached a point of stagnation with the portrait. Jerry's was finished.

"I wish I really looked like that, Mr. Newsome," he said.

"You do when you're at the piano or a girl's around."

The boy laughed. "You know, it's been great fun talking with you. I'm sorry I've got to go back to Harvard soon. You're so understanding. In a way, I don't exist for Mom. I can have anything I want. She smothers me with affection but she hasn't the slightest conception of my inner life."

"It's a common failing with parents, Jerry."

"Gee, I wish you were my Dad. I've never really had one. He was killed when I was a baby."

"I wish you were my son," answered Newsome, gently. "We've never had children, alas."

There was a silence. They looked at each other.

"Then let's pretend that I'm your son," said Jerry. He went up to the artist and stood before him a little embarrassed and his face quivered.

Newsome put a hand on the boy's shoulder and smiled into his young eyes. "That will be very delightful. Let us keep in touch."

There was a silence between them. The artist let fall his hand after pressing the boy's shoulder. The room had darkened, the blood-red Florida sunset flamed through the windows. Newsome long remembered that scene.

III

Mrs. Newsome arrived on the tenth. Mrs. Dugdale drove with Newsome to the airport to meet her coming from New York. The Atlantic crossing had been smooth, the flight perfect. Mrs. Newsome was a small, shy woman. Mrs. Dugdale put her at ease at once. They were given a large corner room overlooking the lawn and pool. Some guests had departed, others had arrived. For a week Mrs. Dugdale had behaved perfectly. She seemed spurred on by Jerry's finished portrait. She was prompt and patient for five consecutive mornings.

A New York ballet company was performing in Miami. Mrs. Dugdale booked seats for her house-party, but some of them were not destined to see it. At five o'clock that afternoon Bobo Gehr appeared, dishevelled, tears streaming down his face.

D

"My darling Marie's dead!" he announced.

"Bobo, what are you saying?" exclaimed Mrs. Dugdale, getting up from a chaise-longue.

"She's dead! Dead! I tell you, my Marie's dead! She went to bed for her siesta. When she didn't ring for tea, as usual, on waking, the maid went in. She didn't answer or move. The maid fetched me—I saw she was dead. The doctor's just been. It was a heart attack!"

He flung himself in a chair, covered his face with his hands and sobbed. It was half an hour before he was capable of returning to *Sunrise*, accompanied by Mrs. Dugdale and Newsome.

IV

Whatever their relationship had been there was no doubt that Bobo's grief was genuine. After the funeral he slept at *El Mirador* for four nights. He haunted Newsome's studio to a point of inconveniencing him. He turned Newsome into a father-confessor. It transpired that on the morning of his wife's death there had been a high-worded duel between them. It had all arisen over the gas bill for the car. In one of her recurrent fits of parsimony, often followed by loose generosity, she had upbraided him for extravagance, for utter indifference to her interests. He had retorted with lively reproaches. Exasperated, he had called her a mean old bitch. "Get out! Pack your bag and get out, you louse!" she had cried. He began to pack. Then she came up into the bedroom and cried, "You can't leave me, Bobo. You can't leave me!" After a time there was a reconciliation, but neither of them had eaten any lunch, they were so upset. "I should never have said what I did. I should have held my tongue. We'd had scenes before, she'd ordered me out before, but she had never really meant it. Calling her a mean bitch upset her. I can't think what came over me. I feel I've killed her. She had that heart attack because of me!" cried Bobo, his face pressed into his hands as he sat in the studio.

"A heart attack at eighty-six can happen to anyone, my good fellow. You must pull yourself together," said Newsome.

"She'd have lived to be a hundred. She'd a wonderful constitution. I killed her, I know I did!" cried Bobo.

He was still distraught and inconsolable after the funeral. The doctor gave him tranquillizers. Newsome went over to see him several times. He always found him seated in the patio by his wife's chair, facing the cage with Timmy, the green budgerigar.

"He talks to me. He says, 'Marie, darling' like she used to. He knows she's gone. I feel she's talking to me through him!" cried Bobo.

He began to drink hard. He had never been a drinker. "I don't know what's going to happen to me—to all this. Her sons have been very good, they've told me to stay on and not to worry about anything yet. Well, I shall know tomorrow. I'm to see poor Marie's Will."

The next day at noon he was back at *El Mirador*. He interrupted a sitting with Mrs. Dugdale.

"I know I'm in the way but I must talk to someone. I've had an awful blow at the attorney's," he said, collapsing in a chair and wiping his face with a black-bordered handkerchief. "Marie made a new Will. She's left me everything she could—the house, furniture, pictures, jewellery, furs and cars. And her cash. She must have been tucking it away for me, saving from her trust. She's left me half a million dollars."

He appeared distressed by the amount. "I won't take it. I won't take it, how can I? I killed her!" he cried.

"Now Bobo, don't be foolish! Half a million dollars isn't so much, after all. Marie wanted you to have it. You know she was really fond of you and that's why she saved the money," said Mrs. Dugdale.

"I called her a mean bitch—I can never forgive myself!" he cried. "Never! Never!"

They did their utmost to pursuade him that he was entitled to the legacy. He listened to them in a state of muddled unbelief.

Very odd, thought Newsome, reflecting on events. Here was a young man who had sold himself to an old woman, obviously anticipating that she could not live long at her age and that he would inherit a comfortable living, and who now became afflicted on receiving more than his expectations.

In the ensuing days it became clear that Bobo had persuaded himself that a great love affair had come to a sudden end. He became tiresome in his recital of poor dear Marie's virtues. He transformed her into a great beauty, a woman of unfathomable generosity. He sat in front of the bird-cage and harassed the budgerigar by inducing it to repeat "Marie, darling".

Then one day he startled them by saying he had released all the birds in the aviary.

"Released them?" asked Mrs. Dugdale. "Bobo, whatever do you mean? You've let them all out?"

"Yes. Some didn't want to go. They're all evil, but I shooed them out! I don't want any birds to be chattering away and interrupting what Marie wants to say to me. Have you ever heard of Pythagoras and the transmigration of souls? Marie's talking to me through Timmy. I don't want to hear any other bird."

"Bobo, are you crazy! Those poor birds! Don't you know that they'll all be killed by the other birds?" asked Mrs. Dugdale.

"What if they are! They're evil birds! They screech and laugh. They hate Timmy because he comforts me," replied Bobo, fiercely.

Mrs. Dugdale and Newsome exchanged glances.

"Look, Bobo, I've got an idea. You shouldn't be in the house alone. Come over to us," said Mrs. Dugdale.

"Thank you, but no. I must stay. I can't leave Timmy."

"Bring Timmy with you."

"That would not do. Marie would come and not find him."

"Would you like Mrs. Newsome and me to come and sleep at your house awhile?" asked Newsome.

The strain left Bobo's face at once. "I should like nothing better! Would you?" he asked. "You see, I belong to nobody. I've not a relation in the whole world!"

So it was agreed. The Newsomes moved to *Sunrise*.

V

They had been there a week when it was discovered that Bobo was visiting a psychoanalyst in Miami.

"My God! If those charlatans get hold of him he's lost!" exclaimed Newsome.

"Don't interfere. If it gives him any comfort, let him do it," said his wife.

A week passed. Bobo seemed calmer. Every night he retired to bed carrying the bird-cage with the green budgerigar. It occupied the bedside table where it had stood when Marie was alive. He brought it with him out on the terrace at breakfast. They all breakfasted together.

Bobo's house was efficiently run by a coloured butler and two maids. In the mornings he sat in the patio reading the newspaper. From time to time he talked to the bird. "Chic-chick," he said, "Marie! Marie!" it replied, its head on one side, climbing up and down one of the wires. Every morning he cleaned the cage, sanded the bottom, and put water and greenstuff in the cups.

He never looked at the long, empty aviary. It was as if it had never existed. There was not a sign of its former hundred birds. Nor did he show any interest in his collection of humming-birds. Newsome looked at the cases in the hall and asked him about various birds. He answered perfunctorily. There was not a vestige of his former passion for them.

Each morning Newsome went back to *El Mirador* and worked on Mrs. Hutton's portrait, then he went up into the tower for the sitting with his hostess. He was happier now. The work progressed. He broke his rule and let Mrs. Dugdale view the canvas. "You've made me very young," she said.

"I see you very young," he replied.

He missed Jerry, whose portrait now hung in the salon. They hoped to meet in London next summer. His wife found friends among the house guests. How easy Americans were to know! She loved the warm days, the pool before lunch when Mrs. Dugdale, the sitting ended, swam with them. But pressed, as always, she sometimes dictated letters to the typist and gave instructions to Miss Fawthorpe while swimming or coming up out of the water, svelte, head encased in a red rubber helmet which made her face petite. She had the figure of a young woman and swam well despite the handicap left by her slight stroke. Just now she was very busy arranging for a garden party for forty children from an orphanage. Every one was to have a present, individually wrapped and labelled.

The butler brought a tray of cocktails to the summer house. Ten guests arrived for lunch, which would be late, for the hostess, disappearing with Adèle into the dressing-room, would take at least half an hour to get ready.

After lunch there was a general siesta but some guests went to the bridge tables. Bobo was a good bridge player but these days he lacked concentration and annoyed his partner by his indifference. Newsome went up to his room in the tower and worked over his canvas. Two more weeks would see it finished. Mrs. Hutton's portrait was almost finished too. By the middle of February they would think of leaving. It had been a wonderful and profitable holiday. The thought of London in the dark and damp, and of surly Lord Hinchlow, made him reluctant to depart.

One afternoon Newsome motored into Miami to see a frame-maker about crating the two portraits for despatch to London. He was sending them both to the Academy Summer Exhibition. Mrs. Dugdale and the Huttons were going over for it.

When Newsome returned his wife was waiting for him, anxiety in her face.

"Henry, the most frightful thing's happened!" she said, "Timmy's escaped!"

"Timmy?"

"Bobo's bird. He's in the most terrible state. Mrs. Dugdale's out and I don't know what to do about him. He's quite demented."

"Where is he?"

"Over at the house. At four o'clock, when we were playing bridge, he suddenly said he couldn't go on. He was certain something dreadful had happened. We told him not to be silly and made him resume playing. It was hopeless. His hand shook and he'd no idea what he was dealing. So we gave up and he went off. François had just brought in the tea tray when Bobo returned. You never saw such a spectacle. He came in like a windstorm, shaking and shouting 'He's gone! He's gone! Marie's got him! She couldn't trust me! She's taken him!' At first we didn't realize what it was all about. Then we heard what had happened. When he got back to the house he went into the patio to feed the bird. The wind must have caught the pedestal table. It had gone over and the cage was on the ground. Its door was open and Timmy had flown. The servants were all out except Lena, the cook. When Bobo went into the kitchen he looked so terrible that she screamed and ran out of the house. She came over here. François, Miss Fawthorpe and I went back with Bobo. We went through all the rooms, hoping the frightened bird might have flown into the house. It wasn't there. Bobo flung himself on the bed, crying and shouting 'Marie's taken Timmy! I knew she wouldn't trust me!' He repeated it over and over. Finally we called the doctor who gave him a sedative. What an afternoon! What a fuss about a ridiculous bird!"

"The poor chap's unbalanced. He's not been normal since his wife's death. He was obsessed by that bird."

"Françoise and Miss Fawthorpe are over there now—until they can get his butler back. I think we should go across," said Mrs. Newsome.

He agreed. They walked over to *Sunrise*. They found Miss Fawthorpe there, cool and capable as usual.

"Where is he?" asked Newsome.

"Upstairs, sleeping. The doctor gave him a shot. The butler's returned."

They went out into the patio. The empty cage was now upright on the flagstone, near the small table. It was easy to see what had happened. A sudden forceful eddy of wind, blowing strongly from the ocean, had overthrown the light pedestal table and the cage. Newsome picked up the cage and examined it. It was in no way damaged. The jolt had unhinged the door and enabled the frightened bird to fly out. It was a stroke of bad fortune that it should have happened at all. The bird-cage was always taken in at sundown, and during the day stood by the patio table where they took breakfast. It was in exactly the position where Newsome had first seen Timmy behind old Mrs. Gehr. Bobo had been most precise about the cage's position. It never varied an inch from day to day. It seemed as if for once the wind had maliciously upset the table.

VI

All the next week, after the tragedy, Bobo was subdued. He was so subdued, so listless, that they felt alarmed. At meals he scarcely talked. The Newsomes now lived at *Sunrise* so that he should not be alone.

"Now Bobo, you're not going to make yourself ill over a silly bird!" said Mrs. Dugdale, playfully.

He flared up. "Silly! You call it silly, do you? You none of you care a damn about poor Marie. Her soul was in that bird but you've none of you any souls—you're only animated bodies!" He jumped up and rushed out of the room.

The next day he apologized. "You're very kind," he said to Newsome. "I don't know what I should have done without you."

He seemed very busy these days, motoring frequently into Miami. He never told them what he was doing. Possibly he had decided to give up the house. One morning a large van arrived. In the hall Bobo stood supervising the removal of the cases of humming-birds.

"I don't want any birds around," he said. "I know Timmy was jealous of them. I've given them to the Museum."

He said no more. One by one the cases disappeared in the van. The great hall looked very empty. One thing he retained, Timmy's cage. Every day it stood in the patio, every evening Bobo took it up to his bedroom. He kept the cage door wide open.

"The Massa's sure strange, suh! I hear him talkin' to the bird-cage as if Timmy war thar!" said Jesse, the butler.

The doctor was still in attendance. Bobo complained of sleeplessness. In the daytime he sat for hours in the patio by the bird-cage, not speaking.

"I'm getting a little unnerved," said Mrs. Newsome. "If only he would talk, or do something!"

"Poor chap! He's certainly taking it very hard," commented her husband. "Well, in a little while we'll be gone. We must stick it out until he's more normal."

"Was he very much in love with his wife?"

Newsome paused. "I really don't know what you'd call it. He quite frankly admitted he'd married the old girl for her money—but in a way I think he must have been fond of her."

"But there was forty-two years' difference between them. I find it incredible!"

"I find many things incredible, my dear. It seems to work both ways. I see in the paper this morning that a Justice of the Supreme Court of the United States, at sixty-three, has married a girl of twenty-three. That's forty years. And it's his third marriage, following a divorce. 'Man is most curiously made', said one of our poets."

VII

One morning while they were dressing there was a tapping on their bedroom door. When Newsome opened it Jesse, the butler, stood there, the whites of his eyes showing in his black face.

"You'll pardon me, suh, but it's Massa Gehr," he said, breathless.

"Yes?"

"I jest took him his marnin' coffee, as he likes, on waking, and he doesn't answer me, he's so fast asleep. I shouted an' I shook him. He jest sleeps."

"A moment. I'll come along," answered Newsome. He put on a dressing-gown, and followed the butler to Bobo's bedroom. The butler drew the Venetian blinds, revealing the bright sunshine over the blue Bay. The room was in perfect order. The bird-cage stood on the bedside table.

Newsome went over to the bed. "Bobo!" he called. "Bobo!"

There was no movement, no answer. The sheet was high up over his face. Newsome pulled it down and shook the sleeper.

Then, seeing no response, he peered down at the calm face. Gently he pushed back an eyelid.

"You must send for the doctor, Jesse," he said, straightening.

"The doctor, suh! Massa Gehr's no dead?"

"I fear so. Let no one in the room until the doctor comes," he said.

CHAPTER 5

I

BOBO GEHR WAS DEAD. The inquest confirmed that he had taken a whole bottle of prolixin, the tranquillizer the doctor had prescribed. A verdict of death from misadventure was returned. He was buried with his wife. There was only a handful of mourners. His stepsons and their wives were not present, it was a long journey to make twice within a few weeks.

Newsome and his wife moved back to *El Mirador*. They were suffering from shock. Newsome could not help liking the odd little man. He had been friendly and generous. The fault that had undermined his life lay deeper than weakness of character, for in some ways he was tenacious as well as gifted. He was psychologically unbalanced, with no controlling faith except material security, a vain thing in a mutable world. He had cast his line and caught something powerful enough to drown him. Where reality had failed, illusion took possession and destroyed him.

There was much speculation as to what would happen to *Sunrise* and its contents, and the fortune he had inherited from Marie. No one knew whether the probate on her estate had been settled yet. It was Mr. Hutton who came with the news that it had. He had gone into Miami, paid a dollar at the County Judge's Office, and read the Will. *Sunrise* had been assessed at eighty thousand dollars, Mrs. Gehr's jewellery at fifty thousand. All told, Bobo had inherited a clear, tax-paid, estate of some four hundred thousand dollars. He would not have been able to keep up *Sunrise* in its former style but he certainly would not have been pinched. What he had played for he had got, and lost.

One morning Newsome was called to the telephone. A voice asked—"Am I speaking with Mr. Henry Newsome, of the Savile Club, London?"

"Yes," said Newsome, surprised.

"You are the Royal Academician who has painted a portrait of Mrs. Dugdale, your hostess?"

"I am, why are you asking?"

"You were a friend of the late Mr. Robinson Gehr. I am James Halliday of Halliday, Sansom and Oppenheim. We are attorneys for the estate of the late Mr. Gehr. I would, at your convenience, like to see you. I could come to you, or you to me."

"Is it in order for me to ask in what manner I am concerned with Mr. Gehr's estate?" asked Newsome.

"Yes. You are a legatee. I would rather not say more over the telephone."

"Very well. I will come to see you. Is this morning suitable— say, eleven?"

"Sure! Our office is in Scheerman Building, Delroy Boulevard."

"I know it," said Newsome. "I waited once in Mr. Gehr's car while he went in to see you."

"Good. At eleven, then?"

Newsome put down the receiver. He found his wife sewing under an orange tree and told her the news.

"Does that mean he's left us something? How extraordinary!" said Mrs. Newsome, dropping her sewing. "I wonder what!"

"I hope not that bird-cage!" laughed Newsome. "I hope it's a piece of his wife's jewellery for you. What an extraordinary man!"

II

Newsome returned at noon. He found the house-party in the pool, including his wife and hostess. It was a hot sticky day with no air. As he hoped, his wife had said nothing. He gulped down two cocktails from the tray. He was sweating heavily. His wife got out of the pool and came up to him, dripping. "Well?" she asked.

"It's not a piece of jewellery," he said quietly. "Get dressed and come to our room. I don't want to talk here."

He was standing by the window looking down on the garden when she came in. "Well, what has he left us? I can't wait," she asked.

"Sit down. You may faint."

She sat down. He took a chair, placed it in front of him, looked at her for a few moments and then spoke.

"My dear girl, don't think I'm out of my wits. Bobo Gehr's left us everything!"

"Everything?"

"Everything! House, contents, jewellery, furs, cars, shares, cash—everything! It was a thirty-line Will only. He made it two weeks before he died."

"Everything! But it is quite unbelievable!" cried Mrs. Newsome.

"My whole time here has been somewhat unbelievable—the whole set-up, and this climate in winter."

"Did the lawyer give you any idea how much it all comes to?"

"Yes. He said that, after Probate duty, etc., the estate was worth around one hundred and eighty thousand dollars—some seventy thousand pounds. It depends partly on what the house and contents fetch. Anyhow, it's a staggering sum!"

"Did he leave anything to relations?"

"Apparently he had none. I am the sole legatee."

"To the servants?"

"Nothing. We must look after that," said Newsome.

"I still can't believe it!"

"Nor I. And to think we owe it all to that green budgerigar!"

"What do you mean?" asked Mrs. Newsome.

"If that bird hadn't escaped Bobo would be alive."

III

For a week it was a sensation in Coconut Grove, then the lime-light was switched elsewhere. A business tycoon, living on a fifty-acre estate, shot himself. It seemed clear suicide. It proved to be suicide and murder. It was a *crime passionel*. He had dis-covered that his wife was unfaithful. He had shot her first and then himself. Her body, missing for four days, was found in the "deep freeze" where he had stuffed her. Then an enormous fire, north of Miami, took the headlines.

After considering the matter Newsome decided, while *Sunrise* was up for sale, to live there until the end of April. There seemed no reason to hurry back to the English winter. This was their great opportunity. But what about Lord Hinchlow's portrait, asked his wife. It was due for the Summer Academy.

"Hang Lord Hinchlow or rather I won't 'hang' him. He kept me waiting long enough. I'll keep him waiting. That'll be a new experience for his lordship—no one's ever dared to snap their fingers at him!"

So they settled in at *Sunrise*. The pool of life grew placid again. The days were halcyon, the velvet nights were spangled with stars and full of hidden scents. They were fussed over by the soft-footed, soft-voiced Jesse, who rolled his eyes and said "Yassuh" and "No suh" and "No ma'am."

They had been installed a week when, one morning, Mrs. Newsome went into the back room where her husband was painting a flower composition.

"I want you to come with me," she said.

"What is it?"

"Come with me!" she said, laconically.

He got up and followed her. She led him out to the patio and halted by the door.

"Look!" she said, softly.

He looked. In the corner, on the pedestal table, stood the bird-cage. In the cage, on the perch, sat the green budgerigar.

"Bless me! It's Timmy—he's returned!" he exclaimed.

After a few moments of wonder he stealthily approached, and closed the door of the cage.

BOOK 2

The Swallow

CHAPTER 1

1

MONSIEUR EMILE VILLARDON found at last a place in which to park his small Renault car. The side street was crowded with shoppers and he was dismayed to see that the shops were still full although it was past eleven o'clock. Shopping was something of a nightmare these days in Paris, which had one million too many people in it, he complained. If you went early to the butcher's, the greengrocer's, the baker's, you stood in a mob of women, expert in getting served out of turn; if you went late then the best cuts, the freshest vegetables, the kind of bread one liked, were gone. Even at eleven o'clock, when all the women ought to be home cooking the day's lunch, the counters were crowded.

Monsieur Villardon got out of his car, picked up a cloth bag, felt in his pocket to make sure he had his shopping list, and began his quest. He worked his way from shop to shop. He came out of the butcher's with something he did not really want, after an interminable wait. He had picked over the lettuces in the greengrocer's and emerged with a shrivelled specimen; all the best had gone an hour ago. At the grocer's his favourite cheese was out of stock, also the canned soup he wanted. His eye glanced along the shelves. He collected six tins and put them in his bag. More and more he was living on tinned foods. They were easier to buy, easier to cook, but he was not happy over his choice, he preferred fresh things, richer in vitamins. Tinned foods were resorted to by lazy housewives, bachelors and widowers. He was in the last category. He cooked, he ate, he washed up alone. It was no kind of life at all, but this was the life he had been living these last three years since the death of Sophie. During her life the cuisine had not been much better. She disliked the kitchen. Her repertoire had consisted of six dishes, over and over again. He knew the day of the week by the dish she served. Happily, at the insurance

65

office where he had worked, they had a staff dining-canteen. There he had variety, the dishes were hot, and they talked over their food. At home Sophie had never talked at table. She propped up her latest novel brought back from the subscription library, and shovelled the food into her mouth, hardly aware of what she was eating. It was the same with her clothes. She had worn anything, anyhow. Her hair had always looked as if she had come in out of the wind.

The shopping list finished, Emile got back into his car. He lived in a grey apartment-block off the Boulevard Maillot. He was on the third floor, the windows looked into a dark court-yard. He had always intended leaving the place but his wife had objected to the trouble of moving. Indifferent to daylight, she had lived with the light on. She sewed, read, cooked and even slept with the light on. Their electricity bill had been ridiculous.

Emile climbed the stairs, opened the door and deposited the cloth bag on the table. He sorted out the contents and then placed them in the refrigerator and on the shelves in the kitchen. The cat came in and bothered him. He knew what it wanted. He took the milk jug out of the refrigerator, filled a saucer and put it down for the cat. He noticed that the jug was almost empty. He would have to go out again for some milk. Also, somehow, he had forgotten the butter.

Dismayed, he noticed that the woman had not been in to clean. The pots he had left for her in the sink were unwashed. She came in three times a week, Tuesday, Thursday and Saturday for an hour, if she came at all. She was a woman who seemed to be visited by recurrent domestic tragedies, a sprained ankle, a small boy with mumps, a husband with lumbago, a sick sister who had come on a visit and just could not be left. He would have dismissed her, but knew he might fare worse. He had dismissed five in three years. Two more had simply ceased to come in.

Monsieur Villardon's sister, Fanny, paid him boisterous visits at unpredictable intervals, and told him that he lived in a state of filth. Nevertheless, he was greatly relieved when she came in just after he had put away the groceries. She began at once to tidy the place.

"How long have you been sleeping in these sheets—they're black! Why hasn't that woman changed them?" she demanded, stripping the bed. She went to the linen cupboard to get clean ones.

"I don't understand," she said, looking at the shelves. "You used to have a lot more sheets. That was one thing Sophie was particular about—the linen. She hemmed and embroidered beautifully. I'll say that of her."

"I suppose the sheets got lost in the laundry," said Emile.

"That's taking a charitable view!"

"Oh, I think the woman's honest."

"Well, I don't! You should keep a list, and check the laundry when it returns," said his sister, making the bed. This finished, she stood up, paused, and looked at him with kind eyes. "Emile, this is no way to live. You're going downhill. Look at those shoes! It's time you threw them away. They're disgraceful! You want someone to look after you. You ought to get married again. Mousing around in this fashion is ridiculous!"

"Who's going to marry an old man of over sixty?"

"You're not an old man. You're not at all bad-looking. I'm fifty-six and I consider myself a young woman."

"You are, my dear. Jean's a very lucky fellow."

"Just because you were unlucky once there's no reason why you shouldn't do better next time. Life begins tomorrow, I say."

"I don't think you should talk like that of poor Sophie," said Emile. "Anyhow, I'll never marry again. It's too great a risk at my age—and only someone desperate would take me on. Out of the frying-pan into the fire."

"I'd sooner be burnt up in the fire than live in a dirty frying-pan," retorted Fanny. "Now give me a hand with this rug—it's not been shaken for a month. I can't stay, Emile, I'm meeting Marie Dufresne for lunch at Printemps, and then we're going to a cinema."

When Fanny had departed, having effected a swift transformation in the apartment, Emile sat down for a moment before getting his lunch. He felt tired. Fanny was a dynamic woman, kind, downright but exhausting. Her enjoyment of life dismayed him. At thirty she had given up a career as a school-teacher to marry Jean, who worked in a bank. They had three children, a boy and two girls. She kept house, looked after them, cooked, dressmade, and yet always had time to be going around. She went canoeing on the Seine with Jean, loved a game of skittles, and roller-skated with the children at the local rink. Emile had seen more of her since Sophie's death. They had never got on together and she had kept away. "A lazy puss!" said Fanny. "Vulgar!" said Sophie.

His wife's photograph stood in a leather frame on a side table. She had been a very pretty woman. Everyone agreed on that. Her health had always been poor. "She enjoyed being ill," said Fanny, caustically. That was being unfair. They had had no children. She had never wanted children. "They pull you down," she said. He would have liked two or three children. He looked enviously on Fanny and Jean. They were not threatened with a lonely old age.

Emile got up and went into the kitchen. He began to lay plates, a knife and fork, a bottle of wine, on the kitchen table. It was covered with an oilcloth. He paused, looking at the table. No, he must not get into this lazy way of eating, pigging it in the kitchen. There was no dignity in living like this. He went into the dining-room, took a tablecloth out of the sideboard and laid the table properly, with a cut-glass wineglass for his wine and a clean napkin. He brought the plates, knife, fork, out of the kitchen and placed them neatly on the white cloth. He took a small vase of flowers off a shelf and put it in the centre. He looked at the table, pleased with the effect. One must not get slovenly. Fanny was quite right, he must throw away his old shoes and get a new pair.

There was something his sister did not understand. Life had been more difficult since he had been pensioned off at the office, Time hung heavily on his hands. He played a little tennis, golf and bowls but discovered that he was always in the company of other pensionnaires. There was no one young around, they were all at business. The talk about past events, misfortunes, ill-health and general dissatisfaction with life, bored him. He had enjoyed having young people around him in their large office, alert, ambitious youngsters, smart clerks and pretty typists. Now he was in a backwater. It was a blow when they retired him at sixty. It was all nonsense, he was good for another ten years. But that was the rule and out he went, as others had gone before him.

He returned to the kitchen, opened a glass jar of tongue and a tin of beans which he heated up in a saucepan. He tore off the withered outer leaves of the lettuce, sliced a tomato, mixed a dressing of oil and vinegar. The beans heated, he emptied them on to a dish. Then he carried his lunch into the dining-room. The cat mewed around him. Milk was not enough. He got up, went back into the kitchen, cut her a slice of tongue and put it on a plate, which she walked round suspiciously several times.

"That's all I've got for you just now," he said, and went back to the dining-room, picking up the newspaper, which he propped up against a toast rack. He read while he ate, with growing impatience about a political squabble. Perhaps it was real, perhaps it was not. The newspapers had to fill up with reading stuff, to carry the advertisements. In any case it did not matter, the politicians were all calling one another names as they had a hundred years back and would for a hundred hence.

His lunch finished, Emile drank a second glass of wine. It helped him to sleep. He got up, removed the dishes, washed them and then went into the bedroom and took off his disreputable shoes. He would have his usual nap. At four o'clock he would go out, buy some milk and butter. Perhaps also he would get a new pair of shoes for Fanny's sake.

Emile had just placed himself on the bed when the bell rang. It was most unusual. The bell seldom rang these days, never in the afternoon. It could not be the charwoman, she came in the mornings, and had a key. He hesitated about getting up. It was probably a tout hawking something. The bell rang again, then again. The caller was persistent. Emile got up, buttoned his waistcoat, and the top of his trousers which he had let out, put on some slippers, and, still in his shirt sleeves, went to the door and opened it suspiciously.

"Emile!" said a voice.

"*Mon Dieu!* Etienne!" cried Emile.

He opened wide the door. They fell into a tight embrace, kissing each other. They had served in the infantry together in the Great War and came out unscathed through the hell of Verdun. Etienne Dunois had been the best man at his wedding thirty-five years ago. He was his oldest, dearest surviving friend. But these years he seldom saw him. His business had taken him to Lyons.

"I'm here for two weeks, on business, very unexpectedly," said Etienne, standing back and looking at his friend. "Have I broken your nap?"

"No—where's your bag?"

"In the taxi. I've just arrived. I thought I might find you in and we'll dine tonight."

"You go down now and get your bag. You're staying here, if you don't mind camping. I've only a woman that doesn't come in," said Emile, his face beaming.

"You're sure it's convenient?"

"Sure!"

"I was hoping that perhaps you could," laughed Etienne, giving Emile's ear a tug. "I'll go and get my bag."

He turned and went down the stairs. Emile watched him, standing at the door. Etienne was very agile at sixty-five. They hadn't retired him. He was thinner and taller but he wore glasses, whereas he himself could read and write without them. He waited by the door until his friend came up again, carrying a bag. He was not at all puffed by three flights.

"How's Françoise?" asked Emile as he closed the hall door.

"Fine—she sends her love."

"And Louise, Theodore, Julie?" naming the children.

"Fine, Emile, thanks. Julie's had her second child. Theodore's expecting an addition. Louise's eldest, Jean, has graduated."

"Well now, would you believe it! A father three times and a grandfather five! You're a lucky fellow, Etienne!"

"I am! Do you remember how we sat in a trench, wet to the skin, and said if ever we came through, we'd have three boys and three girls each—we forgot the grandchildren!"

"They all forgot me," said Emile, quietly.

"Ah, yes, yes. I've been very lucky," commented Etienne, conscious he had been too exuberant and tactless.

Emile opened a door. "This will be your room—I'll make up the bed. There's a door direct into the bathroom." He drew up a Venetian blind. It let in only a little light. He switched on a chandelier, opened a wardrobe. "There are plenty of hangers."

Etienne opened his bag. Emile pulled out some drawers for his things.

"How are you liking a retired life?" asked Etienne.

"I'm not. I'm bored to death. I'm going downhill, old boy. The less I do the less I want to do."

"Oh, nonsense! You're a pretty resourceful fellow, I'm sure!" replied Etienne cheerfully, hanging a suit.

II

In the course of the next few days it became clear to Etienne that his friend *was* going downhill. He appeared listless. Twice in a cinema he had fallen asleep. He noticed that he could not concentrate on a newspaper. And there was no ignoring the fact that the apartment was run down. There were rents in the bedsheets, holes in the towels. The lavatory wanted a handle on the chain. There had been no toilet paper one morning. The two easy chairs in the sitting-room required new covers. The slats in one of the Venetian blinds hung askew. Nothing gave such a dilapidated air to a room as a broken blind. Then the food. Their breakfasts were good. Emile made excellent coffee and toast. He made it while Etienne was in the bathroom and he would not let him do a thing in the kitchen. Happily Etienne lunched out, being on business all day.

There had been two evenings when Emile had insisted on their dining in. "It's more cosy than going out," he said. The dinner proved disastrous. The steak was uneatable, the vegetables had come out of a tin. The sweet, an apple tart, had been bought and was tasteless, leathery and full of glucose. On the pretext that he really could not let Emile do so much work in the kitchen, Etienne insisted that they went to a restaurant. They had a fight over the bill each time, and came to an alternating arrangement. All this perturbed Etienne, coming from a home in which the cooking was excellent and varied. There was also something else, there was laughter at the table. Now that the children were married they had friends in. They dined with each other, had bridge-parties. The current of life flowed cheerily. Poor Emile's abode was like a deserted monastery. Etienne knew his friend's marriage had not been happy. Sophie had been peevish and self-absorbed. But at least there was another live person in the house and things were taken care of.

One evening, after dining in a restaurant, Etienne delicately broached the subject on his mind.

"Have you tried getting a good housekeeper?" he asked, having lit a cigar, and toying with his liqueur.

Emile was silent for a few moments, drew slowly on his cigar and then spoke. "I've tried twice. One drank, the other wanted to get into bed with me. In both cases the bills were frightful. Good housekeepers went out with horse cabs."

Emile revolved his cigar slowly between his fingers. He liked the aroma. They had dined well. "I had another experience," he continued. "The domestic agency recommended a man-servant. He was a paragon. He cooked marvellously, he was quick and clean and very honest. The place shone. I was in clover. He had only two faults—and they weren't things I could really complain about. He was a good-looking lad, always smartly dressed. He had wavy chestnut-brown hair and on it he used an awful hair cream. It smelt of cheap scent. The other thing I didn't like was the hours he kept. I used to hear him coming in at two and three in the morning—I'm a bad sleeper, you know. As he was never late in the morning with breakfast I felt I had no right to complain. I made a joke about his hours, just to let him know I knew. He smiled at me— he had a nice smile—it bowled over the concierge's daughter— and said 'I'm always very quiet, m'sieur. If you sleep badly you should take a sleeping-pill.' It was rather impertinent, I thought, but he said it so nicely that I felt perhaps I was wrong. Sometimes I heard movements in the apartment—he was going to the bathroom, I told myself. Then one night I was certain I heard voices. There was a light in the hall. It was five a.m. I got up. He was in his pyjamas and he was letting someone out. I told him what I thought, and that I couldn't have that sort of thing. He looked at me quite calmly and said 'M'sieur, I recommended you to take a sleeping-pill. As for what you say, I have as much right to lead my own life as you have. I've not inconvenienced you or robbed you and I've done my work conscientiously.' Of course, I got rid of him. He had the impertinence to send me a Christmas card! After that it's been a series of 'dailies'. I didn't know there were so many sluts in the world."

Etienne called the waiter and ordered more coffee and liqueurs. There was a long comfortable silence between the two friends. Then, after lighting another cigar, Etienne spoke.

"Emile, *mon cher*, I've been thinking a lot about you these days. I'm not happy about you. I'm going to make a suggestion."

Emile glanced at him sharply, and said—"I hope, like all the others, you're not going to urge me to get married again."

"Yes, I am," answered Etienne. "It's the obvious and sensible thing. It's idiotic to go on like this. You'll turn mental if you continue living alone."

"I should turn mental if I had a wife on my back! I don't have to disguise from you that my last marriage was a failure."

"We knew that, Françoise and I."

"What I'm going to say to you is a terrible thing, but it's a fact I can't ignore. Sophie's death was a happy release for me. Looking back I don't know how I stood it all those years. She never made a cosy home for me. She was always discontented. She refused to have children. For the last fifteen years we never slept together. She never wanted to go anywhere. She sat and read those trashy novels until you'd have thought her eyes would fall out. All she thought of was saving. Her one extravagance was electric light. She kept all the windows closed and all the lights on. She turned the place into a glaring bird-cage."

"But didn't you put your foot down? If you give way to some women they're relentless tyrants," observed Etienne. "I only once had trouble that way. Françoise is as sensible a woman as ever lived, but about one thing she had an obsession. You'll scarcely believe me when I tell you what it was. She violently objected to me sleeping in a nightgown! She begged me to wear pyjamas—hateful things. It came to a point where she actually bought me a pair and said she wouldn't sleep with me unless I wore them."

"Did you?"

"I certainly did not! I said that if I couldn't wear a nightgown I wouldn't wear anything. I carried out my threat. I got into bed naked. That ended the trouble!" exclaimed Etienne, taking a long pull at his cigar.

"I notice you wear a nightgown. I'm surprised you can still get them. Odd of you—but we're all odd in one way or another!" commented Emile.

"Let's return to the subject, *mon vieux*. I'm of the opinion you should marry again—a nice little woman who would sweeten your last years."

"Thank you. Once was enough. Start all over again at sixty-one? I should be mad!"

"There are women and women. There are some very nice widows around, *mon cher*."

"Oh, have you one in mind?" growled Emile, a little out of patience with his friend.

"I have," said Etienne, quietly. "A very nice little woman. She's a widow, and like you, lonely."

"So she's asked you to find her a husband! Don't waste any time on me. Quite frankly, I'm not her or your man," said Emile, drawing hard on his cigar and sending the smoke out in a strong puff that expressed his determination.

"She has not said a word to me," replied Etienne. "But I know she's lonely. She has more reason to feel lonely than you have."

"How do you come to think that?"

"Because, *mon vieux*, she had a long and very happy married life. I lunched with her yesterday. I have a feeling that if she could marry happily again she would—and the fellow would be lucky."

"How well do you know her?"

"Pretty well—over thirty years. She's Eloise Vaux, my cousin."

"Oh, you've a family interest in her!"

"Now don't be sarcastic. I only wish to do two lonely and very nice persons a service," said Etienne, smiling at his friend.

"How old is she?"

"Fifty-five, and a grandmother."

"A grandmother!"

"She married at nineteen—a friend of mine, Henri Vaux, a chemist. They had a son and a daughter. The boy was killed in the last war. The daughter's happily married and has a child. Eloise has been a widow four years. She is still a pretty woman, slim and chic—with a sense of humour."

"Has she any money?" asked Emile, curtly.

"A little."

"If the woman has money and the man hasn't, it's quite fatal for him," said Emile.

"It can be fatal for both. I once heard a woman say that to be the widow of a rich man was the best thing in the world because she was free and the man couldn't change his mind. It's silly to say you can't be happy with money, whichever one has it. I know you can. My Françoise has some, I haven't. In Eloise's case the risk doesn't arise. She has to be careful with what she has. Now what about it? Let me introduce you. You could meet each other without any thought of anything more. Let me ask her to lunch with us, one day."

"No!" said Emile, firmly. "In the first place I'm not marrying anyone—not if she has all the virtues! Also, it would be very embarrassing. No!"

"You're afraid?"

"I'm not afraid of any woman. I just don't want to raise any false hopes. She'd know I was a widower, you'd have to tell her that, and also she'd know that I knew she was a widow."

There was a silence between the two friends.

"If you met a really nice little woman who was a good companion and who would make you a home, would you consider marrying?" asked Etienne.

"The proposition has too many if's, *mon cher*. You don't

realize what I went through," replied Emile. "I'm lonely, certainly, and I'm not living as I like, but I haven't a peevish hypochondriacal woman on my back."

"Eloise certainly doesn't fit that category. She's a very charming woman and made Henri very happy. I see no reason why you should not know the delights of a good home. Look, I've got an idea," said Etienne. "You don't want to risk anything, neither does she for that matter. Suppose you could see her without meeting her if you didn't wish to—would you take a look?"

Emile said nothing for a while. He moved uneasily in his chair. Then he looked at his friend suspiciously. "What's in your mind?"

"I've got a plan. Let me think it over."

"You're wasting your time, Etienne."

"There would be no waste of time if I could make you happy and see you living like a civilized man," said Etienne, quietly, putting his hand on his friend's knee.

CHAPTER 2

I

TWO DAYS BEFORE Etienne was due to return to Lyons he said to Emile, as they dined at Prunier's, "Well, I've seen the lady!"

"Who?"

"My cousin, Eloise Vaux, about whom I talked to you. I was very frank with her. Like you, she doesn't want to commit herself and she's somewhat embarrassed. So this is what I've arranged—"

"One minute," said Emile. "Just what does she know of me? You've not turned me into an Adonis?"

"On the contrary—you'll turn out better than I've painted you. Let me tell you, *mon vieux*, it took some time for me to persuade her to have a look at you!"

"And how's she going to do that?"

"This is the plan. You don't even have to admit you've seen each other. You know where the Rue du Colisée intersects the Rue de Ponthieu? There are two cafés on opposite corners. Next Friday night at nine o'clock she will go to the Café Plon, it's on the right-hand side as you come from the Champs Elysées, and in the inside room she'll take a coffee. You will go in and take one at the opposite side of the saloon. You will see a lady wearing a white hat with a swallow on it. That will be Eloise."

"And what do I do then?"

"If you like the look of her you will get up, go across to her, raise your hat, and in your best manner say 'Madame Vaux? I am Emile Villardon, Etienne's friend'. And for God's sake wear your best clothes!"

"And what if she doesn't like me?"

"Knowing Eloise, I don't think she'll fail to let you know— tactfully. You will ask her to have a drink with you. She will, of course, accept, your being her cousin's old friend—and then *le bon Dieu* takes care of the rest!"

77

"I don't quite know what you're letting me in for. Perhaps I'll not turn up," said Emile.

"Then you'll be very ungallant, and very rude to me. *Mon Dieu!* She's not a praying mantis! She's a very pretty, attractive woman with lots of sense."

"With lots of sense she wouldn't take on a battered old wreck like me—what's she going to get out of it?"

"Just what you're going to get, companionship and a happy home."

"You've left one important point unmentioned," said Emile.

"What's that?"

"Sex."

"My good fellow, I'm doing all I can for you, but that's something I'm not touching. That's up to you and Eloise. You can work that out between you. Now, will you go on Friday?"

"Must I commit myself?"

"No—even if you don't go there are no eggs broken, though it would be ungracious of you, after the trouble I'm taking."

"Very well. Perhaps I'll go," said Emile, reluctantly.

II

Etienne departed. For the next two days Emile was in a state of mental ferment. On Thursday morning he had decided he would not go to the Café Plon. On Thursday evening he thought that would be churlish, besides, he would like to look at Madame Vaux and see just what Etienne's cousin was like. On Friday morning, the fatal day, he was still undecided. He had his hair cut, the very little that was left over his ears, and collected the suit he had taken to be pressed. He could not eat his lunch. At four o'clock, unable to take his nap, he went to the bowling club and played badly for an hour. At seven o'clock he had a bath and got into a dressing-gown. He clipped some hairs in his nostrils and ears, trimmed his white moustache, then went into the kitchen to make himself a sandwich, but had no appetite.

"You're a silly old fool!" he said to himself, stumbling over the cat. "And she may not turn up. I don't even know her address!"

At half-past eight, dressed, he looked at himself in the mirror. Well, he wasn't too bad for his age. He did not stoop, his teeth were good, his eyes clear. He hated the brown spots that had come on the backs of his hands. "Age," said the doctor he consulted. "There's nothing to be done about them." He changed his tie twice, finally selecting a demure one into which he stuck a pearl pin. Then he took it out of the tie. It was one poor Sophie had given him on their twenty-fifth marriage anniversary. This was not an occasion for it.

He put on a light tan overcoat and took an umbrella. It was a cool evening of early spring. He went to the Metro and got out at Franklin-Roosevelt. As he walked towards the Rue du Colisée his hands and feet were cold. Nerves. He came to the crossroads. There was the café. For a moment he hesitated by the chairs and round-top tables. The cool night had driven the customers inside. He walked in and, without looking around, chose an empty corner seat and ordered a Pernod. Then he summoned courage to survey the saloon. It was quite full. Up at the bar every seat was taken. His eyes carefully travelled round the room. There was no woman sitting alone, no one with a swallow in a white hat. He looked at his watch. He was early, it was three minutes to nine. It was unlikely she would be prompt. Out of sheer coquetry she would keep him waiting.

The waiter brought his drink. From where he sat he could see anyone who came in at the door. He would be able to see her enter. He had bought an evening paper and pretended to read. At a quarter-past nine she had not appeared. He drank and read and waited. People came in at the door endlessly. But there was no woman in a swallow hat, no woman of any kind that fitted Etienne's account. He waited. He finished his drink and paper. It was now ten minutes to ten. He would go. It wasn't dignified to hang on like this. She had made a fool of him. She was probably at home laughing to herself at the thought of him waiting in the café. He folded his paper, put a tip in the saucer and drew on his gloves. He would wait until ten o'clock to make it a round hour. What a letter he would write to Etienne who was the cause of this!

At ten o'clock he got up and walked out. He paused for a moment thinking he would take a taxi home. Then something he saw made his heart stop. In red lights across the way, on the opposite corner, was the *Café Plon*! He had been waiting in the wrong café. Etienne had said "on the right", and it was on the left. He had not thought of looking for the name of the café he had entered.

Should he go in? It was not likely she would be still there, if she had come. She would have left, as angry as he was. After a few moments' hesitation he crossed the road and entered the Café Plon. It was full. He found an empty table just inside. He sat down, took off his gloves, and gave an order. Then he looked around, certain it was useless. Suddenly, half-way down, on a red plush banquette backed by a large gilt mirror, he saw a white hat with a swallow on it.

For a few moments he could not see clearly, as a line of customers obstructed the view of her face, and only the top of the hat was visible. Then as they moved he saw her face. She was alone and sat quietly looking in front of her. She had a round face with light brown hair drawn back over small ears that carried a pearl in each lobe. She wore a high necked grey silk bodice with a pendant of brilliants. Her complexion was fresh, her nose straight, and her eyebrows, arched, were well marked. She was a very pleasant-looking woman. It was almost impossible to believe that she was fifty-five, a grand-mother. She could have passed for a woman of forty-five.

His drink came, he was too agitated to touch it. If he did not move soon the lady might leave, tired of waiting. He got up and threaded his way through the tables towards the red banquette. She looked up at his approach.

"Madame Vaux?" he asked, hat in hand, bowing slightly.

"Yes?"

"I am Emile Villardon—Etienne's friend."

Was it possible he had blushed? His face felt very hot, his voice sounded unnatural.

"*Mais Oui!* He spoke of you," she said with a warm smile.

Then, after a pause, as he stood, self-conscious, before her—
"Won't you sit down, M'sieur Villardon?" She moved a little
to the right to make a place for him.

He sat down slowly, disposing of hat and umbrella.

"I must apologize," he began. "I have made the most stupid
mistake—I've been sitting for an hour in the wrong café, across
the way. Etienne said 'on the right' and I was foolish enough not
to look at the name of the café."

She laughed gaily, her eyes twinkling. "How extraordinary!
I thought perhaps you had come here and had gone," she
said.

"Gone?"

"Yes. You remember the arrangement. If you didn't like the
look of me you wouldn't speak," she said, without a trace of
embarrassment. "Also the traffic—it's often difficult to be on
time in Paris."

"Yes, yes, it is," he said, gratified by the turn she had given
to her comment. There was a silence. "Will you have a drink?"
he asked, a desperate remark, since he saw she had one.

"Thank you, I have one. And you?" she replied.

"Thank you, I have just ordered one. The waiter will bring
it over." He called the waiter and instructed him.

She had pretty hands. He had not dared to look at the colour
of her eyes, which had sweeping eyelashes. Her bodice fitted
her perfectly. She had a good bosom and neck, but slender. He
was relieved. He detested bosomy plump women. There was a
decided air about her. Etienne had not exaggerated. She was
chic. He became conscious of another thing, she had a most
pleasant, modulated speaking voice.

They discussed Etienne and Françoise, and their children.
They agreed that they were *très sympathiques*. He had seen her
eyes now. They were grey, with much animation. The subject
of Etienne and family exhausted, there were a few moments of
silence. She broke it with a question.

"Do you like music, M'sieur Villardon?"

"To be honest, I'm afraid I don't."

She laughed easily. "What a relief! Neither do I, so we need
not bore each other by talking about opera and opera stars, and

F

how they thrilled one as Mimi or failed as Carmen. The truth is I have no ear!"

"The truth is, Madame Vaux, if I may say so, you have a very pretty ear!"

He was surprised at himself. She raised a hand to the lobe of her ear and touched the pearl. "Well, my earrings are pretty. They are a present from Henri, my late husband."

"Ah, you are a widow?" he said. The moment the words had been spoken he knew the question was utterly fatuous. He knew perfectly well she was a widow. If she had not been, she would not be sitting here.

Madame Vaux ignored the silly question. "Henri had very good taste," she said. "I was never nervous when he was going to buy me something—he knew exactly what suited me. You have been a widower three years, Etienne told me, so you will understand what a loss I suffered."

"Indeed! Indeed! If I may say so, you are too young a woman to lose a husband," he said.

"Not young. How old do you think I am?" she asked, looking at him with dancing eyes.

"I should say—I should say, maybe forty-five?"

She threw back her head and laughed, "Oh, come now, M'sieur Villardon! You know I'm a grandmother, Etienne told you!"

"Yes, but there are grandmothers of forty-five."

"True. Well, I'm fifty-five. How old are you?"

"Sixty-one."

"Then I should say we have both taken good care of ourselves, and *le bon Dieu* has been kind!" she said and finished her drink.

He called the waiter and ordered fresh drinks. What a very sensible woman. No humbug about age!

"I hope your marriage was as happy as mine. I've a very lovely daughter and son-in-law."

"Er—yes, yes. Alas, I have no children," he said. Then Etienne had not told her the truth about his marriage. He became conscious of the perfume she wore. It pleased him. It was feminine and discreet.

Their conversation proceeded easily. He was surprised when
Madame Vaux pushed back a lacy cuff and glanced at a little
gold wrist-watch. "It's eleven o'clock, I think, M'sieur Villardon, I should be going."

"Eleven o'clock, is it possible! It has been a most enjoyable
hour, *madame*," he said.

"I too have enjoyed it," she replied, picking up a grey glove.

He called the waiter and settled the bill, brushing away her
offer. She rose. It was an anxious moment. He had wondered
about her height. Some women had surprisingly long or short
legs. You could not tell when they were sitting. Madame Vaux
was of medium height. Moreover, she was just the right height,
a little shorter than he. He liked the feminine way in which she
made a brief inspection of herself in the mirror as she turned
by the table.

"You will please let me take you home?" he said.

"That is very kind of you," she answered, and led the way
out. His last curiosity was satisfied, more than satisfied. Her
feet were dainty. She was light on them. Her shoes, while
fashionable, were sensible. How he had suffered from Sophie's
idiotic shoes, so high and pinheeled that she could not cross a
few cobbles.

They found a taxi immediately. In it a silence descended on
them. They spoke in monosyllables. The address she had given
was near his. He would keep the taxi and go on.

They arrived, got out, and entered a dimly lit little hall. She
rang for the lift.

"It has been a very pleasant evening, *m'sieur*."

"*Madame*," he said, taking her hand, "It has been such a
very pleasant evening for me also that I would like to repeat it.
Will you give me the pleasure of dining with me one evening?"

She looked at him with her beautiful frank eyes. "*Mais oui!*
I should like that very much!" she replied, vivaciously.

"Monday?"

"I'm so sorry."

"Wednesday?" he suggested.

"I am so sorry. I am engaged until Friday."

"Then shall we say Friday? May I call for you at eight

o'clock—then I shan't get to the wrong place!" he said, with a little laugh.

"That will be very nice. Thank you," she replied.

The lift had descended. He took off his hat.

"*Bon soir, m'sieur.*"

"*Bon soir, madame.*"

He waited until the lift started, then he went out to his taxi. What a sensible, pleasant woman! She could not dine on Monday or Wednesday. He must wait until Friday. He admired her the more for her dignified restraint.

III

They dined on Friday. They dined the following Tuesday. They dined regularly three times a week for the next month. Then she invited him to dine with her in her apartment. This relieved a slight anxiety he had. It was an opportunity for testing her cooking. The dinner was superb. They had reached the stage of calling each other Emile and Eloise. The original purpose of their coming together had not been mentioned by either of them. Once, he had made an allusion to the burden of loneliness that resulted from the loss of one's life partner. She had wholly agreed. "The happier one was, the greater the loss," she commented. He could not claim a parallel experience but tactfully agreed.

He began to be worried about his position. He could not go on seeing Eloise with such frequency, with such growing friendship, without facing the fact that he would have to make a definite move. It was impossible to attempt a sort of brother-and-sister relationship. Everything he saw and learned about Eloise increased his certainty that here was an admirable woman who might grace his home, set it in order, and make him an excellent companion. But marriage was more than companionship. It entailed deep obligations, a surrender of independence. It was also, to his serious nature, an irrevocable bond. How much was he in love with her, she with him? Youthful ecstasy was behind them, passion certainly. Physical pleasures? That was a question to which he could find no assured answer. It was one thing to admire a woman, to enjoy her company, but another to go to bed with her, get up with her, and mutually experience day after day all the physical and mental intimacies of married life. When one was young, hot-blooded, the unconscious victim of glandular pressures that were confused with romantic sentiments, caution played no rôle. The physical urge of youth brooked no impediment of thought. Now, the blood, cooled with experience, one thought and thought to a point of cowardice.

There was a moment one morning, when he was in the kitchen frying two eggs for breakfast, that he saw himself as a conceited egotist. What had made him take it for granted that the choice of the next step lay with him? Eloise might turn him down. There had been no sign that she had ever seen him in an heroic light. "Emile, you are a great fool!" he said to himself. He said it aloud. He repeated it as he turned the eggs over. Talking to himself had become a growing habit in his loneliness.

While eating his breakfast he came to a resolution. He sat back in his chair, in a posture of determination. He was dining with Eloise tonight. "Tonight I will find just where I stand. I will settle my fate!" As he said this aloud he brought down his fist with such a bang on the table that it rattled the china and the cat ran into the kitchen.

IV

He was reckless in ordering their dinner at the Café de Paris.

"Do you like caviare, Eloise?"

"Yes, I do."

"So do I!" he said, and gave an order for caviare.

When the wine list came he turned it over and studied it carefully.

"I hope you like champagne?"

"Indeed. But, Emile, is it your birthday?"

He smiled and ordered a Veuve Clicquot. It had been understood between them that they would dine modestly as befitted their incomes. She had firmly insisted that they would entertain

each other in turn. Caviare and champagne were extrava-
gances in their mode of life.

"*Chère* Eloise," he replied, "It is not my birthday but it is an
occasion just as momentous. But later. Tell me, what have you
been doing—did you go to the Salvator Dali exhibition?"

"Yes."

"And what did you think of it?"

"He is a genius who makes a very unsuccessful attempt to
persuade people he's mad. If I had the money I would have
bought two of his things!"

They found much to talk about. They dined well. They
finished with coffee and liqueurs.

"You asked me, Eloise, when I was ordering, whether it was
my birthday. No, that is on July 19th. Today is February 10th,
but it may be just as momentous. I ordered champagne because
I wanted to find courage to ask you if you would consider
marrying me." His voice was not steady but he had not hesitated.

Eloise put a hand on his arm and smiled at him.

"I don't have to consider it. I've been considering it for some
time—for myself. I expected you would say this one day." She
stopped and then said, "We're both rather nervous about it,
aren't we? We've both seen life go behind us. At our age there's
no margin for error. When one has had a happy married life,
as I have had, one thinks twice before asking for a renewal of
Fate's kindness. We hope we can make a success of another
marriage—but we're both set in our ways. Habits are like ivy,
they eat into the fabric of one's life, and tearing them out is
pretty ruthless. I am a little afraid, and I think you are."

"I am, and I am not," he said. He was not hampered by any
memory of lost felicity but only by fear of a second failure.

"You used the word 'consider'. Here's what I've considered,
cher Emile. I may shock you. I think we should make an experi-
ment—" She paused, then added—"We should make a trial
of it."

He was puzzled by her words. She saw it on his face. She
gave his arm a little shake, then calmly, in a low quiet voice she
said, "In Sweden it is a habit, I am told, for young couples,

before they embark on matrimony, to go on a trial trip to find out just how they suit one another for a life journey. I am willing, if you are willing, for us to have a trial trip, with no obligation on either of us. We can do it very privately, we are both independent."

He made no answer for a few moments. He just looked at her, serene, smiling, her hand still resting on his arm. When he did speak he could hardly believe his own ears, his words seemed so utterly idiotic and flippant.

"I'm getting a new car next week. We could go away in that," he said.

A little ripple of laughter swept over her pretty face. "What a very delightful idea, *cher* Emile!" she cried, "Let us go to the Riviera!"

CHAPTER 3

I

THEY PLANNED for two weeks and set off for the south with no fixed itinerary. They drove leisurely. Emile found that Eloise could drive, so they took the wheel in turn. The first evening after visiting the lovely cathedrals at Sens and Auxerre they stayed at Autun, a sleepy little old town. There was an inn, a former coaching station, which attracted their attention.

"What are we going to do about our names?" asked Emile.

"Why not Monsieur and Madame Villardon?—I may as well get used to it, and it's easy for you to remember!" said Eloise.

The hotel was not full. They took a room with a bath. The boots went out to collect their bags. They followed him up a wooden staircase and down a long corridor. He unlocked a door. The room was shuttered. He opened the shutters. It was an old-fashioned room with a faded flowered wallpaper. Most of the space was occupied by a large double bed, *un lit matrimonial*, from the days when single beds would have been considered an affront to conjugal rights. Two large white pillows lay side by side. There was a red silk eiderdown. The bed had brass rails. Emile went in to look at the bathroom. There was a roomy bath, with a clumsy white marble wash-basin with long-handled taps, a porcelain bidet, a closet with a pull-chain. The whole suite had not altered much since the days of Victor Hugo.

When Emile returned into the bedroom and the boots had gone, he found Eloise pressing down the bed, testing its softness.

"Do you mind?" he asked, watching her.

"Mind what?"

"A double bed—perhaps you prefer a single bed."

"I've always been used to a double bed. I sleep in one now. So why change!"

She moved towards him, patted his cheek lightly and proceeded to take off her hat. Then she went into the bathroom and shut the door. Emile stood still for a moment, looking at their portmanteaux side by side. He opened his, took out his pyjamas and placed them under one of the pillows. He then went to the window and looked down into the courtyard. It had grown dark outside. He drew the blind. Why should he feel like a conspirator? It was ridiculous. He admired Eloise more and more. She was so easy and self-possessed.

They went down to dinner. It was a good dinner, well served. There were only ten persons in the dining-room. No-one took any notice of them. Later they had a short walk round the *Place*. There was really nothing to see, everything was closed up. The town was dead, the wind cold, but a starry sky promised a good morrow. They retired early and went to bed.

II

The trial trip began auspiciously. They loved seeing the same things. The new car ran well, they were lucky with the weather, and oh, how lucky in themselves! A forgotten happiness returned to Emile. It was all that life should be and had not been. They lingered in Avignon three days, they lingered four in Aix-en-Provence. A ballet company was performing, also they saw an excellent comedy. At noon it was warm enough to take an *apéritif* at a café on the Avenue Mirabeau, watching the people sauntering under the sunlit leafless plane trees. At Bandol they found a charming little hotel facing the sea. Here they took a suite, with a small sitting-room done up in noisy chintz but with very comfortable armchairs. They wheeled these out on to the balcony during the day. Sometimes in the evenings after dinner they stayed in. Eloise took out her sewing-bag. Emile read the newspaper. To his delight she liked him to smoke his pipe. Poor Sophie had never been able to tolerate his pipe, it made her cough. For some reason he obtained the greatest pleasure in seeing Eloise open her sewing-bag. It was round, made of green leather with a top drawn together by a red cord. When she opened it up he saw neat little reels of cotton and silks, a gay kaleidoscope of utilities. He watched her with quick fingers pick out a reel, break off a length of cotton, thread it in a needle, without glasses, and then proceed to sew. He watched her deft needle in wonder and delight. It was home. She had gone over his wardrobe. His shirts had missing buttons replaced, she re-buttonholed his cardigan. When she picked up his socks she burst into laughter.

"Emile!" she cried derisively, spreading a hand inside a sock, revealing his lumpy darning. "You poor thing! Is this the best you can do? Why didn't you get your woman to darn for you!"

"One of them took my darning—four pairs of socks and a vest—and never appeared again. They were almost new socks, so I did my own after that," he replied.

Eloise unpicked the sock and redarned it. It was profession-ally done. He looked at her neat darning. "My dear, you are a very accomplished woman, you must have been well brought up. You can cook, you can darn, you can drive a car, you can play bridge. Your handwriting is beautifully legible, unlike mine. I am wondering what else I shall discover," he said.

"I'll show you, M'sieur Villardon!"

She picked up his pyjama jacket, then searched in her sewing-bag for some coloured silk threads and tried them against the lilac jacket. Satisfied, she selected a length, threaded a needle, and spread the pocket of the jacket on a little wooden hoop.

"This is quite unnecessary but I'm going to embroider your initials just to demonstrate that your wonder-woman can embroider! And Emile, what are your initials? You can't be simply Emile Villardon."

"I am Emile Hyacinthe Villardon but I keep quiet about Hyacinthe. I never liked the name. It makes me sound like a dewdrop."

"Then we'll have E.V. only," said Eloise.

He watched her intently, putting down his paper from time to time. How quick and clever she was with her needle! Never in his life had he had his initials embroidered on anything. He bought his shirts ready-made. When at last the E was finished, she smoothed off the jacket and displayed it to him. He put down his pipe and paper, got up, went over to her and, stooping, kissed her brow. "If this sort of thing goes on you'll turn me into a giddy old man. Initials on my pyjamas. Just fancy!" he exclaimed, holding up the jacket.

"Emile, I've something to tell you," said Eloise. "Our landlady is eaten up with curiosity!"

"I like Madame Colet—she runs this place perfectly."

"I agree, but she has sharp eyes. She is a little too curious, she wants to know what you do, where we live, how long we've been married."

"What did you say?"

"I told her a nice little fat lie. I said we had two children, married, but no grandchildren. I thought that would satisfy her. It's very fortunate that our initial is the same."

"The same?"

"My dear man—V! We're Vaux and Villardon."

"So it is. How very convenient!"

"Yes, very. You see there's V on all my toilet articles, which I'm sure she's examined."

He had walked to the window and studied the lights and the reflection on the water where the boats lay huddled together. Then he turned and looked down on her in silence for a few moments.

"My dear, I don't like your having to lie about us. There's one way to avoid all this, Eloise. Will you marry me?" he asked.

She sat with her back towards him, beginning the V on his jacket.

"Is that how you feel?—our fortnight's not yet up," she said quietly.

"Our fortnight? Oh, be damned to the fortnight! Eloise, what do you say?"

She stood up, straightened her dress and then went over to the window where he stood. She placed both her hands on his shoulders and looked at his serious face.

"I'll say with you, be damned to the fortnight. I think we're old enough to know our minds!" she said, her eyes laughing into his.

He held her to him and kissed her.

"But I think," she said, drawing a finger across his brow, "we should go on with our honeymoon, it's such a success, and I'd like to see Cap D'Antibes!"

"My girl, you shall see it, and any other place!" he replied fervently.

III

Early in April, back in Paris, they were married, quietly, at the Mairie. The wedding party was a very small one. Etienne and Françoise came up from Lyons. There were Emile's sister Fanny and her husband, Eloise's daughter and her husband, and an old office friend of Emile's, with his wife.

The evening before the wedding, just as Emile was leaving her after they had spent the day furnishing the new little apartment overlooking the Bois de Boulogne, he asked, "What are you going to wear tomorrow?"

"That will be a surprise for you—a new costume, of course! It will be very sober—grey," she replied.

"Ah, then it will go with something I want you to wear—that charming little white hat with the swallow, in which I first saw you at the Café Plon."

And to please him she wore it.

BOOK 3

The Crimson Parrot

CHAPTER 1

I

"TO BE YOUNG was very heaven." Indeed, indeed, Mr. Wordsworth. I know it is very hackneyed—music, novels, plays and films and poems have worked it to death, with its gondolas, moonlight, honeymooners, but can Venice ever really lose its allure? Certainly, if you are young it cannot. For a time you are walking on another planet, even if there is not a pretty girl at your side; with one, of course, it is near delirium. I am not thinking of a Venetian; any girl is enchanting in Venice.

I was twenty-four when I saw Venice for the first time. Youth was in its air, magic lay upon its waters. I had never been in love, if by that we mean sexual desire sublimated. I had emerged from a very filthy war and some of its filth had touched me. A lad likely to be dead soon is not finical about the dishes he tastes. "Keep yourself clean for your fiancée," said the chaplain, but if the odds were against your ever seeing your fiancée, or acquiring one, the slut in a French back street filled a heady need.

A devoted old aunt had given me fifty pounds when I came back from the first World War. With that, and my army gratuity, I postponed reading for the Bar and took a three months' holiday; an imprudence, financially. I never regretted it despite the dire warnings of my family. I was a good-looking lad. Envious colleagues told me that I was endowed with plenty of "sex appeal", and credited me with being the Don Juan that I was not.

I had two letters of introduction when I went to Venice. One was to an elderly gentleman who was a bachelor baronet of the old school. He had delightful manners, was well-read and entertained generously. He lived in a slip of a house off the Calle Morosini. Two servants looked after him, an old gondolier, who rowed no more, and the wife, an excellent cook. My host had "gone over" as they termed it. He had become a Roman Catholic with the exaggerated devotion that seems to afflict proselytes. He owned numerous Madonnas, both pictures and statues. The most noticeable feature of his luxuriously furnished house was the hundreds of gilded cherubs he had collected. They filled the tables and shelves, draped the mirrors and windows and hung from the ceilings like stalactites. As a result he was nicknamed Cherubini, though in no way addicted to that composer's works.

Amid a congregation of water-colour-painting ladies, pale gentle souls living on restricted incomes, was Lady Gwendoline Thelton. She did not paint, nor was she poor. She presided over the female lovers of Venice. By virtue of birth—she was a duke's daughter—she took precedence of all in the British colony. It was, alas, a dying community. Thrones had fallen, kingdoms had passed away and incomes had been severely reduced. The reign of the English milords in Italy was over, as that of other grandees. There was a Spanish Royalty, a Hapsburg-Braganza, Don Carlos, but being very old and deaf he made no social appearances. There was an English peer, self-exiled after an unfortunate episode, whom Lady Gwendoline looked right past. Being lavish, and living in a beautiful *palazzo*, he never lacked guests at his table or on the boat on which he sailed the lagoons.

The smaller fry met at Florian's, lunched, dined, played bridge and went to concerts and theatres. In the summer they had *capannas* on the Lido. They sniffed at the luxurious Excelsior Palace, with its film stars and international beauties, which they declared raffish and found too expensive. There was a small colony of professional artists that had no social life. They were engrossed in their work. They painted endless pictures that seldom caught Venice, or purchasers. They lived mostly across on the Giudecca, the cheap and rather inaccessible part of Venice.

I found a delightful little *villino* on the Zattere, then a less-known district lying between the Grand Canal and the Giudecca, near the old Customs House with its globe and the great dome of the church of Santa Maria della Salute. The Zattere had a long quay with moorings, and the Gesuati Church. It faced the broad channel of the Giudecca that led to Porto Maghera and the wharves on the mainland across the lagoon. In those days this area was a no-man's-land. The port channel was a source of delight to dwellers on the Zattere. Liners, traders, tankers, even sailing vessels, glided soundlessly by. From my upper floor I had an endless pageant of Adriatic shipping. Venice has never lost her maritime character. The ships from Alexandria, Beirut, Constantinople, Tunis, Athens, Spalato, Taranto, Messina, Syracuse, Naples, Genoa, Marseilles, and from London, Southampton and Liverpool, carried their names on bow and stern.

My little *villino*, set back, had a small garden. The kitchen and dining-room fronted this; my salon and two bedrooms were above. I found an excellent old housekeeper, Anna, widow of a gondolier. She had only one failing. I came to notice that I was feeding a large family. When I went downstairs a host of strangers, old men, old women, young women, young men and children, rose up and bowed. They were either Anna's sisters, brothers, sons, daughters, in-laws or only neighbours and friends with numerous children. As a result my food bills were quite ridiculous for one young man and one old woman; a platoon of soldiers would not have eaten more. I was warned that it was the custom. Otherwise Anna was scrupulously honest and frugal. She insisted on burning a candle in her bedroom, explaining that electricity was terribly expensive. Actually it was her fear of suddenly being in the dark. The current, a result of the war, we were told, was eccentric. Three, four or five times in the night we would find ourselves plunged into darkness.

The Zattere had a claim to fame which attracted British visitors. A plaque proclaimed on a house, later a *pensione*, that Mr. Ruskin had lived there while working on his famous book, *The Stones of Venice*. As "Cherubini" observed, it would have been more appropriate if he had called it *The Bones of Venice* since he dissected the past so meticulously. Another title to fame was wholly ignored. On an old stone archway an inscription proclaimed that there had lived Cardinal Bembo, poet,

G

philosopher, statesman, man of letters. He had been the friend of Petrarch, the counsellor of the deposed Queen of Cyprus, long resident at Asolo, and a lover of Lucrezia Borgia. He had just missed being elected Pope but he became secretary to Leo X.

A little way along the Zattere, seen from the arch of a bridge, was one of the loveliest vistas of Venice. It was much painted, and caused miles of film to be exposed by delighted photographers. It was the Rio di San Trovaso, a long narrow canal contained between red brick walls, stone-topped, with a causeway on either side flanked by the gothic windows of small palaces and houses. But what gave the greatest enchantment to the view was in the foreground, a red-pantiled wooden chalet and boathouse beside a *squero*, a boat-builder's wharf that sloped down to the canal. Behind these rose the window and gable of the church, backed by a tall *campanile* with open belfry, its square tower crowned by an octagonal chamber surmounted by a cross. Around these buildings were trees, hanging oleander and pepper, a green trellis between blue sky and reflective water. Sometimes on the mud of the *squero* there was an upturned gondola whose flat bottom surprised the tourist. The graceful swan, reversed, was just a long tub.

Thus happily housed in the spring of the year, young, eager, unworried, I seemed to touch the pinnacle of ecstasy. I wandered in the great Piazza. I was even raw enough to let myself be photographed feeding the pigeons. I scribbled on numerous postcards those words of delight and coy provocation—"Wish you were here"—in which tourists indulge. I sat and gossiped at Florian's Café, for by this time I had met an agreeable circle of fellow-sojourners. I listened to the noonday gun, and the crash of bells in the great campanile, and watched those greedy pigeons rise in a sudden flurry of alarm, as if they had never heard it all for three hundred and sixty-five days through innumerable years.

As the sea grew warmer I swam at the Lido whose miles of sands were not then cluttered by lurid bathing establishments. I returned to the Piazza for tea, to watch the golden glory of sunset fall upon the angels, pinnacles, oriental domes, mosaics and bronze horses of St. Mark's façade. Often in that ravishing half-light which visits the city just after sundown, when the shops turn on their bright lights and the vesper bells are ringing, I took a gondola, but this was later in my sojourn when I could always command a pretty companion.

The truth is never told about the gondola or the gondolier. One recovered from the first shock of its funereal blackness, enforced by a sumptuary law passed in the seventeeth-century to check the gaudy extravagance of their decoration, but I never could understand why the gondola enjoyed world-wide fame as the peerless conveyance for lovers. It is nothing of the kind. Every word, every intimacy, is heard and seen by the gondolier behind. You are as exposed as a de-shelled snail. The fact that a good gondolier emulates the monkeys of Nikko and is expected to hear, see and speak no evil, is no compensation.

I had been in Venice two weeks when I met Sandro Giustiniani. As a boy he had stayed at a neighbour's house in Farnham, where we lived, having come to England to learn the language. We became great friends and for a whole summer we rode, swam and played tennis together. He was very popular, being a slender, very handsome youth with a quick mind and excellent manners. He came of an ancient Venetian family which had given a Doge to the Venetian Republic and built one of the most beautiful palaces off the Grand Canal. I was walking across the Piazza one morning when I heard steps behind me and someone call me. I turned and it was Sandro. With a shout he embraced me fervidly. We had not met for six years. In England we had been adolescents, now we were young men of the world with a war behind us. He had served in a crack cavalry regiment on the Piave. He was now even more attractive than I had remembered: a blond Venetian, broad-shouldered, narrow hipped. Nature had designed him for a lady-killer, which he was.

It was a great stroke of luck for me. In one bound I was in the exclusive circle of the Venetian aristocracy, diminished and impoverished but fiercely proud. I entered *palazzi* I should never have seen but for Sandro, who was evidently the golden boy of Venice. Nevertheless, he exercised a quiet judgement.

That year, in a sort of post-war delirium, the international riff-raff of Europe and America descended on Venice. They were headed by an ugly, vulgar little woman, Milly, out of the Middle West, whose dynamic energy created an atmosphere of *carnevale*. She was adept in baiting her following with blown-upon, impoverished princes, marquises, counts and barons often hovering on the borderline of gigolos. With these were noisy rich American women of tarnished reputations, loosely married or divorced, accompanied by gimlet-eyed youths, beach bodies by day and lechers by night. Now and then a real royalty appeared, lured by the loan of a palace rented by some moneyed matron who paid the bills. Milly was a tireless entrepreneur. She organized balls, nocturnal swimming-parties, and treasure hunts. She called dukes and duchesses by their Christian names. No celebrity dared to snub her. She was the agent of a new god, Publicity, whose domain was the gossip columns of the popular press. "Names make news" ran the slogan. It did not matter what news. Gossip-writers kept near to Milly, who was a cornucopia of "copy".

Sandro, polite, discerning, steered his own course, kept to his own circle. By virtue of his introductions I was given the freedom of a Venetian society rarely in the news. In the high summer when the tourists seized Venice they retreated to their country properties in the Veneto. Many of them let their palaces, happy to augment their incomes, but the letting implied no social relations with the tenants. They left details to the agent and disappeared.

It was through Sandro that I met Clementina. Her full name was like a song. Clementina Maria Rondanelli da Valmontona. Her father, whom I never met, was Prince Rondanelli. He stayed on his estate in Valmontona where he lived in a medieval castle among the vineyards. He watched over a flourishing wine business. Clementina spent the early summer in Venice with her grandmother, the Dowager Princess Rondanelli da Valmontona. Clementina was twenty-one, a distant cousin of Sandro's. She was a sylph, blue-eyed, with a mass of brown hair that draped her shoulders. Her eyes were big under long upturned lashes, her nose was delightfully *retroussé* and gave her a pert look. Despite her name, there was little that was Italian about her appearance. She had a fair golden skin, bronzed with swimming. I was not surprised when I learned that in the family tree there had been a Hohenzollern princess. From her, it seemed, had come Clementina's hair, eyes and skin. Otherwise she was Italian, vivid, vivacious, a chatterer, impetuous in thought and movement. She was chaperoned—very loosely, since the old Princess was a recluse—by an elderly aunt, a fat easy-going creature who had a passion for talking French and eating peppermint creams. Clementina disposed of her with little effort, since she was always too slow in the up-take. "*Cara*, what did you say? *Cara*, do you think you should? *Cara*, we must ask your grandmother, I think." It was the case of the humming-bird and the old crow. I had no trouble with the Countess Contarini. I shamelessly flattered her. I practised my French on her, and fed her with peppermint creams. "I know you are a steady boy. Young Englishmen are more trustworthy than Italian boys. You will look after Clementina," she said.

I did, insofar as Clementina would allow anyone to look after her. "Don't be an ass, she's an incorrigible flirt, and remorseless," warned Sandro, who teased her. I had plenty of competition. A swarm of glamorous young Italians formed a court around her, but for some reason she showed me preference. She pretended to teach me Italian. The lessons never lasted long, she was too impatient and would break into laughter at some gaffe of mine. She nicknamed me *Sposo*—"You always suppose so much." I was not aware until then that I did over-work the word—"Suppose we have a swim" "Suppose we eat at the Fenice" "Suppose we go out to Torcello". After that I carefully avoided the word but her nickname stuck. There was a little joke in the name, which she loved, for *Sposo* in Italian meant 'betrothed' or 'bridegroom'.

How the young can suffer. She kept me in heaven and hell. It was the intoxicating headiness of youth, her fresh beauty, her tireless vivacity, the splendid setting, a fantasia of sea, sky, lagoon, of arched bridges, narrow canals, sunlight, moonlight, bells in high belfries, birds singing lustily in cages hung out of windows in pink and ochre courts, the gold and flamingo of sunset, the band in the Piazza at night, the string orchestras at the cafés, the shops of the teeming Merceria—it was all these plus the most wayward lovely nymph a lad ever paid court to.

She was a fearless swimmer. We would go to the Lido, take a catamaran and row out over the blue placid sea. Then she would dive and keep underwater so long that I was sure she had drowned, and, diving, I would make a frantic search. She would come up, shout with laughter at my panting quest, slide over me, and swim off like a dolphin. Once on the catamaran she scratched the tan on my back with her sharp nail.

"Now everyone will know!" she said.

"Know what? What have you written?" I asked.

"*I love my Sposo*. That is very proper, yes?"

"How much do you love me?" I demanded.

"A leetle, sometime, when I am sad."

"Clementina, you are never sad!"

"Oh yes, sometime. Sometime when I am too much in love I cry!" she said simply.

"Have you ever cried for me?" I asked.

She looked at me with her big blue eyes. "You would like to know! Suppose I did?" she said, with a ripple of laughter, using my word.

I knew it was nonsense. I knew she never cried. She was not that kind.

One day, playfully, on the Lido sand as we lay sunning after bathing, I tied a blue ribbon off a chocolate box round her toe. She had pretty feet.

"You have no idea what you're doing! In Venice that means I shall have a boy baby," she said. "Blue is for a *maschio*."

"I have no pink ribbon for another toe," I said.

"One day we shall be old and fat and we shall have grandchildren. Won't that be awful!" she cried.

"Grandparents don't seem to find it awful."

She rolled over on her stomach and lay with her chin on my leg. "I want to die young," she said.

"That is very wicked of you," I replied, trying to be severe.

"I am very wicked!"

I laughed and pulled her hair. She looked at me reproach-fully. "You never take me seriously," she said.

Alas, I was taking her too seriously. By now I was madly in love with her. She had become an obsession. I thought of her, going to sleep. I thought of her, waking. Sometimes, when her slim body lay in the sand before me, I ached with longing to gather her up in my arms and carry her away. It was not only her body, her hair, her eyes and hands that were entrancing. It was also her impish ways and sharp mind. I taught her to sing *Oh my darling Clementine*. She rapidly learned every verse and would sing them, bubbling with mischief. *You are lost and gone for ever, dreadful sorry, Clementine!*

I was never quite sure whether I had any preference among the court of young Italians she commanded. She flashed among us like a tropical bird.

One evening, leaving a dance, I got permission from the Countess Contarini to escort her home. The sporting old girl took another gondola. It was nearly midnight but Venice was still alive on this warm May evening. Our gondolier was an oldish man, dressed in a white blouse and with a broad-brimmed straw hat sporting a long red ribbon. I ordered him to make a *gita* for an hour. Long experienced, he knew exactly what to do. He rowed out of the Grand Canal, where our host's *palazzo* stood behind its striped posts, and turned off into the small tortuous side-canals.

We lay back on the divan-like cushions. The silence of the dark waterway closed us in. On either side rose, sheer, the ochre façades of old houses, shuttered, with gothic white marble windows, and balconies on which were red and white gerani-ums and brilliant cinerarias. Occasionally a lighted room threw a shaft of light across the glimmering water. At a turning the gondolier uttered his warning melancholy cry that had been heard down the centuries. We listened for echoes from ghosts of the past, all the long-dead lovers who had floated through the night.

We did not talk. My arm had gone stealthily behind Clemen-tina and she leaned easily against me in a scented softness that matched the velvet night. Presently my lips were on hers, unresisting. It was the first time in three weeks that she had let me kiss her, she had always been mockingly evasive. Now her surrender was responsive to my ardour. We rode through the night in silent ecstasy. The old gondolier behind made not a sound. There was only the dip of his oar. The gondola's steel-toothed prow, shining above the black water, proudly glided along the narrow *rio*. I knew then that all that the poets had written about Venice, about love in a gondola, was true.

II

It was to Clementina that I owed my introduction to Princess Rondanelli da Valmontona. The old lady had asked her to bring me to tea. The Rondanelli *palazzo* was quite near to me on the Zattere. It was a characteristic palace, a huge block, four stories high, its windows facing the Giudecca. On the first floor was the great salon, with a long balustraded open balcony of white stone and six immense windows with pointed Venetian gothic arches. Two large wings of the palace, running backward, enclosed a vine-green courtyard with a trickling central fountain and, beyond, a trellised iron gateway giving on to a back-canal.

We crossed a deep entrance hall and mounted a wide stair-case of shallow stone steps to the first floor, the *piano nobile*. Two large mahogany doors opened noiselessly when we rang. A young servant in a white brass-buttoned jacket, white-gloved, conducted us across a small hall, opened a door and announced us. We were in an immense salon that ran, front to back, through the palace. It had a high coffered ceiling with painted panels of allegorical figures. The long walls were hung with tapestries and life-sized portraits in heavy elaborate gilt frames. A grand piano stood in one corner loaded with silver photo frames. The furnishings were massive, with old-fashioned crimson damask that had long lost its freshness.

The old princess rose from a chair at the far end of the salon, her back to the light. She stood motionless and stately as we made the long journey down the highly polished marble floor towards her. As we drew near I saw she was white-haired, dressed wholly in black save for a collarette of fine lace.

Clementina went forward and kissed her and then introduced me. I bowed over the thin cold hand offered to me. She was a beautiful old lady. I was surprised to learn she was eighty-four. She spoke very good English. "I lived in London for four years when my husband was naval attaché at the Italian Embassy," she told me. She had lived in Paris, Washington, Athens, Constantinople and Rome. She had been a widow for almost fifteen years. Her husband had been an admiral in the Italian navy.

The footman brought in a large silver tea tray. "I shall give you English tea," said the princess, with a smile. "We Italians are coffee-drinkers but I acquired the tea habit in London."

She was very interested to learn that I was living on the Zattere. "Then we are neighbours! Any afternoon that you want a cup of tea do come in, but I warn you that you may find a lot of old ladies here—we play bridge three times a week. Tea is served at five."

As we were leaving, going down the stairs, Clementina said, "Thank God—you've made a hit! Grandma Emilia is very stiff about visiting tourists. Now you'll have to go to tea. If you don't she'll feel insulted."

III

We had been together for over a month when one day the blow fell. "My mother's sent for me, Sposo. I have to go to Fiuggi, she's taking a cure there."

"When will you be back?" I asked, anxiously.

We were lying on the sand outside the Rondanelli *capanna*. The sun was very hot and we were roasting ourselves after a long swim. There were three other boys and two girls there, our usual set.

"I'm not coming back, not this summer."

She turned, raised herself on one shoulder and looked at me. She must have seen the dismay on my face as I lay back on the sand. She ran a finger down my nose. "Poor Sposo! Will you miss me?" she asked.

"No, you will be very quickly forgotten," I said, to mask my desperation.

"Little liar!" she cried, shovelling sand on my belly. "You'll go all over Venice crying *Oh my darling, oh my darling, oh my darling Clementine!*"

She sang the words I had taught her. Then she stopped halfway, seeing something in my eyes. "Poor Sposo! I shall miss you too," she said quickly, almost in a whisper. Then she got up, gave her hand to Marcello Brandini, and ran into the sea with him.

There were four more days, days of happiness and misery. On the last evening we took a gondola again, leaving Aunt Contarini chatting at Florian's. We promised to be back in an hour. We found a gondola at the station by the bridge on the Calle Larga. We rode past the Fenice Theatre, along the back canals. Clementina was very silent for a while. There was not a sound except the faint lap-lap of the water on the prow, and the dipping of the oar. She lay in my arms, unresisting when I kissed her, her fingers gently combing my hair. At last we ordered the gondolier to return, for Aunt Contarini was waiting and we had been away more than an hour. Presently I heard a little choking noise. I looked closely at her face in the dim light and saw tears well in her eyes and spill over on to her cheeks. I gathered her closer, very moved.

"Clementina!" I whispered, wiping a tear away with a finger.

She tried to smile at me, her eyes luminous with tears.

"Sposo, I do love you, and I shall never, never see you again!" she said, and pressed her lips on my mouth as I held her tighter in a movement of desperate protest.

"Nonsense, I shall come to Venice again. I'll come next year. I'll come every year that you come!" I cried.

She shook her head. Then she sat up and smoothed back her hair.

"I know that things are never the same twice—I won't be I, and you won't be you!" she said tensely.

"But that is ridiculous, Clementina!"

"It is not ridiculous, Sposo. Life does things to you. This is Venice. Venice is all illusion!"

I tried to laugh at her but she had sent a little cold wind round my heart. Defiant, I thought of asking her to marry me but saw the absurdity of such a thing. Her family would not let her. I was a foreigner with no social position, no money, and of a different religion. I had not even a profession yet. In a month my money would run out.

We rode back in silence, our hands interlocked.

IV

After the departure of Clementina I stayed on for three weeks, but Venice was not the same without her, though her friends were just as hospitable. I found poor Marcello Brandini as depressed as I was. He, too, was in love with Clementina. We consoled each other.

I made several calls on the charming old Princess Rondanelli. It was comforting to visit the *palazzo* where Clementina's lovely ghost haunted the rooms. The Countess Contarini lived with the princess. I gathered that she was a poor relation who had become a kind of lady-in-waiting. One evening as I was leaving I got her to show me the room in which Clementina stayed on her visits. It was at the back, overlooking the courtyard and the fountain. The room was quite unlike any other in the palace, for she had furnished it in the modern style. It was very dainty and bright. On a table there were photographs of her parents, the present Prince and Princess Rondanelli, of her home, Castello Valmontona, a large medieval-looking castle with a machicolated tower and battlements. For a few moments I sat in her chair. The old countess smiled at me indulgently. She knew how much I was in love.

When I had tea with the old princess there was always a spectacular ending. The sun was setting in a great blaze of golden light beyond the tall gothic windows. The salon grew dark, with the ancestors in the heavy frames somewhat menacing in the gloom. Then a door opened at the far end of the salon and the white-jacketed footman entered. He put a blue shawl over his arm and took out the parrot that lived in a large cage on a pedestal table. Then he slowly advanced down the salon towards the great windows, opened them, went out on to the balcony, spread the shawl, and left the parrot on it. The bird spread its great crimson wings against the sunset and began to screech and chatter. Voices below, young voices, answered. The parrot, very voluble, carried on an excited conversation, walking up and down the wide parapet and fluttering its wings. For about fifteen minutes the voluble parrot talked and screeched, evidently giving much amusement below. As it was in Italian I could not follow. Then the footman came back, took the parrot off the balcony and returned it to its cage.

"Beppe is a very wicked bird," said the princess. "I would not keep him but my dear husband, who bought him, loved him. He went everywhere with him."

I did not know why she called poor Beppe a very wicked bird just because he created a little commotion. Poor bird, there was not much excitement for him cooped up in his cage in that long silent salon.

The ceremony of the parrot, as I came to regard it, was the signal for me to make my farewell. Only once on these visits did the old princess make any reference to Clementina. I said I had had a letter from her.

"She is a very sweet child. I enjoy her visits. But she is rather wild. That will pass. I hope she will make a good marriage," said the princess.

I was a little sad when I paid my last visit. She was always so charming to me and her talk of past events and people was full of interest. She had been a lady-in-waiting to Queen Margherita. I knew that I might never see her again. She was eighty-four. At that age twelve months can change everything.

CHAPTER 2

I

I DID NOT KNOW THEN and I would not have believed anyone who prophesied it, that forty years would pass before I saw Venice again. When the train had carried me over that long bridge crossing the lagoon to the mainland, after my first visit, I had watched Venice fade, tumult in my heart, and was determined to come back and see Clementina again.

I did not go to the Bar, I went into the Colonial Service and for the rest of my life was sent all over the world. I wrote to Clementina from my first post in Nassau. She answered. Then, after a silence, I wrote again. I could not come to Venice, as I hoped, I was being posted to Fiji, of all places. A dire fate was sending me as far away as possible. It was in Fiji, a year later, that I had a letter informing me that she was marrying Marcello Brandini. "You'll remember him, he could double his thumbs back. I am very happy."

I wrote a suitable letter. She had been right about Venice—it was a city of illusion. Ironically my predecessor on Fiji had left in my palm-shaded chalet a battered novel. The scene was set in Venice. The title was *The City of Beautiful Nonsense*. And now, forty years on, I was at last in Venice again, not in the early summer but in the autumn. The place had not changed much. There were too many tourists crowding the Piazza but in these days of an affluent democracy tourists are everywhere, since to stay home is to lose face with the Joneses. There were too many motor-boats rushing up and down the canals, creating a disastrous wash that was undermining the old palaces. But the essential Venice was the same, the Venice of the noonday gun on the Customs House, of the Piazza with the café orchestras, of the pink and crimson sunsets, the Campanile bell, the black gondolas, the noise of footsteps up and down the little humpbacked bridges, St. Theodore and his crocodile on the column, Sansovino's Library with its white stone Olympian statues against the sky.

I stayed in a small hotel off the Calle Larga. It had a terrace built out over the Grand Canal, across whose green flood rose the majestic dome of Santa Maria della Salute, with the Madonna's halo electrically illuminated. It was for me, however, a Venice of ghosts. My youth, long lost, came back with sad eyes, conscious of the lost years. The melancholy memories of *tempi passati*, of dreams that had faded out of sight down the river of Life, were evoked by a *calle*, a *rio*, the façade of a church glimmering in the twilight.

One night, going back to my hotel from the Piazza, where I had sat listening to the band, I passed over the *ponte* by the rococo church of San Moisé. It was still a station for gondoliers, and as I started over the bridge there came the old familiar solicitation—*Gondola, gondola, signore?* He was a young gondolier, muscular under his white singlet. It was late and I had no intention of taking a gondola ride, but a sudden impulse caused me to step down into his boat. It was here, all those years ago, about this time, that I had made a *gita* with Clementina on that last night in Venice.

"Take me round by the Teatro Fenice," I said. If I had added—"The way we went forty years ago, before you were born," he would have thought me crazy.

He went under the bridge, lowering his head, into the blackness of the narrow canal. He began to tell me the names of the places we passed, seeking to please a tourist, but I checked him.

"*Silenzio, per piacere.*" I said over my shoulder.

"*Si, si, signore!*" he responded.

I asked for silence, it was foolish, but it was a sweet foolishness I had embarked on, to evoke the past, one's youth, that heady first love. We came eventually to a turning by the round tower of the Fenice Theatre. It rose, very tall in the pale moonlight of the September night. It was here, just here, that I had wiped a tear from her cheek and she had said "Sposo, I do love you!"

Clementina. Where was she, what had been her fate as Clementina Brandini—a happy wife, a mother? With a shock I realized she might now be a grandmother, if alive. I was a grandfather, a widower. I had been happily married, with two children, a son and a daughter. My boy had been killed in North Africa, my daughter was married to a doctor, the happy mother of two boys. Tomorrow, I told myself, I would go over to the Zattere, look at my old *villino*, and then at the Palazzo Rondanelli, where Clementina had stayed with her grandmother. Certainly the old princess had long been dead. I wondered what had happened to the great crimson parrot that the footman took out on to the balcony at sunset. I had heard that parrots could live to be eighty. It might still be alive, a link with my youth and Clementina. I wondered who lived in the *palazzo* now. Perhaps it had been divided up into apartments, as had happened to so many of these vast old palaces. I would go and enquire.

It was nearly midnight when my gondola arrived back in the Calle Larga. What a long time off was one's youth! I recalled Browning's *A Toccata of Galuppi's*, the musings of that old Venetian composer,

Dear dead women with such hair too, what's become of all the gold
Used to hang and brush their bosoms? I feel chilly and grown old.

Clementina's hair was not gold, or Titian red. It was a dark chestnut, lighter where the sun had bleached it. Lovely hair.

I slowly got out of the gondola. The black headed young gondolier waited for payment. I took out my wallet.

"Are you single or married?" I asked.

"Single, *signore*. But I have a *fidanzata*, and if the season is good I hope—"

The suggestion was cleverly made, and not lost on me. If the tips were generous he would be able to get married. I gave him a good tip. He thanked me with a flashing smile. The race of gondoliers should be kept going, I thought.

II

I did not get over to the Zattere the next day. I wrote letters all the morning, ending with an *apéritif* in the sunshine at Florian's. A shabby artist came up to me, hawking his gaudy paintings of Venice. I waved him away, recollecting that two hundred years ago another Venetian artist, Francesco Guardi, had hawked his paintings at Florian's. In the afternoon, after a short siesta, I went to the Ducal Palace to see the exhibition of Tintoretto's works. It was a superb collection. At six o'clock I walked towards the Palazzo Davanti. There I had an Austrian friend, a cultivated elderly man whom I had known years ago when we were both *en poste* in Berne. Like me, he was retired. He had taken an apartment in the floor of the palace for the season. We had run into each other on the Piazza and he had invited me to his party. When I arrived, there were about twenty guests, Americans, French, English and Italians. We chatted with each other in a mixture of languages. I had a little shock on looking out of the salon's windows. There was the Fenice Theatre and the narrow canal, the canal of my last journey with Clementina forty years ago. I found myself talking to a good-looking young Italian. He asked me if I knew Venice well. I said not very well but that many years ago I had lived on the Zattere.

"The Zattere!" he exclaimed, and turned to a smart young woman at his side, calling her. "My wife, Contessa Collini," he said, introducing me. "*Cara*, this gentlemen once lived on the Zattere!"

"You did!" she exclaimed, vivaciously. "We live there now. Where did you stay?"

"In a little *villino* set back in a garden—" I began.

"I know it! Near the place where Ruskin stayed. We live a short way along, in the Palazzo Rondanelli."

They must have seen the surprise in my face.

"Do you know it?" asked her husband.

"Many years ago I used to visit the Princess Rondanelli da Valmontona. She was a very old lady. She had a very pretty granddaughter with whom I fell in love," I answered.

"Not Clementina?" asked the countess.

"Yes."

"My mother! I inherited the *palazzo* from her!" cried the countess, clutching her young husband's arm in excitement. "You are English?"

"Yes," I said, telling them my name, quite overcome by this coincidence.

The little countess looked at me with her pretty dark eyes searchingly. "Are you Sposo?" she asked.

"Good heavens! How should you know that? It was the nickname your mother gave me."

"My mother had a photo album. It was full of snaps, some taken in Venice when she was a girl. She showed me some of you, Sposo, the English boy. You were very handsome and nice, and she was in love with you. How extraordinary to meet Sposo!"

"I gather your mother is dead?" I asked.

"Yes, six years ago."

"And your father—wasn't he Marcello Brandini?"

"Yes. He's alive. He's coming to us next week," said Count Collini.

"The old Principessa, I recall her so well. She was then eighty-four," I said.

"She died at ninety. I can just remember her old parrot!" exclaimed the countess.

"Beppe, the wicked!"

"You knew him! He died fifteen years after my great-grand-mother."

"Your father says he was a monster—a most embarrassing bird," said Count Collini.

"He was a magnificent parrot. I never knew why he was called wicked," I commented.

"You must come and visit us, our host must bring you," said the pretty young countess. "We'll make a date."

I was pleased to know that I was to enter the Palazzo Ron-danelli again. I wanted to talk of Clementina. I wondered if she had had other children as lovely as this vivacious young woman. I wanted to know about her life down the years.

III

One afternoon I went with my Austrian friend to a cocktail party given by the Collinis in the old Palazzo Rondanelli. They lived in only part of the palace now, the floors were let off in apartments. The servant problem was here in Venice also, and the mounting cost of living. But the great salon was as beautiful as ever with its gothic windows and balcony overlooking the Giudecca canal. The windows were open, and I walked out on to the balcony. I thought of Beppe, the crimson parrot, parading and screeching in the sunset. One other thing had not changed. A young footman in a white uniform and white gloves served the cocktails.

My young hostess came out on the balcony to me. "I want to show you something," she said. I followed her in. She took me across to a bookcase with some photograph frames on it.

"There's great-grandmother," she said. "Of course younger than when you knew her—in Court dress. And here's the old admiral, my great-grandfather. Here are my grandfather and his wife—isn't she lovely? And here's my mother—Clementina. Do you recognize her?"

"Of course I do! What a beautiful woman!" I exclaimed.

I looked. It was Clementina, and it was not Clementina. She was a woman of about fifty, robust, but with the same clear eyes. In the strange alchemy of Time the sylph had been lost, with the fresh grace of her young beauty, but something remained of the girl who had hypnotized me in that enchanted Venetian summer. I looked long and a little sadly. She was gone from the scene and I was here in the salon where she had talked and laughed. I learned that she had had two sons and one daughter, my hostess. Her life had been very happy. She had seen her grandchildren, one of whom, my hostess's bright little boy, was present, dressed in a white sailor suit, carrying around the *petits fours*.

Presently my host came up and talked to me. "I suppose you remember the old lady's chair—we've kept it, in the same place. I'm told she sat in it like a reigning queen, and was very formidable."

I looked across at the highbacked velvet-covered *settecento* chair in which she had sat by the tea-table.

"I never found her formidable. She was always very gracious to me," I replied. "May I ask you a question?"

"Yes."

"Beppe—why was he always called a wicked parrot?"

"Ah! I never knew the bird—died before I was on the scene, but my father-in-law has told me about him. He was bought by the old admiral in Malta. He had reason for thinking he had once belonged to a British sailor. The admiral worshipped that bird, largely because of its vocabulary! Living for years on Italian battleships, he had picked up things you don't say in drawing-rooms. He had a filthy repertoire that distressed the old princess. They used to put him out on that balcony—"

"I well remember that," I said. "Every day after tea, the servant took him out, and he used to screech and chatter."

"Yes, the neighbours complained that their children used to gather below the balcony, and provoke him, to hear him swear at them luridly in nautical Italian. But that wasn't the worst. He once disgraced his ship. The Fleet was here in Venice on one occasion and a visiting British royalty came on board. After lunch he went up and spoke to Beppe. The accent must have aroused some memory in Beppe's past. What he said in answer to the greeting brought a look of consternation on the faces of the royal guest and his wife. Later, one of our officers translated for the admiral what he had said."

"What had he said?" I asked.

Count Collini looked round and drew me aside, lowering his voice. "He said to His Royal Highness—'You bloody old stinker!'"

BOOK 4

The Pelican

CHAPTER 1

I

THERE IS SUCH A THING as love at first sight. Tom Little, an American in the United States Air Force stationed in England in 1943, saw and fell in love with an English girl. He was coming out of a cinema in Derby when he saw her. It was only a quick glimpse, but her face and its expression hit him so hard that he was dazed. Before he could do anything about it he had lost her.

He joined his comrades in a car that took them back to their base. "What's the matter? Are you sickening for something?" asked one of them, observing his silence. He made no answer because he was sick at heart and could think of no cure. He had lost the girl for ever, it would seem. At twenty-one the blows of Fate seem heavy, darkness falls on the young heart with a velvet and total blackness.

It was absurd that he should be hit so hard in a few seconds by the face of a girl coming out of a cinema into the darkened street of a Midland provincial town in England. There were thousands of girls with pretty faces away back home in an even smaller town on the Gulf of Mexico, and being in love with any one of them would not involve him in all manner of difficulties that came with love in a foreign country. Perhaps if he saw her again the effect would not be the same. There was often a special enchantment in the half-seen that vanished at the full view. And what was the use? A swift death most probably awaited him and his buddies unless he had exceptional luck.

The next day he began to wonder if he really was sickening. He could not get that girl's face out of his mind. It would be of no use haunting that cinema in Derby; there was a complete blackout each night. It was now October and the days were short.

Three days later, on a Saturday afternoon he joined some of the boys again and went into Derby. They prowled listlessly about. Some of them hooked giggling girls, loud-voiced and common. The end of their adventure was pretty certain. The crude details always came out with the morning coffee. It was like playing an old gramophone record.

At one point he unshipped himself from his companions and went into a teashop. He asked for coffee and a doughnut. There weren't any doughnuts in Derby. You could buy a Rolls-Royce, made there, but you couldn't get a doughnut. The sniffy waitresses were accustomed to this vain order. A currant bun was served, the currants almost invisible.

When the coffee was brought with the bun, he looked at it and smiled at the waitress pathetically. But his smile changed to one of astonishment. His mouth opened and his eyes went into a stare. It was the girl of the cinema! Before he could find any words she had gone.

This was what they called the "working of Fate". True, there weren't many teashops in Derby, but that he should have chosen this one suggested more than chance. For a time he touched neither coffee nor bun. Was she really as wonderful as a heated memory had made out? She was. He had not been fooling himself. There was something in her face, the tilt of her nose and chin, the colour of her eyes and the fresh complexion such as he had never seen in any other girl in the whole world.

His hand trembled when he picked up the teaspoon. He stirred and stirred, his mind going round with the coffee. What did he do now that he was so near and so far? He had not yet been given a check. Would she be the one to give him it? He waited and waited. Presently she came to a nearby table. Now for the first time he could take a long careful look. Everything he had thought was true. She was fair and graceful and the way the blonde hair fluffed over her ears and round her neck shook him. He watched her delicate fingers writing an order on a pad. And then he saw something that made his heart stop. There was a ring on her finger. She might be engaged or married. On what finger did English girls, married or engaged, wear their rings? As the query arose she left the table and passed by his. Meeting his eyes, she gave him a smile and was gone. So she had noticed him! Idiot, he said to himself, all she had seen was a face above a brown uniform. "Give the boys a smile. They're a long way from home, and soon they may be dead." That was the formula for the hour. There would be another dozen faces after his at the table, and they would be all alike to her.

He lingered over his coffee and ate the last crumbs of his bun. He thought of ordering another coffee. It was poor stuff. Then he remembered there was a notice saying only one coffee and bun could be served per person. So he watched for her return and put up his hand for the check. To his immense relief, she came to his table, and began to write his check. Desperate, he forced words to his lips.

"I saw you the other night coming out of the cinema."

"Oh yes!"

"Did you like the picture?"

"It was all right," she answered.

"My name's Tom Little," he said.

"Yes?"

She tore off the check, put it on the table, smiled at him and was gone.

He got up and went to the cash-desk, dazed. What now? He was as far off as ever. No, he was farther off, for he had made an attempt and failed.

"What time do you close?" he asked the cash girl.

She glanced at a clock. "In half an hour—six o'clock," she replied.

He went out into the dark street. A cold wind was blowing. It seemed to get right into his heart. He told himself that he could not be crazy enough to hang around for half an hour to see her come out. But he was. There was a passage at the side of the shop. She might come out of a side door. He took up a position that commanded both exits.

At six the last customers left, a chink of light showing as they came out of the heavily shrouded door. He wondered if in the darkness he would be able to recognize her. He waited and waited. At about a quarter-past six some girls came out, obviously waitresses. She was not among them. One of the girls, when she saw him peering at them, said, "Good evening!" and smiled. He looked away. She giggled with the other girls and walked on. He felt rather ashamed of himself yet he stayed.

He had waited about three-quarters of an hour when two more girls came out. She was one of them. They began to walk down the street, chatting. And now? He had not foreseen that she might have a companion. What a lovely little figure she had, enveloped in a transparent raincoat. He kept an exact distance behind them and could hear them talking gaily. They came to a bus stop and halted. If they got on a bus he must follow with no idea where it went. His hands were moist in his pockets. Then luck was with him. The girls said goodbye as a bus came up and only one got on it. His girl remained on the pavement. She began to walk away. He hurried after her.

"If you please, miss—can I talk to you? I was in the café—"

She stopped and faced him. "How dare you! What do you think I am—a pick-up? Didn't your mother teach you any manners?"

She was very angry and her eyes burnt him. He felt dumb. Then he found words to say:

"I'm sorry, miss. I saw you in a cinema, and then just now in the café—and you sort of bowled me over. I am a harmless guy, really."

She looked at him. He was a big lad, pink-faced. She thought she saw his mouth tremble.

"I accept your apology. Goodnight!" she said.

"But can't I—won't you—"

She halted again and gave him a freezing look. "Look, Mr. American, you're making yourself a nuisance. Get back to your camp. My father works in the shop over there. I'm going to him and we're going home together. So be off!"

"Please, can I meet your father?" he asked.

She was about to step off the kerb, and he was going to lose her. She turned and stared at him. He saw now how very young she was, not more than twenty. She just came up to his shoulder. A wisp of blonde hair escaped from a soft felt hat and fell over her brow. She was enchanting, even with a look of anger in her eyes.

"Well, you have a nerve! What do you think my father'll say to you?" she cried.

"I'll risk that. I've got to know you—I just have!" he said in a strained voice.

She crossed the road, ignoring him, and entered a shop. He followed her in and paused inside the door. It was a hardware shop. They were closing down. There was a man waiting, in a macintosh, with a hat on. The girl walked up to him, kissed him, and began to tell him something. Obviously it was about the soldier annoying her. The man left his daughter and came towards the door.

"What do you want? Get out or I'll call the police!" he cried. He looked at the boy's face and saw it was tense. He was a tall lad about twenty-one, a good-looking dark youngster, strong and shapely. "You should know you can't come over here and pick up girls in the street, not any nice girls. You may do it in America but not here!" he said. "You've frightened my daughter!"

"I am very sorry, sir. I don't pick up girls, here or in the States. I've never done this before. I guess I'm a bit crazy just now. You can't know what it's like to be in a strange country and be lonely and never see a nice girl to talk to!"

The man looked at the boy and was moved by the unhappiness in his face.

"I do know—I was once a lonely young soldier in France," he said. "What is your name?"

"Tom Little, sir."

The man laughed as he told him his name. "Well, that's a bit odd! Mine's Small—and we're neither of us little nor small! Where do you live?"

"Near St. Petersburg—on the Mexican Gulf. It's in Florida."

"You're a long way from home, my lad!"

"I sure am! And it's the first time away from my folks," he said, forcing a sad little smile.

Mr. Small turned to his daughter and looked at her with an amused expression. "I'd like, my dear, to introduce you to a nice young American, Mr. Tom Little," he said. He turned to the soldier. "This is my daughter, Alice Small."

There was an awkward pause. The boy saluted. Alice put forth a hand. "Pleased to know you, Mr. Little," she said. He took her hand.

"And ah'm sure pleased too!" he said, his face puckered in a big smile.

"What time do you have to be back in camp?" asked Mr. Small.

"Ten o'clock."

"Then I suggest you come home with us and have a bit of supper."

Tom Little could hardly believe it. "That's mighty kind of you, sir," he replied.

They left the shop and walked through the empty darkened streets. "Don't like these moonless nights—the Nazis like them for bombing," observed Mr. Small.

"So do we," said Tom Little.

"Oh, what are you?"

"Navigator in a bomber."

"It's all a senseless business, isn't it?"

"It sure is. Ah sometimes think that we humans are plain crazy."

Mr. Small smiled and quoted some verses—

> *Yes, quaint and curious war is!*
> *You shoot a fellow down*
> *You'd treat if met where any bar is,*
> *Or help to half-a-crown.*

"Our Thomas Hardy wrote that during the Boer War. And here we are, at it again." He had just lost one son and had another serving. He was a little bitter.

They came to a street with a long row of houses set behind gardens. Mr. Small opened the front door and walked down a passage into a dining-room where a middle-aged woman rose to greet him.

"Mary, this is an American boy who's been chasing Alice, so we've captured him and brought him home to have a bit of supper, to see if we can tame him!"

"Isn't that nice! You're very welcome," said Mrs. Small.

That was how Tom Little entered the family and found the best wife in the world.

II

They had been married twelve years and had one son, Jeremy, aged eleven, having lost a little girl at birth. They were a happy family. It had not been easy for Alice Little at first. She found herself, far away from home in a strange land, speaking a language almost the same but sometimes with confusing differences. Also there were different customs. When Tom had flown back to Derby immediately after being demobilized and had married Alice, deeply in love with the girl he had "picked up" one dark night, there were many prophets of doom. Dire stories came back home of these Anglo-American marriages. The young wives grew homesick and deserted their husbands. Some of them discovered they had been grossly deceived by glamorous talk about their future homes. They found themselves domestic drudges in dreary little American towns, smitten with arctic blizzards in winter and boiled alive in summer. Some had no homes of their own, and the girls were thrust into the crowded, poverty-stricken tenements of parents who were hostile.

Some of the girls picked up were mere sluts in England and remained sluts in America. Some of the husbands were lechers and good-for-nothings. The wartime shotgun marriages went on the rocks. The lads, so glamorous in uniform, proved louts in civvies. The pretty "floosie" could neither cook, sew nor wash, and was only happy at the cinema or on the dance floor. They bred indiscriminately. To escape the smell and noise of babies, the husbands haunted the bars.

These histories had all been brought to Alice Small as a warning. But she had faith in her young husband and embarked on the great adventure. She was lovingly received by Tom's parents, brothers and sisters. The American families, she found, lived gaily and with a thoughtless extravagance that amazed her. Almost everything seemed on the hire-purchase. They all had large automobiles on which the instalments never ceased, for a new one replaced the old one before it was paid for. They went in and out of jobs with acrobatic agility. They had strange streaks of religious fanaticism, measured everything by dollars, became hysterical over politics but were always generous, sociable and charitable. They lived with gusto and courage.

Tom was employed in his father's market-garden business. It was enterprising, run on scientific lines. They cultivated fifteen acres, some of it under glass, and had orange groves inland. It was a prosperous business, employing three white truckers and twenty negroes. But it was a night-and-day job, the weather their taskmaster, "freezes", droughts and windstorms ever lurking under that great blue sky. Once in a while there was a hurricane.

Tom found a little four-roomed bungalow down by the coast, twelve miles out of St. Petersburg. He had a passion for the sea, boats and fishing. Its position seemed ideal for his hobby. It was on the high bank of a creek near the sea inlet. They looked out over the Mexican Gulf with its vast radiant sky and deep blue sea. Around the bungalow there was a small garden, dug out of the coralstone with which the houses were built. There was a great banyan tree that had driven its branches down into the earth, the live oaks had hanging greyish creeper, a casuarina tree, a mauve jacaranda tree, a magnolia, oleanders, tall palms, some cypress, a fig tree, and a small grove of grapefruit and orange trees, two acres in all. Over part of the bungalow's roof and along a low wall trailed the brilliant orange flame-vine.

There was a short wooden jetty built between great wooden posts, and a low boathouse and toolshed in which Tom housed a boat with an outboard motor. It was an earthly paradise— with a green hell not far away. A large mangrove growth struck down its contorted branches into the muddy and brackish water where strange things slithered and squeaked. Behind the swamp lay the scrub with palmettos and dwarf pine trees. The liana-matted jungle ran for miles inland, little changed since the Indians and Spanish conquistadores had contended for Florida.

They were isolated, two miles from a small settlement, mostly of fishermen of Greek origin, with some shops, a mail office, a schoolhouse and three churches. They were nine miles from the market gardens over a flat sandy road threading a waste of pines and palmettos and scrub oaks. The bungalow was their own, bought for them by Tom's father, a hardworking, taciturn but good-hearted man.

One of the features of their jetty home was the birds. The catbirds, small and grey, blithe singers; the yellow-throats, scarlet tanagers and cardinals, the flycatcher phoebus and the ruby-crowned kinglets abounded. Of all these birds, the most familiar, and full of character, were the pelicans. Alice was fascinated by them. They were very fond of the jetty posts, which were flat-topped. They sat there and contemplated the world like philosophers. A little along the coast they nested in the mangrove swamp.

At the mouth of the creek the fishing boats were tied up by a long jetty. They usually came in towards dusk with their day's haul. The pelicans awaited their return, certain to be rewarded by "trash" fish thrown out from the catch. During most of the day the pelicans sailed up and down over the sea, where they dived or floated, or else sat calmly on the jetty posts. Alice noticed that they all faced the same way. They were highly regimented. They flew in single file, or sometimes in a V formation, often in a wide echelon, reminding Alice of Air Force manoeuvres. Clumsy at taking off, they alighted on the water like skiers, their webbed feet thrust forward, churning up a watery barrier before they settled. When they dived they plummeted with a great splash, coming down from thirty or forty feet in a bomber's dive that sank them in the water.

"Don't they hurt themselves?" asked Alice.

"No, they are a sort of pneumatic bird. They've a network of air sacs through their bones and under their skins," said Tom. "It's curious how they're both clever and clumsy. They patter along the water for quite a distance before they're airborne, like top-heavy old hydroplanes. But once they're up, my! how they go, with the wind astern, flapping and planing, with an eight-foot wingspread. If you watch you'll notice that when they're bucking a head-wind they come down and skim over the sea. The water friction reduces the wind force and the small upright draught from the waves gives them enough lift to glide steadily, with an occasional flap to keep up momentum. Pelicans can teach us quite a thing or two about flying—but a gull can beat 'em any day. You'll always see gulls hanging around pelicans. When the old bird lifts up his bill to drain a catch of fish the gull slips in, snatches it before he can swallow, and there's just nothing the poor old pelican can do about it!"

Every morning and evening there were pelicans standing motionless on the posts. They seemed to be deep in thought. The crowns of their small heads made them look like venerable old men. In due time Alice became familiar with their characteristics. They let her approach closely, watching her tranquilly. With their downy necks and broad wings they were rather like swans, with long bills and pouches added, grey instead of white. Unlike swans, they were very sociable. Alice loved them when they yawned, as if bored with life. They revealed a large deep sack which was really a fishing scoop.

"You've heard the old limerick?" asked Tom—

> *What a wonderful bird is the pelican*
> *Whose bill can hold more than his belly can;*
> *He can hold in his beak*
> *Enough food for a week—*
> *I'm blest if I see how the hell he can!*

"Well, it's all wrong! He never holds fish in his pouch. He swallows it very quickly, and he couldn't hold enough in it for a week. A pelican eats four pounds of fish a day. In a week that's twenty-eight pounds, over twice his weight. Nor is he such a pious bird as they make out."

"Pious—I've never heard him called pious!" said Alice.

"Well, a kind of symbol of piety. They got it around in the Middle Ages that pelicans fed their young on their own blood by puncturing their breasts with their beaks. By that the pelican became a sort of symbol of Christ's suffering, and was shown in heraldry as representing piety and charity. Actually, to feed their young, pelicans regurgitate their food in the form of pap. They hold it in their gullets while the fledglings dip in.

But I'm not running down the pelican. He's a grand old bird!"

More and more Alice wondered at her husband's knowledge of things. He seemed to know everything about fishes. He could readily name most birds, trees, plants, flowers, shells and even the stars that looked so near in the clear night sky. He was capable with his hands, a good fisherman and shot. He sometimes terrified Alice with his underwater swimming, armed with snorkel and spear gun. When the marine motor broke down he could always repair it. He had taught Jeremy to be a fearless and adept swimmer. But he could not add up, eat his food slowly, or wash without making a fearful mess. He did not like music, the only serious difference in their tastes. He was also reckless with money. He spent everything as soon as it came into his hands.

They were serenely happy. He was a virile and tender lover, and ever ready to give her a hand in the house. Quite tireless, he worked from dawn to sundown.

Alice quickly settled down in the new community. Many things were strange, including the language. The native Americans, Crackers, as they called them, had a curious accent. They were great gossipers, full of wise saws, and friendly.

They had arrived in October so she did not experience the fearful heat that afflicted her in summer. The winter days were like those of a perfect June in England, except for short spells when the temperature fell, occasionally near freezing point, but this lasted only a day or two. They swam in the warm sea through all the winter months.

Alice had noticed on arrival that all the windows and doors were screened. She was to learn how necessary this was. In June came a plague of insects, or "bugs" as the natives called them. There were flying beetles an inch long, but she loved to watch the great lizards basking or darting across the coralstone. The palms quivered in the heat under the scalding sun. Over the hammock, as they called the wild land, the hawk cried or swooped on the quail and rabbits. Once they saw an alligator lazing in the creek. There was shade under the live oaks, dripping with moss, and the magnolia trees, but the open spaces

I

and the roads burnt one up. Sometimes she longed for the lush green coolness of England, the rocky dales of Derbyshire, great trees, and the wind sighing through them on the uplands. The cypress and mangrove swamps had no peace in them. They were evil, with tangled roots coming up from the slimy ooze, with watersnakes, with a dense vegetation murderously struggling for life. Yet great beauty lay around their nestling bungalow, the blue of the sea, the trees with golden oranges, grapefruit, avocado pears, kumquats, pears and figs. There was the daily pageant of the sunset, with the great open sky in crimson flame, dying in celestial magnificence, and, in the fading purple afterglow, the brilliant stars and the deep silence over the flat land.

They had been married a year when their felicity was crowned with the birth of Jeremy. He was sturdy, fair, happy-natured. In his fourth year they took him to England for a two months' visit to his grandparents in Derby.

"Happy?" asked Alice's father, nursing the boy.

"Wonderfully!"

"Hm. And to think you'd have turned Tom down if it hadn't been for me!" he said, chuckling.

III

In the fifth year they lost a child, a girl, an hour after birth. Little Jeremy flourished. He was strong and intelligent. He lived in and out of the water, naked and brown. He followed his father like a shadow. Presently his mother took him daily to the village school until, aged ten, he was given a bicycle. One morning he came in from the jetty.

"Mom!" he said. "A pelican spoke to me! He's been talking to me for a week, but I didn't realize it."

"Don't be absurd! You know pelicans can't talk."

"He's got a squeak-talk, Mom."

She laughed. Late that afternoon when her husband came in from a fishing expedition Jeremy repeated his story. "Pop, when I say 'Hello' he says 'Hello' back. He's been saying it for a week—I'm sure he has!"

"How do you know it's the same pelican?"

"He sits on the same post always and I can tell him by the look on his face," replied Jeremy.

"Now don't be silly, my boy. All pelicans look alike. You can't tell one pelican from another."

"Their babies know their Moms and Pops don't they?" asked Jeremy, unconvinced.

"All young 'uns know their parents."

"Do they smell them?"

"Well, I wouldn't say that—perhaps they do, perhaps they don't. Do you smell me?" asked his father, laughing.

Jeremy was not satisfied.

"Look son, you'll find some 'trash' fish in the bottom of the boat. Go and take it to your friend and make him say 'Please' before you throw it to him," said Little, cutting himself a slice of cake.

Jeremy slid off his chair. Tom and Alice exchanged looks.

"Son, you're sure crazy. I'll give you a nickel for every word that old bird says."

"Come with me, Pop, and hear him," said Jeremy.

Little went with his son, got the fish and proceeded to the jetty. There was a solitary pelican standing on a post, his long grey beak resting on his chest, his small yellowy poll sunk between his shoulders. At their approach the pelican raised his long neck, turned round and regarded them quizzically.

"Hello!" said Jeremy.

The pelican squawked, and looked down benevolently at the small boy. Whatever gifts nature had bestowed on the bird, a voice was not one of them.

"Would you like a fish?" asked Jeremy.

The pelican squawked again.

"Then you say 'If you please'," cried Jeremy, holding up a fish.

The pelican spread its grey wings, folded them, and squawked.

"There, Pop! That's three nickels!"

"I don't call that talking!"

"But he answered me three times!"

"Very well, give him the fish."

The pelican caught three fish. A fourth he retrieved from the water. He flew back to the post, the fish in his beak, and then swallowed it.

They had returned half-way down the jetty when the pelican took off, planed overhead, and then settled on the boards just behind them, ungainly on his webbed feet. He began to walk with them. Little turned and looked down at the bird.

"Hey you! There's no more fish!" he cried.

The pelican looked up, with amused eyes.

Jeremy turned and said—"If you'll come tomorrow you'll get some more fish," and then to his father's amazement Jeremy put out a hand and touched the top of the bird's head, smoothing it. It stood placidly looking at the boy.

"Well, he's sure tame!" observed his father.

As they walked away the pelican watched them for a while. Then it took off, rising high in the air, flapping and planing, a dark body in the fading sky, disappearing down the coast.

A week later when Little returned home for lunch his wife said, as he came in from the back courtyard, "I want you to come and look at Jeremy. He and that pelican have gone into business together!"

She led him into the living-room and up to the window. He looked out. There was Jeremy, with hatchet in hand, chopping a branch off a pine tree. He was naked except for a slip on his loins, like a young Indian out of the brushwood. One sturdy leg was braced against the trunk that shook under the blows of the hatchet. On one of the swaying branches stood a pelican, its wings spread to keep its balance. Both boy and bird were deeply in earnest.

"They've been having a long conversation all the morning," said Mrs. Little. "The pelican seems to be works manager, squawking instructions to Jeremy."

They watched. It was a singular sight. Boy and pelican were on the most confidential terms. When not swaying on the branch the bird stood on the ground, solemnly watching his companion's attack on the log.

"I believe it's the same pelican—the one Jeremy talks to down on the jetty!" said Little.

"I'm certain it is. He walked with Jeremy right up to our door about an hour ago. He haunts the place when Jeremy's around," said his wife.

ONE MORNING the Littles were preparing to go out fishing for the day. Jeremy, an adept helmsman, brought the boat alongside the jetty. Mrs. Little and her husband began to load it with lunch basket and tackle. Suddenly out of the sky a pelican sailed in and settled on a post. It watched the proceedings calmly. Jeremy saluted it. "Hello!" he cried to his old friend. There came an answering squawk.

"Pop, don't you think we should give him a name?" asked Jeremy.

"Well, that's an idea," answered his father.

"But we don't know whether he's a lady or a gentleman," said Mrs. Little.

"Oh, I'm sure he's a gentleman. He's such good manners, hasn't he, Pop?" cried Jeremy.

"For some reason he always reminds me of William Wordsworth," said Mrs. Little.

Jeremy was familiar with Wordsworth. His mother had read to him some of the poems. He could recite the whole of *The Idle Shepherd-Boys*.

> *"A Poet, one who loves the brooks*
> *Far better than the sages' books,"*

quoted Mrs. Little.

"That seems to fit him pretty well. He's a nice poetical-looking old bird—let's call him William," said Little.

So he was called William, and as William he was destined to make a stir in the world.

"Are you coming with us, we're going fishing!" cried Jeremy to his friend on the post. "Come on, William, you'll have a good time!"

William extended his wings, reared up, seemed to hesitate and then flew down to the boat, landing on the fore-deck.

Mrs. Little looked at her husband. "Nobody would believe it unless they saw it!" she said.

The engine spluttered, picked up, and they moved forwards. It was a pleasant morning in May. William took up a position for'ard, the breeze fluttering the yellowish feathers on the top of his venerable head. He obviously enjoyed the movement.

II

William became a regular passenger on the motor-boat. The noise of the engine seemed to fascinate him. He would make his way astern and stand watching the wash. Away from the coast he flew off fishing on his own, coming down to float on the sea. There were a few occasions when, encountering a flock of pelicans, William joined them, entering in perfect formation. But he always came home with the launch, taking up his favourite position on the prow. Later he watched from the post in anticipation of the unloading and the share-out.

One day the jetty was being repaired and several planks had been taken up. William observed the work, visibly annoyed, flying off and on to his post. Then he followed Jeremy, and coming to a gap, was perplexed. Jeremy stooped down, picked him up and hopped over with him. After that William had complete confidence in his friend and let himself be picked up and carried. He weighed about ten pounds, as much as Jeremy could carry comfortably.

There was one occasion when he followed Jeremy into the kitchen. Perhaps he could smell fish frying. The coloured help, Lizzie, who came in each day, fled into the living-room, where she found Mrs. Little. "Mes Little," she said, rolling her eyes. "I jes don't work in de kitchen wi thet heathen bird aroun'. No, Mes', he's possessed of a sperit!"

The offensive William was evicted. A week later as they sat down for lunch at one end of the living-room, Jeremy came in from the garden carrying William.

"Oh, no, Jeremy! Put that bird outside. We're going to eat," said Mrs. Little.

"But, Mom, can't he sit at table?" asked Jeremy.

"With a bib and spoon, I suppose?" said his father, ironically.

"I'm sure he'll behave, Pop. Won't you, William?" Jeremy asked, addressing the pelican as he placed him on a chair in front of the table. William rested his yellow-lined bill on his downy chest, his bright round eyes deeply observant.

"Well, anybody might think we'd got the Archbishop of Canterbury to lunch!" exclaimed Mrs. Little.

"Ask him to say Grace," said Tom Little. "Look, son, we can't have William in the house—he'll be getting into bed with us next!"

"Oh Pop! Please let him stay. I'm sure he'll behave!" cried Jeremy.

"Very well, this once. I don't know who's the crazier, that bird or us!" said his father.

All through lunch William never moved. He watched everything and seemed to be considering some deep problem.

III

Two weeks after coming to lunch, William, who had been missing for three days—something never solved—appeared on his post, contemplating the creek. Jeremy went up to him. The pelican squawked. "William, where've you been?" he asked. He had an orange in his hand and playfully threw it at the pelican. He was dumbfounded to see William deftly catch it in his bill, hold it in the air for a few seconds, then let it fall into the sea. Jeremy hurried off at once to the garden. Here he picked up three fallen oranges and came back with them down the jetty.

"Catch, William!" he called, and threw one towards the pelican. William caught it, held it, and dropped it in the water. Jeremy threw a second orange, then a third. They were both caught, briefly retained and then dropped. Four catches and not a miss.

This astounding feat was reported to Little when he came home. "He must have been disappointed. He thought they were fish," he commented.

Jeremy was not pleased by this aspersion on William's

intelligence. He was far too wise to mistake an orange for a fish. The next day when William came across to the stone terrace in search of his friend, Jeremy rushed into the room and collected the net containing half a dozen of his mother's tennis balls. He carried them out on to the lawn and stood about six yards in front of William.

"Hey! Catch!" he cried, and threw one.

William caught it perfectly. For a few moments he kept the ball in his beak, then dropped it and watched it bounce away, imperturbable. The act was repeated with the five balls. Only once did William fail a catch, and then it was Jeremy's fault, he threw the ball wide.

Collecting the six balls Jeremy threw them again. They were all caught by William, who squawked with delight.

"You don't think they're fish, do you?" said Jeremy, patting William's head. The pelican looked at him calmly as if to say, "Don't be silly!"

By now they were inseparable. As soon as Jeremy appeared on the jetty William would turn round on his post to look at him. Often there were half a dozen pelicans sitting there, awaiting the evening return of the fishing boats. They were so much alike that it would have been impossible to identify William had he not turned and given a squawk of welcome. He flew off with the other birds when the boats came in, catching with them the "trash" fish thrown out at the jetty. After feeding, with much flapping of wings and swift pouncings, the pelicans went off down coast in the sunset light, a single file of dark forms, bills horizontally forward, great wings slowly and rhythmically flapping, feet drawn up. They were bound for the mango swamp where they nested.

"Do you think William's married?" asked Jeremy one evening, watching their homeward flight.

"Quite likely," replied his father.

"With a wife and family?"

"Probably."

There was a silence while Jeremy was thinking.

"He doesn't spend much time at home, Pop, does he?" he asked solemnly.

"Seems not. Perhaps he's a bad husband."

"Oh, no, Pop. I'm sure he has a kind heart," said Jeremy, always William's champion.

Tom Little looked at his boy's solemn face and ran a hand through his fair curls. "Maybe you're right, son. But there's one thing we'll never know—what he's thinking about in that dome of his!"

IV

On Saturday morning Mrs. Little was in her car, to run down to the grocer's. Jeremy came into the courtyard with William waddling behind.

"Can I come with you?" he asked.

"Yes, get in," she replied, starting the engine.

"Can I bring William?"

"Gracious no!"

"I'm sure he'll be good, Mom. He hates being left."

Mrs. Little hesitated. "Oh, bring him then," she said, seeing Jeremy's pleading look.

"Come on! You're going for a ride!" said Jeremy, picking up William and placing him on the seat between them.

William made no fuss and sedately looked out through the windscreen. At the grocer's store he created something of a sensation. Children collected round the car and talked to him. Jeremy swelled with pride at the attention William received. When the grocer came out of the shop carrying a parcel for Mrs. Little and placed it in the back of the car, he started on seeing a pelican standing on the seat beside Jeremy.

"My! My!" he exclaimed. "In all my life I've never seen a pelican in an automobile before!"

"He lives with us!" said Jeremy proudly.

"Can he drive?" asked the grocer, with mock seriousness.

"No, but I think he could learn. William can learn anything!" said Jeremy. "He plays tennis!"

"Now, Jeremy, don't exaggerate! He catches tennis balls," explained Mrs. Little getting into the car.

"Tennis balls! I suppose he can hold more of them in

his bill than his belly can," cried the grocer, facetiously.

"My Pop says that isn't true. A pelican eats four pounds of fish in a day. That's twenty-eight pounds in a week, and that's over twice what he weighs," said Jeremy, breathlessly.

"Is that so, young man? Well, well, I've learned something about pelicans this morning I didn't know! Many thanks. Come again!" said the grocer.

They drove off.

"Everyone likes William, Mom, and I'm sure he likes motoring."

"Maybe, Jeremy, But we're not going to be toting William around with us—people will think we're crazy."

Jeremy made no reply. He put an arm around William to steady him on a corner.

v

It was not long before the whole district knew about the Littles' pelican. Children called and asked if they might see William. Others asked permission to take photographs and movies. The tennis-ball act was a favourite shot. William duly performed. He was very good-natured. He posed with Jeremy and let the children pat his head.

The Littles had built a swimming-pool. It was not long before William joined Jeremy in it. He would paddle around contentedly while his friend dived under and around him. But a day came when William fell under suspicion. He was accused of theft and murder. Little had made a basin with a fountain in the middle of the lawn and stocked it with two dozen goldfish. They flourished for a couple of months. Then one day there was not a single goldfish in the pool.

"Ah sees thet William walkin' round' the rim. Ah knew he was ketchin' somethin'," said Lizzie, the coloured help, William's sworn enemy.

"Then why didn't you go and stop him?" asked Mrs. Little.

"Thet bird! He's sure evil! Ah jes wouldn't cross him. He'd be puttin' a spell on me," replied Lizzie, the whites of her eyes enlarged.

For a month William lay under the charge of gobbling up the goldfish. Jeremy stoutly denied any such crime. Then one day Little came home and William was exonerated. "I've been talking to Jimmy Blair about goldfish. He says you just can't keep them around here. The herons come and catch them. I expect that's what happened to our goldfish, there are herons up the creek."

CHAPTER 3

I

THE SUMMER WAS inordinately hot. Never before had Alice Little experienced such heat. There was no respite at night though they lay naked on the bed. The frogs croaked incessantly down in the ditches along the creek. It was almost a heat bleat, as if they too lacked air. The owls hooted. Strange noises and stirrings quivered in the hot air. The day broke with a dank heat-mist and there was moisture on everything, but it was gone before the light was full and the sky again became a brazen bowl. As one looked at the palms through the rising air they seemed to quiver in the heat. Nothing stirred in the hammock for a space. The chuff-chuff of a motor-boat going out to sea pulsed through the silent morning. A mocking-bird began to sing lustily, with mellifluous flutings. Mrs. Little always liked the wording of the State's official recognition of this bird—"Whereas the melody of its music had delighted the hearts of residents and visitors to Florida, from the time of the rugged pioneers to the present day, and whereas this bird of matchless charm is found throughout the State—Therefore, on the Resolution of the Legislature of the State of Florida, it is resolved that the mocking-bird is hereby designated the State Bird of the State of Florida, and that it be placed upon the arms of the State".

Jeremy was a little aggrieved by this. He thought the State bird should be a pelican, but Louisiana had annexed it for its own State bird.

This morning, as Mrs. Little listened, the song grew faint and then stopped, as if the mocking-bird, too, had been overcome by heat. As the morning mist lifted the distant sea was a cobalt blue with not a white reefer to be seen on the silken water. She went into the kitchen to get breakfast. She could hear Tom running the cold shower, which was anything but cold. Jeremy was up, in his swimming shorts, sitting on the step playing a mouth organ.

"Oh, stop it, Jeremy!" said Mrs. Little, irritably, and then added, conscious of being sharp, "Or play it somewhere else."

She made the coffee, pushed back a damp wisp of hair, and carried it into the living-room. Her husband came in with a towel round his hips. She glanced at him, his torso a triangle from broad shoulders to narrow waist. The deep bronze of his skin afflicted her as if it radiated heat.

"It can't possibly get any hotter than this, can it?" she asked, sitting down. "And it's only seven o'clock!"

Little looked at the barometer on the wall. It was 99 degrees Fahrenheit. But he saw something else that he did not like. The mercury had fallen very low. It was ominous. He had been through two hurricanes. He said nothing to his wife about the lowness of the barometer. The Weather Bureau would send out its radio warning if a hurricane threatened.

He sat down and poured the coffee. "Cheer up, my girl! Next summer we'll be in England and perhaps it will be raining on us," he said with a smile.

"I'd like a little of that rain now. I've never known it to be as hot as this."

The holiday in England next year, how she longed for it! It was seven years since she had been home. Jeremy was then only four and her parents were anxious to see him again. Each year they put by a little for the expensive journey. They planned to leave in July and stay three months. She was happy here, she had a good husband, a fine little son, and had received much kindness from everybody, but an ache for England at the bottom of her heart was never quite repressed.

To her surprise her husband was back from the nurseries at half-past eleven. The moment he came in she saw from his face that something had happened.

"You've not heard—on the radio?" he asked.

"No, I've not had it on."

"They've sent out a warning. There's a hurricane blowing up the Gulf. It may be here in fifteen hours. They want us all to leave the coast. We must batten down everything and make all ready. They've got the flags out already."

"The flags?"

"Hurricane warning flags—red and white with black centres. They're opening the schools and churches for refuge places. I've been lucky enough to get a room in an hotel in St. Petersburg—we must leave in two or three hours."

"Leave! But why can't we stay here?"

"It might not be safe. We're on the coast. Luckily we're coralstone but a wind could take the roof off, or the sea come up, or something flying around could break us open. You can't predict what a hurricane will do. Fill the car with clothes and some food. And run water in the bath and in the buckets. We might need it when we come back if the mains are burst."

He turned to Jeremy. "Come on, boy—help me with the shutters, and we must take the boat higher up the creek," he called, going out.

They all worked desperately for two hours. They stored water, packed away glass, pushed heavy furniture up against the outside door, made fast the wooden shutters, turned off gas, water and electricity. As they took the boat up the creek they saw flocks of birds wheeling in the air. "They know what's coming," said Little.

"What'll William do, Pop?" asked Jeremy.

"I don't know. Everything has to look after itself."

The sea had turned the colour of lead. It had a sullen light upon its slowly heaving mass. Immense angry clouds piled up, grey and white, and touched with sinister light. There was not a breath of wind. The still scene was heavy with drama.

High up the creek they made fast the boat, and covered up the outboard motor. On the way back to the house there was a sudden downpour. It was not just rain. It came down as if someone had emptied a bucket on them. They were drenched. Then the rain was gone as completely and quickly as it had come. But out at sea, under a blue-black horizon, there was a yellow wall of racing water that mounted and then crashed on the leaden glaze of the sea with a horrifying noise. Then once again a sinister silence.

Back at the house, they changed their clothes, put on oilskins and began carrying the last things to the car. But they were not in time. The light suddenly went and the heavens opened. They were blinded by the torrent of rain, and with it a savage wind hammered at the house and howled through the trees. It almost wrenched the open door of the car out of Little's hand. Jeremy, half blinded, about to follow his mother in the car, suddenly saw something through the rain. It was William trying to make his way towards him. Jeremy rushed and gathered up the bird.

"You can't bring that bird!" yelled Little, over the roar of wind and water.

"Pop! I must! I must!" shouted Jeremy, lashed with rain. "He'll die. He'll die!"

Hastily Little pushed his son and bird into the car, slammed the door, and jumped into the driving-seat. Mrs. Little, looking back over her shoulder, saw a rather frightened wet face pressed against a drenched bird in her son's lap.

"I don't know what you think we're going to do with him!" shouted Little, as they turned into the road.

"I'll look after him!" said Jeremy, earnestly. "Thanks, Pop!"

Little drove blindly, a sheet of water down the windscreen blotting out all vision. Sometimes it seemed as if the wind would lift the car off the road. They were nearly hit by a flying palm frond. At one place, where the road bordered the sea, the foaming water washed the wheels. The hurricane was sending its forerunner. Little grew anxious but said nothing. He knew what hurricanes could do. His grandfather had miraculously survived the Galveston visitation in 1900 when three thousand homes had been washed away and six thousand people killed in a few hours. His grandfather told how he had gathered forty persons in his house on higher ground, and that two adjacent houses, uprooted by wind and water, crashed into them and threw them all into a raging cauldron where all but five perished.

St. Petersburg was twelve miles away. Two miles outside the town a sheet of galvanized tin, torn off a roof, flew through the air like a piece of paper and missed the car by a couple of yards. He knew an old man who had had both legs sheared off in that manner. The hurricane must have travelled much quicker than predicted. The outer tornado had arrived. It was almost dark at four o'clock. The town, as they entered it, was deserted. Not a person or car was on the roads, the shop windows were boarded up, the offices closed. Everyone had rushed home to batten down.

When they reached the hotel a strange sight awaited them in the lounge. It was crammed with people sitting on their baggage, refugees from the coast like themselves. As they got out of their car the wind had almost carried them away, the downpour drenched them. They arrived, dripping, at the reception desk. The clerk was giving them the room key when he saw Jeremy holding the pelican.

"Hey! What've you there! A pelican! My God, what you folks bring! Cats, dogs, rabbits, mice, snakes, canaries—say, this place isn't a zoo! That bird can't come in here!" he cried.

"But if we keep it in our room—" began Little.

"No, sir! No animals in here. They all have to go into the garage."

The clerk was adamant. When they had brought in their luggage, Jeremy and his father went back to the car with William and drove to the hotel garage. Like the lounge, it was crammed—a still more amazing sight. On the roofs and bonnets of the cars and on the floor were boxes covered with wire, cages containing canaries, budgerigars, parrots, tame rabbits, tame mice. There were baskets with things alive in them pushing snouts and paws through the crevices. Half a dozen harassed youths were trying to pack in the cars. It took half an hour for Little to get a place. Many of the cars had dogs locked up in them. Above the roar of wind and drumming of rain rose the noise of yapping dogs, whining animals and birds screeching. The dark garage had become a little inferno. It was here they left William, very calm, on a waterproof on the back seat. He looked scornfully at the bedlam around him. Little locked the car, leaving the rear window open a little for air.

They had not been half an hour in their room when the hurricane hit them. There was a deafening uproar. A hundred-mile-an-hour wind screamed and hammered the great building with demoniac rage. Water, streaming down the windows, made them opaque. The day was blacker than black night. They

K

had to shout at each other over the uproar of wind and rain. There were terrifying crashes and bangs. Suddenly all the lights went out. They were in total darkness. The electric light had failed. Alice Little groped for a bag and produced two torches. "I've packed some sandwiches also," she shouted, putting them out on the dressing-table. "And a flask of coffee."

"Splendid!" shouted her husband. "I don't think there'll be any dinner served."

They sat for an hour in the darkness, the demon storm howling about them. Presently Little felt his foot slither. He looked down with a torch. There was a pool of water round his chair. It came from the wall under the window. The terrific wind pressure was forcing the rain through the window frames.

At seven o'clock Little said he would go and investigate about dinner. He took a torch and went down the corridor. Many of the bedroom doors were open as if the occupants craved company. Candles were lit in some of the rooms.

The elevators were not running. He sought the staircase. There were people wandering about in the darkness like lost spirits. Suddenly there was a tremendous tearing noise and a great crashing of glass. The wind had blown in two long windows at the end of the corridor. A horizontal sheet of water came in, knocking down a man and woman. The woman was screaming, her face running with blood, cut by the flying glass. They helped her into an adjacent bedroom. There was no telephone service. Little volunteered to search for a doctor. He was wet to the skin and went through the torrent again to reach the stairs. They were on the eighth floor. People were groping their way up and down the stairs. When at last he reached the lounge it was like a scene in Hades. Everywhere figures crouched in the dim light of the wavering candles which they tried to protect from the draughts that beat on the flames. He was unable to find a doctor. While he enquired, a man had an epileptic fit on the carpet.

There would be no dinner. The kitchens were out of service. They would try to serve soup in paper cups and perhaps sandwiches. At one end of the lounge a group was dismally singing hymns, as if it expected the end of the world. Little slowly made his way back to their room. In the bathroom he took off his clothes and wrapped himself in a blanket. They ate their sandwiches in darkness. They did not go to bed but dozed uneasily, Jeremy and his mother on one bed, Little on the other. At four o'clock in the morning the storm abated. Little got up and looked out. There was an angry gash of red in the east, but neither wind nor rain. The hurricane had moved on.

Little decided not to leave until after lunch. There might be wreckage on the road and it would be wise to give time for its clearance. He tried to telephone to his parents but could not get through. All the lines were down. They found William bedded down on the back seat of the car and in no way agitated. He squawked when Jeremy addressed him and lifted him out. He spread his wings, ruffled his feathers and waddled a few steps.

"He must be hungry, Pop," said Jeremy.

"I'm afraid he's got to go hungry until he can do his own fishing," replied Little.

The hotel served a scrap lunch. The lounge had emptied, also the garage. The assorted pets had gone home. When the Littles left about two o'clock the town had come to life; they were taking down the boards from the shop windows. Some of the streets were flooded, the drains choked. Here and there a tree had been blown down. It was not until they had left the town that the havoc became visible. Telephone and power lines were down, their great posts leaning drunkenly at all angles, or flat on the ground. Then, as they neared the coast road, the signs of devastation were everywhere. A billion tons of water sucked up as rain vapour had been dumped on the land in eight hours. Steel highway-signs were twisted into strips of soft lead. The hurricane had lopped off the heads of trees like a boy with a stick in a thistle-field. In places the road had been washed away and they had great difficulty in proceeding. A large three-storey wooden house had been lifted off its brick foundation, carried into a field, and dumped like a paper bag. The sea still boiled. It had bitten away great pieces of the shore. Everywhere there were uprooted trees, tumbled hoardings and fences. A row of wooden houses had lost their roofs as if a scythe had swept them. A large boat, upside down, lay over a poultry coop five hundred yards from the shore.

Three miles from home they were held up by a line of cars. Little got out to investigate. There was a complete road block. A huge live oak had been uprooted and lay in a tangle of riven branches across the road. It was impossible to proceed further. They decided to leave the car and walk. It might be hours before the demolition squad arrived. Jeremy lifted up William.

"You're not going to carry him. He's too heavy," said Little. "Put him down."

"But he can't walk all that way, Pop."

"Don't be ridiculous. He can fly. We've had quite enough of William—there are other things to think of. Put him down!" said Little, angrily.

"Jeremy, don't be absurd. He must look after himself," said Mrs. Little.

Jeremy put William on the bonnet of the car. The pelican stood there watching them walk away.

They started out on the battered road, leaving the locked car with the others that had been abandoned for the same reason. When they had gone some way Jeremy looked back. What he saw made him jump with excitement. William was in the air.

"Look, Pop! He's flying!" he cried.

They looked. The pelican was high up, his long beak forward, his wings slowly flapping, in steady flight with intervals of planing. He was going out to sea. Obviously he was looking for food.

"Well, I will say one thing for him—he behaved beautifully," said Little.

At last they drew near to the house. With relief Little saw that it was intact. He opened the gate into the courtyard and had to force it. Gravel had piled up against it. Through the gate he drew a sharp breath. An enormous branch of a live oak had been torn away from the trunk. It lay, black, splintered, not two yards from the house. If it had fallen across the house it would have demolished the roof. It had torn down the side wall of the courtyard. A small branch had been thrown on to the back window and had shattered it. There were four roof tiles on the ground.

Little unlocked the door and went in. There was a hot damp smell. The hall floor was covered with black sand and mud two inches thick, the carpet invisible. They came into the large living-room, again over a bed of wet filth. A side window had given way and there was a pool of water along the wall. Over all there was a mass of shattered plaster. They looked up. Water had been driven in under the roof of the ceiling, which had fallen. Through broken laths and a hole in the roof they saw the sky.

Mrs. Little collapsed on a chair and burst into tears.

II

Little by little they discovered the extent of the havoc. The lawn had disappeared under a matting of sand and broken branches. All the shrubs had been uprooted. A foot of filth was built up against the front door. As Little stepped out he saw that the toolshed had been carried away and lay smashed against the banyan tree. The tree had stood firm but it was skeletal, its branches like writhing snakes, stripped of all leaves. He squelched ankle-deep down the lawn. At the bottom he saw that four planks had been wrenched off the jetty and had vanished. The mimosa, the jessamine and honeysuckle over the house were gone. The water-stained walls stood naked to the sky. All round were palm-fronds ten foot long. Seven palm-trees were down. He went up the creek. There his heart sank. The boat had gone. A titanic force had wrenched the bolted iron stanchions from their seatings. Over the whole scene there was a warm miasma, a stench of rotting things, a putrescence of animal bodies. He looked and saw the reason. He was in a graveyard of drowned creatures—cormorants, a blue heron, white egrets, wood-rats, black-fox squirrels, rabbits, a banded mocassin-snake, a king-snake, coots, and innumerable small birds, battered and pulped by the storm. This part of the creek was higher ground and they had converged on it, driven by the rising waters.

Three days later their boat was reported. It was found right up the creek, in the middle of a field, its prow smashed in. The adjacent field held thirty drowned cattle. The devastation ran for miles inland, up and down the coast. Market gardens, farms, orchards, orange groves and plantations were stripped or ruined by salt water, or had the top-soil carried off. The Little nurseries were heavily damaged, partly flooded. An acre of glass had been demolished. Everywhere the power and telegraph lines lay roped over buildings and trees. The sea had smashed hundreds of water-craft to matchwood. Millions and millions of dollars had been lost.

One thing was very clear to the Littles. There could be no holiday in England next year. It would take months to repair the house, clear the land and gardens, and replant. It would be years before the shrubs, bushes, trees and normal vegetation could be restored.

Four days passed without any sign of William. There were no birds visible at all, not even the seagulls, usually so ubiquitous. Jeremy watched the battered jetty. Seven of the posts were awry but William's favourite post had received no damage. A week passed. Would he ever come again?

"Perhaps he's searching for his family," said Little. On the eighth day three pelicans settled on the posts. Jeremy rushed down to the jetty calling William's name but none responded. Then one morning he was sawing up a branch by the banyan tree when a shadow passed over him. He looked up and a pelican alighted on a wrecked garden chair near him.

"William!" he cried, dropping the saw.

The pelican squawked and danced a bit on the chair back. Jeremy rushed into the house.

"Mom! Mom!" he cried, "William's back! Come and see! It's William!"

Mrs. Little went out into the garden with the excited boy. Yes, there was no doubt, it was William. He let Jeremy stroke his head.

"Now where've you been! What have you been up to?" demanded Jeremy, stroking the bird's back.

William just looked wise and said nothing.

III

On a beautiful morning in March when the sea was like a blue
lake, and brilliant sunshine filled a cloudless sky, Mr. Little
opened a letter that gave him a surprise. It was from the Nature
Film Corporation of Hollywood. They were planning a series
of features on the bird, animal and marine life of each State.
They were coming to Florida and had heard of a singular pelican called William, owned by Mr. Little. Would he be willing
to let them make a film on location? If suitable arrangements
could be made they would pay a fee of three thousand dollars.
Little burst into laughter. His wife looked up from the breakfast
table.

"How would you like to see William a film star?" asked
Little, passing the letter to his wife. "We'd have one problem—
how could we guarantee that he would be on the set when he
was wanted?"

"Oh Pop! I'm sure he would be. William's always very
obliging," said Jeremy.

"I think it would be most amusing—and three thousand
dollars!" said Alice Little. "Tom, we could go to England!"

He looked at his wife. "That's quite an idea," he said. "I'll
write them."

IV

The film people arrived in June. Before their arrival they had
submitted a provisional script. William was to be "shot" on a
fishing trip, catching tennis balls, walking about the garden,
lunching at table, and going to the grocer's. Jeremy would be
in all these shots. William was to be shown as one of the family.

One day in early June two vans drew up to the house loaded
with apparatus. There were a director, an assistant director,
two camera men, an electrician, some odd men, and a very
smart young woman with the script. The convoy created such a
sensation in the district that Mrs. Little had quite a business
keeping people away.

The filming went on for a week. The director was delighted

with Jeremy. He found him a "natural", quick on instruction and photogenic. Despite all the fuss and the strange people around, William was quite unperturbed. He had never had so much fish thrown to him in his life.

There were two incidents that gave them all alarm. One day William did not turn up. They waited from dawn till sunset. There was no sign of him. Something like panic spread over the scene, with the star actor missing. His conduct was inexplicable. They were half-way through the shooting and all had gone so well, with few "retakes".

The next day William returned, but late in the afternoon, perhaps anticipating the return of the fishermen on the creek. Two days later he became temperamental. He refused to catch the tennis balls. Jeremy threw them and threw them. William remained completely indifferent. They had to postpone the act to another day. All was then well, except that he missed the fifth ball. On a retake he was perfect. He more than redeemed himself with a flawless performance in the visit to the grocer's store, and the high spot, lunch with the family. The script-writer had a suggestion. Could not William wear a bib at table? So they tied a bib round his neck. He accepted it with good humour and looked more like a bishop than ever.

The trial projections were more than satisfactory. Some of the close-ups were superb. "I'm blessed if that bird hasn't got a camera sense!" said one of the operators. They were very pleased with Jeremy also. When the shootings were all over, executed with untiring patience, and the "run-through" had been passed, and the vans had departed, the Little family was exhausted. William seemed in no way affected. He sat on his post contemplating the world around him, leaving it from time to time to investigate what Jeremy was doing.

V

The night before their flight to England Jeremy could not sleep. He got up soon after dawn on a bright July morning, roamed the garden, went to the creek, and then down to the beach. The long white rollers of a calm blue sea were pounding the sands. There were gulls overhead and quick-footed little sandpipers along the shore, but no pelicans in sight. He wondered if William would come in time to say Goodbye.

He could eat no breakfast and was unusually quiet. A car was coming for them at ten o'clock to take them to Tampa airport, en route for New York and London. He put down his teacup and looked at his father. "Pop, how long do pelicans live?" he asked.

"I'm told they can live twenty or thirty years."

"And how old do you think William is?"

Little knew what was in the boy's mind. "I don't know, son, he's a young bird, perhaps only five or six years. You don't have to worry your head about William. He'll be here when we get back," he replied, assuringly.

"Lizzie might shoo him away. She's scared of William."

"Don't worry, Jeremy. If William comes looking for you, Lizzie won't shoo him. I've promised her ten dollars if he's around when we return," said Mrs. Little.

"Oh, thanks, Mom!" cried Jeremy.

The car arrived at ten o'clock. The chauffeur packed in their three suitcases. They said goodbye to Lizzie, who was in charge for three months. As Mrs. Little was getting into the car she looked for Jeremy.

"Now where's Jeremy?" she asked her husband.

"I don't know. He was here a minute ago," he replied. He went back into the hall. "Jeremy! Jeremy! We're waiting!" he called.

There was no reply. He walked into the living-room. The boy was not there. He looked out of the window into the garden. Then he saw him out on the jetty, his small body silhouetted against the bright sky. He knew then what Jeremy was doing. He went back to the car in the courtyard.

"He'll be here in a minute. He's out on the jetty. I guess he's saying Goodbye," said Little to his wife.

Jeremy stood briefly on the jetty. He knew they were waiting for him. He had run out in case William was there but the post was empty. There was only the great sky and the sea.

"Goodbye! Goodbye, William! Wait for me, we'll be back in September. Goodbye!" he called.

He raised his hand. There was nothing but the sound of the sea. He paused a moment, then he turned and ran up the jetty back to the house, and out to the car.

They started. Lizzie waved. Jeremy sat next to his mother. She saw he was near to tears. She said nothing. She put an arm around him, and kissed his rumpled hair.

BOOK 5

The Bluebird

CHAPTER 1

1

I HAVE ALWAYS looked with wonder and some envy on persons who receive legacies. There seems to be a special dispensation of Providence governing the lives of some people. With no effort on their part, they inherit property, *objets d'art*, little souvenirs, or, best of all, hard cash. Maiden aunts appear to be the requisite equipment of well-planned lives. Providence has provided them and arranged the span of their mortality in order to meet various crises in the lives of the legatees.

Observing these recipients of such bounty, and familiar with their characteristics, I have come to see that there is no "damn merit" in the business. You are a born receiver or you are not. The fault, dear fellow-creature, is not in ourselves but in our stars that we aren't legatees. Failing well-endowed parents, rich aunts and uncles, or eccentric relations, who pass over those nearest but not dearest, to those farthest, in the disposal of their goods, there are those singular friends, or even mere acquaintances, who do the oddest things with their money.

For some reason I have had no experience of these unpredictable donors. The old gentleman who broke his leg by a fall in Pall Mall, for whom I procured a taxi and a doctor, and on whom I called subsequently in his nursing-home, though a lonely bachelor, and rich, did not leave me ten or even one thousand pounds. He left sixty thousand to the Missions to Seamen. I did not get a sixpence of his large fortune although he was very appreciative, he said, of all I had done for him.

Then there was the blind old lady living in some poverty, as we thought, to whom I went once a week for her last four years to read to her, being a kind young man. "Beware of pity," they say, but I have been all my life a man of kindly sentiment, I can neither kick a dog nor deal with a domineering woman. In the case of the poor blind lady I willingly gave up an evening each week in order to read to her. I am a good reader, I arti-

culate clearly and respond to emotional passages. Sometimes I
brought tears to my own eyes. On these occasions I carried with
me my own bottle of tonic water with which to moisten my
mouth at intervals, so anxious was I not to strain her hospitality.

She was always touchingly grateful for my visits, being a
very lonely person with no relations. When she died I went to
her cremation at Golders Green. I bought the only flowers that
graced her coffin before it slid noiselessly through that grim
aperture. There were only two persons present, myself and an
extremely cheerful young man who proved to be her solicitor.
He came in a light grey suit and did not wear even a black tie.
I went in a black suit. It was a heavy one, the only black one I
possessed. Being a phenomenally hot day in July, I felt I had
anticipated cremation. As I parted from the young man I
remarked on her sad life, her loneliness, her blindness, her very
straitened circumstances, so sad for one who had once been
well-to-do. He looked at me with what seemed a very unsym-
pathetic and even a merry eye.

"Oh, I don't think you need waste any tears over her!" he
exclaimed, brutally. "The old thing liked it that way. She
wasn't going to waste any money on feeding friends or paying
for help. As for being poor, I can tell you she's left a nice little
packet of money!"

This surprising statement was unprofessional, I felt. He was
a junior partner, I learned. His seniors, like me, would have
been shocked, I am sure.

Alerted by his remark, I watched the newspapers. We British,
famed for our reticence to a degree that enrages other nations,
have none in regard to very personal matters. While it is the
height of bad form to mention money when alive, it is the proud
custom to publish to the world what one leaves when one is
dead. It would seem to be a state of vanity beyond the grave
whereby the living can be impressed, were it not that the
deceased has no choice in the matter of publicity. "Did you see
old Smucker's left a hundred thousand pounds?" "Yes, I
thought it wouldn't be more than fifty," comes the reply, with
a note of admiration.

The custom being what it is, I turned daily to the list of Wills, with details, by which the Press satisfies the curiosity of the public. But I found nothing concerning the old lady. All I learned was of the desperate ingenuity that seems to afflict so many who die rich and leave some odd religious cult as a beneficiary. I began to think that that aggressively cheerful young solicitor had been joking. Then, one day, there it was, the Will of the old blind lady I had read to. At first, in the shaking train where I read it, I thought my eyes had deceived me, adding a digit to the figure she had left. I took out my glasses, used only for Death notices in *The Times* and Stock Exchange quotations, and looked again. She had left £37,268! Apart from one legacy of fifty pounds to the Royal Society for the Prevention of Cruelty to Animals, she left the rest to the Policemen's Benevolent Fund.

She had always had a weakness for policemen, understandably. They helped her to cross the road when she went out shopping. She often remarked on the policeman on his beat below her window in Sloane Gardens. He gave her such a feeling of safety in the night when she heard him go by. So the police got the legacy, and I, who had walked with her, read to her and had gone to her funeral, got nothing. I had never expected anything. I am not of that kind. Nevertheless, it would have been nice to be remembered. There was a small bedside clock by Cartier of Paris. It would have made a useful souvenir.

In the matter of legacies there is also the incredible story of my friend Gerald Johnson. He was a good fellow and everyone liked him though he had no special gifts. He was not good-looking nor really intelligent but unfailingly affable and always well-dressed and cheerful. His marriage was a failure, as was his business, largely because he would not attend to it. He was unreliable, unpunctual, and basically insincere. Women had always fallen madly for him. He exercised his sexual prowess with the itinerant activity of a bee collecting honey. I would not call him immoral since he never betrayed any awareness of morals.

Indifferent to money, opposed to work of any kind, everyone

prophesied his ruin. He was often nearly ruined but never quite, and always rose like the phoenix from the ashes of his overdraft at the bank. From a retreat to a small bed-sitting-room in King's Road, Chelsea, he would migrate to Claridge's Hotel in Brook Street. He once told me that he had to dine at the Ritz because his credit was so low elsewhere. He kept his table at the Ritz as he kept his tailor in Savile Row; they could not afford to discontinue his credit, because from time to time he reduced his bill and thus always kept them hoping.

There was a streak of genius in his irresponsibility; most certainly there was in his luck. His elder and younger brothers, unmarried, were killed in the war. This increased his expectations under his mother's Will. She conveniently died the very week it was rumoured that a summons for debt had been served on him. For three years he led the gay life and shared with everybody. Then the stockbroking firm, in which his late father had bought him a partnership, pushed him out. It looked as if he would have to part with his Rolls-Royce, a powerful asset in his social activities, when he met a rich American woman through catching her poodle when it ran out of the Hotel de Paris in Monte Carlo. This began a friendship that lasted only three years. The lady, in middle age, died suddenly. To everyone's astonishment she left Gerald twenty thousand dollars. It was not for the reason many suggested. She was notoriously frigid, with two frustrated ex-husbands.

There were other legacies, natural and, considering their nature, almost unnatural. Three aunts, by death, trickled small sums that covered small crises. He was left a houseful of furniture by a cousin, a Don Juan, with whom he had made many campaigns in far quarters of the world, sharing a bungalow in Kyoto, a house-boat in Kashmir and a villa in Marrakesh. Then his friend Tubby Lytton drank too much one night and fell overboard off his yacht. He left him the yacht, which he promptly sold for fifteen thousand pounds. He gave the bed-ridden former maid of his mother half of it, buying her an annuity, and lost the other half joining a Frenchman who founded a company to introduce the growing of truffles in U.S.A.

Back from Vermont, nigh penniless, he entered a barren passage of his life, being now thirty-five. It was at this period that I came to see more of him, for we lunched at the same club. He had a brother who had a good job in Imperial Chemicals and I suspected that he helped him out. He now lived in a bed-sitting-room in Ebury Street, and then, to economize, moved to a gas-fire back room in Melwood Terrace. Here he was constantly receiving letters, owing to a careless postman, addressed to a couple of maiden ladies of the same name and initials as his own. He was G. A. Johnson and they were Gertrude and A. Johnson. As the house was only across the road he did not trouble to re-address the letters but delivered them to the maid who answered the door. Sometimes he simply put the envelopes in their letter-box. It chanced one day—he told me the story himself—that just as he was about to put some wrongly delivered letters into their box the door opened, and there stood an elderly lady. She was rather stout, with a ruddy complexion and grey hair. A pair of gold-rimmed pince-nez lay on her shelving bosom.

"Oh! are you the gentleman who brings our letters? How careless of that postman—he's a new lad, not like our old Henry who was always so careful. I'm sorry you are troubled in this way," she said, pleasantly.

"It's no trouble at all," replied Gerald.

"There's one thing that puzzles me, Mr. Johnson. Why is it he never delivers any of your letters to us?"

"I think it's because he comes down my side of the street first—anyhow, I don't think you'd find them amusing!"

It was a thing one should not say but it was part of Gerald's charm to be audacious. He had a twinkle in his eye that disarmed everybody. Miss Johnson liked the joke; her face puckered into a smile.

"May I ask—are you Scottish?"

"Well, in about as small a portion as you get with a whisky and soda," responded Gerald.

"Oh—oh, how very funny!" cried Miss Johnson with a giggle. "My sister and I are Scotch, from Dundee."

"A very excellent brand," said Gerald. There was a pause,

L

he raised his hat. When Gerald raised his hat it was like a mention in the Court Circular. You knew he was someone. "Good morning, ma'am!" he said, with a suspicion of a bow, and departed. He felt through the back of his head a pair of keen eyes examining him as he went to the gate.

"Now, if I had attempted to invade her," said Gerald to me, "I should have lost marks. Never exhaust curiosity, my boy!"

A week passed when, delivering another stray letter, the door opened. The timing was so exact that Gerald concluded that the sisters had been watching every morning from behind the bow window curtains.

"Oh, Mr. Johnson—are we troubling you again?" exclaimed Miss Johnson, taking the letter from his hand. At that moment, surely pre-arranged, another lady came into sight in the gloom of the passage.

"This is my sister, Miss Anne, Mr. Johnson."

He bowed and raised his hat.

"You live across the way?" asked Miss Anne. It was a fatuous remark that expected no answer. She was thin, taller, grimmer. She wore her skirts longer, otherwise it was plain that they were sisters. A pendant gold watch dangled on her flat bosom. "You are new to the street?"

"About three months," he replied.

"Ah, we have been here twenty-eight years—we remember the gas-lamps."

"But the pillar-box is the same colour!" added Miss Gertrude with a giggle. "I hope your wife likes the Terrace—we think it rather select."

"Alas, I am alone," said Gerald.

"Oh, a bachelor!" exclaimed Miss Anne.

Gerald made no reply. To inform them that he had been divorced ten years would not have enhanced his standing with these maiden ladies.

"We were wondering, Mr. Johnson, as we are Scotch and neighbours, and you are our sort of unofficial postman, if you would take tea with us one day?" asked Miss Anne, with a controlled smile.

It was a formidable overture but, being a kind man, Gerald

accepted. And that was how it all began. "I felt I was putting my head in an oven with those well-baked old scones, dear boy. But you can never foretell what may result from a little self-sacrifice."

I remarked that I had been sacrificing myself all my life, with no results.

"Ah, my dear fellow, your technique's wrong!"

"Nonsense! I was born unlucky."

Gerald looked at me. "My dear fellow, the theologians would not agree with you. They believe in the will of God. Very strange—by prayer they're always trying to impose their will on Him. Now I believe in Luck. It's like sex-appeal, you have it or you haven't. Look at my teeth!"

I looked at them, they were good but rather set apart.

"You notice they're gappy? That means you're born to good luck."

"You mean people leave you legacies?" I asked, rather acidly.

"Yes, that and other things. It's not my doing. It's Providence."

"You said just now it was gappy teeth."

"Gappy teeth are Providence, my boy."

Regarding his career, I have come to believe it. No one left me legacies. My teeth are close set. When I asked my dentist if he could make my teeth gappy he looked at me as if I wanted him to go out of business.

All that I have related of Gerald Johnson was twenty-five years ago. Personal history confirmed his singular belief.

A friendship developed from that first afternoon tea. Soon he began going to dinner. "I don't mind confessing, my boy, that I was so pressed just then that a free meal was a blessing. And what a meal! Maggie, their housekeeper, was a wonder. A wonder in the service of a pair of wonders!"

II

The history of the two Misses Johnson was remarkable. Clearly they were in comfortable circumstances. Odd in some ways, they had no telephone, no radio, no automobile. They had no cat, dog or canary, but they had put feeding-boxes in the front and and back gardens. They were grossly extravagant in the consumption of newspapers. They read morning, evening, and Sunday newspapers avidly. Oddly enough, the newspapers prominent on a console table in the sitting-room were, among others, *The Financial Times*, *The Investors Chronicle*, and *The Christian Science Monitor*, though they were strict Presbyterians. Their father, after some years in Dundee, where the sisters were born, had bought a small haberdashery business in Battersea. One day the representative of a growing young firm had approached him with an offer for his business. They were more interested in his freehold shop than in the actual business. The site was good. He sold out to them and invested most of the money in the new company. At the time that Gerald came to know the Misses Johnson the shares inherited from their father were almost twenty times their original value. The firm was Messrs. Marks and Spencer. "Our father was rather prejudiced against Jews and said he wouldn't have put his money into the business if there hadn't been a Christian partner. Well, we know nothing about Mr. Spencer but we thank God for Mr. Marks!" declared Miss Gertrude.

Little by little their story as it was revealed to Gerald became more and more remarkable. Within twelve months they had taken such a fancy to him that they persuaded him to move across the road. "Now all the letters will be together," said Miss Gertrude, gaily. He had a beautiful room, excellent service and splendid meals. He paid very modestly for his lodging. "After all, we have the pleasure of your company," they said. They recovered from the shock of learning that he was divorced, being quite certain that Mrs. Johnson must have been an impossible woman. She was, but Gerald had to produce no proof.

Soon after joining the Johnson household an aunt died and left Gerald five thousand pounds. He was so comfortable and so attached to Gertrude and Anne that he remained where he was, though very much on the wing again. He bought a car and took them out for rides. They had never been abroad. He rented a small villa in Rome and persuaded them to pass the winter there. They proved indefatigable sightseers. They even had an audience with the Pope, swallowing their Presbyterian prejudices. They were delighted to find the Holy Father very human, and were sure, despite his beliefs, that he was a good man.

In the fifth year of residence in Melwood Terrace Gerald inherited a thousand pounds from a cousin in Kenya, of whom he was hardly aware. He lost it all in a flutter in tin but was in no way dismayed. "I was a fool not to have consulted Anne," he said to me. For Anne, it transpired, was a financial wizard. She had the Midas touch. She was always going to the South Kensington Post Office to telephone to her broker. When Gerald suggested that she should install the telephone—he greatly needed it himself—she said, "No—you see, Gerald, the walk to the Post Office enables me to examine my impulse." Those walks must have been very profitable.

For ten years Gerald was the pet of the Misses Johnson. "He has opened new windows on our world," they said. Certainly he gave them devoted service but he continued to come and go, never surrendering his liberty. There was a crisis when he fell in love with a French widow encountered on a plane to Paris. For almost a year he was torn between desire and prudence. As he was then forty prudence won. It would have been a financial problem, too. So instead of marriage he had a liaison, which Time cooled off. It seemed incredible that Miss Gertrude and Miss Anne should never have had an inkling of the strain their Gerald was under. They admired him for being so devoted and anxious over the long illness of his dear friend in Paris, and were relieved when "he" got better. Gerald, careless in many ways, never left letters lying around.

There was an unfulfilled ambition in the lives of the sisters. They had an only cousin, married, with six children and ten grandchildren, living in Montreal. There was much correspondence between them and at Christmas time a convoy of presents was sent by Miss Gertrude and Miss Anne to some twenty recipients. The mantelpiece at Melwood Terrace was filled with cards and photos of elderly, middle-aged, young and infantile Canadians.

There was another reason behind the old ladies' desire to cross the Atlantic. Miss Anne had played the American stock-market most successfully. She had very profitable holdings in sound American companies. For some years there had been a cordial correspondence with a Mr. Kent, of the Madison Avenue branch of the Farmers Trust Bank in New York, who bought and sold for her. The letters were not only full of shrewd sense but were excellent examples of flawless typing on that heavy luxurious stationery used by American business houses. New York and Montreal rivalled Paris in the dreams of the two sisters. It was Gerald who gave them the push. "You know Paris and Florence, why not New York and Montreal? You can go over in a comfortable Cunarder, see your Mr. Kent and the skyscrapers and then, overnight, be with your cousin in Montreal. You can come home down the St. Lawrence River in a Canadian Pacific liner to England. Go at the beginning of October, when New York is not too hot, and return early in November during the glory of the Indian summer in the Canadian forests. I'll go with you to New York, I know every-body there, and leave you to go on to Montreal."

The suggestion took root at once. Gerald came home with shipping schedules. There was a whirr of letters between Melwood Terrace and New York and Montreal. Then on a lovely October day, standing on the deck of the *Mauretania*, they saw the great liner turn by the Calshot lightship, pick up speed in the Channel and head for the New World.

No one would believe that Miss Anne was seventy-eight and Miss Gertrude seventy-four. They were like two schoolgirls on holiday. The exhilarating air of New York made them avid sightseers. They went to the top of the Empire State Building, they took a boat trip round Manhattan and were astonished to discover that New York was an island; they lunched with Mr. Kent on the forty-fourth floor of the Rockefeller Plaza, and saw the panorama of The Narrows and the Statue of Liberty from the top of the Bankers Trust in Wall Street. They met Mr. Junius Pierpont Morgan. They lunched with Mrs. Cornelius Vanderbilt in her palace on Fifth Avenue. They felt they had touched the very heart of high finance, Gerald their cicerone.

The visit concluded with purchases of new shares in companies recommended by Mr. Kent. They were overwhelmed with the friendliness and hospitality of everybody.

Gerald saw them off for Montreal at the Grand Central Station. They were in wonderful form. They kissed him and thanked him for all he had done. In American fashion they departed with sprays of orchids pinned on their bosoms. They chatted brightly with the negro "redcap" who took their baggage to their "drawing-room" on the sleeper. Gerald had no idea it was the last time he would see them. After a glorious month in Montreal, fussed over by three generations, they were both killed in a taxi-cab accident. Thus they missed a new world war looming up.

The shock to Gerald was tremendous. He had been genuinely fond of them. They had mothered him as he had never been mothered. Moreover, he was to lose his very comfortable nest at a time when his finances were again low. Then he had a second shock, of a pleasant nature. The two Misses Johnson left an estate of almost one million pounds gross. After legacies to the Canadian relations, the residue of their estates passed to Gerald. He inherited a net sum of about three hundred thousand pounds. Providence and the gappy teeth had come to his rescue magnificently.

Such was the history of Gerald, a born legatee. He enjoyed the war. He became a colonel with a staff appointment in Cairo. His Rolls-Royce went with him. He was very popular, he entertained lavishly. He was photographed with the famous, he was on calling terms with the King, and twice breakfasted with General Montgomery. Just after El Alamein he married his bright A.T.S. driver, a Girton girl, nearly thirty years his junior. He had yet another legacy. A famous bowler left him sixteen cricket balls, each with a silver plate recording bowling feats in Test matches.

One morning in 1952, after he had mowed the lawn at his Sussex house, he told the butler to bring him a whisky and soda. He then went into the library to cool off. When the butler brought the drink he did not answer. He had died in his chair of heart failure. I was a close friend of Gerald's and, considering his wealth, I thought it possible that he had left legacies to those nearest to him. Providence, which has never loved me, passed me over again. Whatever might have been Gerald's intentions as a generous soul, there were no legacies. He had failed to make a Will. The little A.T.S. widow took all and then married a horsey young man within a year. It was ironical to think that those two old ladies had saved all their lives to provide a racing rapscallion with a fortune, for the ex-widow died in childbirth and the horsey youth got everything.

I could provide many examples of the skittishness of Providence towards others and myself in the matter of legacies. Then, at long last, late in life, I had a legacy, of a kind. Here is how it came to me.

CHAPTER 2

I AM OLD ENOUGH to recall a vanished era. At my birth Queen Victoria, a very obstinate old lady, was on the throne. Later, the British were making a mess of the war in South Africa. Her libertine son, Edward, Prince of Wales, was firmly repressed by Mama. My boyhood was passed amid the extravagance of the Edwardian era when the ramparts of exclusive society were being breached by Jewish diamond tycoons from South Africa, under the patronage of King Edward, indulging in a late fling after the death of Mama. There was also the advent of the daughters of rich Americans married to impoverished peers. An evangelist out of Wales, Evan Roberts, called the multitude to repentance. He was a great manipulator of the herd instinct, a forerunner of those hot gospellers, Torrey and Alexander, the Prophet Dowie, Colonel Rutherford and Pastor Charles Russell. At the City Temple R. J. Campbell, a mop-headed Nonconformist divine, discovered the New Theology and released a tidal wave among the theologians. Strange how dated they are now, superseded by film stars, "pop" singers and television performers.

Leaving Oxford in 1922, I joined a banking firm in the City. Two years later I was sent to their branches in Milan and Rome. It was thus I came to know and fall in love with Italy, after the pattern of many Englishmen. I was just in time to see the English there at the height of their prestige. Germany had been defeated, the British Navy was paramount. Amid the shattered currencies the pound was firm. We did not know that we were enjoying a grand sunset. Our politicians had vain dreams of restoring the Pax Britannica forever broken by a mad student at Sarajevo in 1914. I discovered in Rome, Venice, and particularly in Florence that the British colony had not yet realized that the towers were falling, that Dante's fair city would cease to be an English preserve, that the milords would be leaving the villas and palaces, pinched by viciously mounting income-tax and estate duties, and that, later, a paper pound would trick them out of their substance.

For over a hundred years Florence had been the special preserve of a multitude of middle-class, well-bred English-women. Many of them were of slender means. On an income of two hundreds and fifty pounds a year they lived with a couple of maids in small villas, or in two or three large rooms in old palaces. In the vanished Victorian era Elizabeth Barrett Browning lay pallid in the gloomy Casa Guidi. Mr. Ruskin appeared at tea parties. A hundred maiden ladies of impeccable manners dominated the social life. They had their excellent Reading Room, their English Church and their Protestant Burial Ground. They took carriage rides in the Cascini Gardens, they studied art under Italian artists. Many of them, consumptive, were sent to Florence for their health, under the illusion that the climate was kind. The bitter winds from the surrounding mountains, often snow-capped, hurried them into the Protestant Cemetery. In the heat of summer they escaped to Bagni di Lucca. It did not seem possible that within a century their number would be reduced to a couple of score, the palaces and villas know them not, and the tea-rooms echo with strange accents brought across the Atlantic by vigorous, lavish, itinerant Americans.

It was in the years preceding the sunset of the English era, between the Boer War and the first World War, that more Americans began to settle in Florence, sharp sparrows among the seedy old blackbirds. With illimitable incomes, they stopped at nothing. They bought or rented the great villas on the hills, re-roofed them, re-floored them, added bathrooms and swimming-pools, and with irresistible energy and hospitality swamped the local Italian aristocracy. They spent freely in the shops and art galleries.

The English sniffed, tried hard to keep aloof, then, finding themselves by-passed, reluctantly succumbed. It is said that every Christian has at least one pet Jew for a friend. Every Florentine and every Englishman had at least one pet American. Their drawback as friends was that after October they shut down their palaces and villas and trooped back across the Atlantic until the peach-blossom burst forth again in their gardens.

There were a few Americans who, like the English, stayed on and shivered in draughty villas, hotels and pensions. It is an illusion that cannot be dispelled in Europe that there are no poor Americans. They exist and are a tenacious fraternity, frugal and serious-minded. Europe is their honey-pot. They sometimes suffer unrecorded privations to keep their noses close to the fount of art, music and romantic history. For them every brick of Rome is sacred, every vista of Florence paradise, every whiff of Paris intoxicating. They know not and are not known by their rich fellow-countrymen. They are not on the party list, they have no part in the privileged luxury of the Diplomatic Corps, the local tradesmen are indifferent to them since they spend little. They exercise no patronage and support no parasites. Gay young Count Roverigo di Barca knew they were no good for dinner with caviare and champagne. Signor Treventi, the art dealer with enchanting manners, knew they would not buy one of his spurious masters. To both of these gentlemen they were as useless as the British spinsters. All they kept going were second-rate pensions and dreary little apartments.

Among the American widows and maiden ladies, Miss Jane Grant Saunders was well known by sight. She was in no sense a social figure. She was quite unaware whether she was received or not received. She had no idea whether she was snubbed by her rich compatriots or ignored by the poor ones. To Miss Saunders every human being was worthy, every motive honest, every goose a swan. When the tradesmen swindled her she seemed to be conscious only of their enchanting smiles, their exquisite manners. The air she breathed was intoxicating. To live in Florence was to receive a blessing from God. The sky, the river, the galleries, the churches, the market place, the alleys where Dante had walked, Botticelli had dreamed, and Michelangelo had laboured, left her, like Wordsworth's nun, breathless with adoration.

She had given up much, struggled vigorously to live in this

celestial city. She had come to Florence from Baltimore in 1908, at the age of forty. Eighteen years of her life had been spent as a schoolteacher. She had lived with her mother in a squeaky, over-heated, run-up apartment in a dreary street of step-fronted red-brick houses. They had one retainer, an old black Mammy, cook-housekeeper-nurse and dictator.

It was from this devoted negress that Jane had learned the songs that were to bring her a touch of fame. She had published, when thirty years of age, a collection of the negro songs her nurse had sung to her, under the title of *Mammy Songs*. Jane had a gift for playing the guitar as an accompaniment of the songs. It hid the poor quality of her voice. For a time she had quite a vogue singing these songs with guitar accompaniment and autographing her book in Baltimore and the surrounding places. The fees derived from these appearances went to her Italian fund. For she had set her course already. When her mother died she was going to live in Italy. She had chosen Florence for her exact destination. By her desk hung two large photographs, one of the Ponte Vecchio over the Arno, the other of the statue of David by Michelangelo. Mrs. Saunders and Mammy thought the latter rather shocking with its genital frankness.

Jane took lessons in Italian from an Italian fruit merchant who had a shop at the corner of the street. He gave her two hours a week. She did not know that he had a frightful Neapolitan gutter accent. She laboriously translated Dante, and collected addresses of pensions from friends who had made the great pilgrimage to the holy city of art. Jane was a dedicated soul and romance had only touched her once in the person of a young insurance agent. He had clumsily kissed her under the white-globed chandelier just after he had signed the receipt for the annual insurance premium. It was a rather furtive, bungled affair and that evening she found she could not concentrate on Dante. The young man did not appear again for when the premium was due the following year there was a different collector. Jane felt she had been saved from a disaster into which carnal temptation might have led her. Marriage, even if it had come to that, would have meant the end of the Italian dream.

She was forty when her mother died. She wept heavily at the funeral for she had loved her dearly. But all through the sermon in the Baptist church, when she should have been moved by the parson's eloquent tribute to one whom God had called to His bosom, a little imp kept whispering, "Now—at last!" It was wicked but it was human. She had waited so long.

The coal-black Mammy, almost decrepit, went to live with a sister on a small pension. When the estate was settled Jane found she had a private income, after the sale of the house, of about eight hundred dollars a year, or one hundred and sixty pounds. She was assured by a lady who lived in Florence that this sum was adequate for a quiet existence. She was given the name of a pension where she could live for a dollar a day until she found her own little nest.

On July 4th, 1908, she arrived in Florence. The day could not have been more appropriate. In the American calendar it was Independence Day, the anniversary of the day the American nation had started a new life. All graciousness, all smiles, she descended from the railway carriage in which she had sat up all night, scattering to left and right, and over the heads of porters struggling to possess her luggage, a shower of *Grazie* and *Si*. She had the exact phrase ready as she passed through the barrier.

"*Una carrozza, per piacere!*"

It worked. "*Grazie, grazie!*" she said to the porter and over-tipped him. He raised his battered cap. What gallantry!

"*Pensione Favorita,* Lungarno," she cried, sinking back into the leather seat, a pleasant whiff of horse manure in her nostrils.

"*Si, signora!*" cried the coachman, jerking the horse into action over the cobbles.

Signora. Then the dear man thought she was married, otherwise he would have said *Signorina,* the feminine singular diminutive.

It was a lovely day with the sky a Mediterranean blue. The headache from sitting up all night in the train from Paris was gone. The carriage began to thread the streets. She almost fainted from sheer ecstasy when the great black and white façade of the cathedral, the Duomo, came into view with Giotto's soaring *campanile* beside it. She read the street names, saw the bright flower-stands at the corners, the gay parasols over the fruitsellers' barrows, and then, at last, the Arno. She was a little surprised to see it was so muddy in colour, so shrunken in its stony bed. Across the river stood a long line of palaces. It was all so confusing, so breathtaking as she turned this way and that, almost shaken out of her seat by the iron-bound wheels jumping over the tramlines. But the river was the same, the river seen by Dante and Beatrice and Leonardo da Vinci.

The *Pensione Favorita* was on the fourth floor of an old palace overlooking the Arno. Descending from the carriage, Jane rang a bell. Presently a youth in a green apron came running down the stone steps. He was a slender youth with a mass of black curls and dark liquid eyes, so beautiful that for a few moments Jane lost her Italian. She just looked at his smiling face. He could have been a model in Michelangelo's studio.

"*Come si chiama?*" she asked. Had she got it right—What is your name?

It worked. "Luciano, *signora*," he replied with a smile that exposed two rows of snowy teeth. Luciano! The name was music, worthy of an archangel. He lifted her two bags, putting one on his shoulder, and started off up the stairs, light-footed, supple-backed.

She was received in a high dark interior hall by the cheerful proprietress and conducted down a long corridor to a bedroom. It was narrow and cell-like, with an immensely high ceiling. It was, in fact higher than it was long, with part of a painted ceiling covered with sprawling goddesses and an amorous youth, all naked. The bedroom was obviously part of a large salon, divided off.

When Luciano had deposited the baggage and thrown back the wooden shutters, flooding the room with light, he smiled again and gently withdrew.

It was a corner room with windows on two sides. She went to the first, overlooking the Arno. With a deep breath of voice-less delight she threw up her arms like the Adorante. The dream had become a reality. Below ran the dun-coloured Arno. Opposite there was a line of palaces, and, behind, a hill studded with cypresses and embosked villas. Leaning out, away to the right there was a bridge. She knew it at once, as she knew her own front door in Baltimore. It stood arched over the river, the centre part openly arcaded and showing the sky beyond. It was the Ponte Vecchio.

She had hardly recovered from this peerless vista when, looking out of the side window, over the old russet tiles of the houses, there was another—a huge tower, machicolated, surmounted by a belfry. It rose magnificently in the blue noonday sky. It was potent, aggressive in its grim beauty, the repository of much bloody history. It was the tower of the Palazzo Vecchio. Paralysed by its import, she stood motionless until startled by a tap on the door. It was the maid bringing towels. The girl had amazingly long eyelashes, black, sweeping, over beautiful eyes. Stockingless, she had pretty feet, loosely sandalled. Jane asked her her name.

"Beatrice."

Bay-ah-tree-chay. How muscial, and how appropriate in the city of Dante!

When the girl had gone Jane's eyes fell on something, a four-legged stand covered over with a towel. She lifted the cloth, revealing a white enamel tin tray. How thoughtful of them, and necessary in a hot climate. It was a footbath.

Two days later, while using it, the maid came in, burst into uncontrollable laughter, and withdrew. Puzzled by this strange conduct, Jane rang the bell and asked why she was so amused. The explanation, given with spurts of laughter, was in an Italian she could not understand. "*Un bidè*," repeated the maid and then, seeing she was not understood, she demonstrated its use. Jane's face turned crimson. When the girl departed she hid the thing under the luggage rack.

These Latins were extraordinary people. They were Catholics, of course. She had been told that nuns had to take a bath in their shifts, yet women used these contrivances. And the things that happened to one! A mere letter in Italian made all the difference. She had gone into the *Signori* instead of the *Sig-*

nore and saw at once that it was differently equipped. Also that business with the egg at breakfast. In her best Italian she had ordered *Un uva bollito, pane e caffè*. It seemed very simple—a boiled egg, bread and coffee. But the maid stared at her, uncomprehending.

"*Un uva bollito?*" she repeated.

"*Sì,*" said Jane, and seeing how stupid the dear girl was, she made in the air the shape of an egg—without effect.

The maid withdrew and there was a long wait until Signora Porzi, the proprietress, appeared.

"What is it your wish to order, Signora Saunders?" she asked.

"*Un uva bollito, pane e caffè,*" said Jane, with emphasis.

Signora Porzi smiled gently. "Please, you have asked for a boiled grape! *Uva* is grape, *uovo* is an egg," she explained.

But oh the joy of living in Italy. The warm radiant mornings, the noisy happy people, the flowers everywhere, the open cafés in the squares, the great cool galleries full of world-famed treasures, the flaming sunsets down the Arno, the brilliant stars over Brunelleschi's great dome, a catch of music from an unseen guitar, the *campanile's* solemn bell.

Although Jane Saunders had arrived in Florence on Independence Day, she walked into a warren of the English at her pension. The only American there, she was aloofly inspected by two dozen British women in the dining-room. They were mostly ancient mothers and daughters, lonely old ladies, sedate spinsters, all soberly dressed and mouse-quiet, nibbling away before their bottles of Chianti and San Pellegrino water. She learned that the more active and moneyed had moved up into the hill towns for the summer. No one stayed in Florence in the heat of July if they could afford to leave it. They all came back in the autumn.

Little by little Jane came to know her fellow pensionnaires. Once she had broken through their reserve, she found them mellow and warm. It was her first experience of the English at close quarters. It took time to know them, but how easy and quiet in their manners they were, and what astonishing reserves of knowledge they had! Mostly they were middle-class, widows and daughters of army colonels, solicitors, clergymen and defunct country squires.

After a time she was taken visiting. She drank tea in small apartments filled with English antique furniture, with English prints on the walls, and almost always a photograph of the Hall, Manor House, Rectory or house in which they had been born. They all had small private incomes, spoke a careful grammatical Italian, knew the names of flowers. They had usually one Italian maid who put on a white cap, apron, and cotton gloves, when she took round the teacups.

There was a small current of scandal. There was a fashionable lady who had been a King's mistress, called on. There was a rich American woman, not called on. She was living in a large villa with her Italian chauffeur. There was an English aristocrat, very handsome and hospitable, who would not be coming back to his large apartment. Jane never discovered the reason. The ladies, when asked, said, "Well—" and never continued.

Within six months Jane found what she searched for, a tiny apartment of her own. It was a gem, two rooms only, on the fifth floor of an old palace. The stairs were quite formidable but the view when you arrived was rewarding. There was a little terrace, ten feet long and four feet wide, filled with pots of geraniums and one small orange tree. Across the rooftops one saw the upper part of Giotto's tower, and the marble-ribbed dome of the Duomo. Very near, there was a sixteenth-century *campanile* with an old cracked bell that rang ferociously for mass at dawn and for vespers at sunset. It rattled Jane's windows but it soon ceased to bother her, and after a time she loved it.

She furnished her little apartment with odds and ends in the Florentine style. Just before Christmas she gave a housewarming party and everyone she invited came, mostly those she had come to know in the *pensione*, except four for whom the stairs were too much. Determined old Mrs. Hamilton-Drummond, eighty-four, said the stairs were not worth mentioning. Jane delighted the company by singing some Mammy songs accompanied by her guitar.

Within a year she was completely Italianate. She chatted

with the shopkeepers in the vernacular, she had a cheery word and a candy for every child who watched for the Signora Americana. She did errands for old ladies. Sometimes she relieved Mr. Brownlow, the organist at the English church. All the cabmen saluted her. Tall, robust, large-footed, large-hearted, voluble in ramshackle Italian with a Neapolitan accent, she was a figure in Florentine life. She was completely happy.

CHAPTER 3

I

IT WAS IN 1926 that I first visited Venice. I had been through it in the train several times, going back to Rome from Trieste, where we had a branch of our bank. Unhappily, I never had time to break my journey and stay in the city. In the autumn of 1926 I was entitled to a holiday, and this time, coming from Trieste, I stopped at Venice. To see it for the first time is to arrive on another planet, I had been told. The statement is not an exaggeration. A friend had given me the address of the *Pensione Seguso*. It had the merit, he said, of being on the Zattere, and got the maximum autumn sunshine, a consideration now that it was the end of September. My friend who had given me the address had had a love affair with an Italian girl who lived near there. From a nearby *villino* that he had taken he often went to eat in the *Seguso*. He was a gourmet, I trusted his recommendation.

I took my first gondola ride and presently found myself deposited on a small quay near a little bridge. The modest-fronted *pensione* was kept by the three Seguso sisters, from whom it took its name. The youngest attended to the desk and the visitors. She spoke a little English. The middle one was general manager of the place, a pleasant bustling woman of about forty. The eldest sister was the cook, seldom seen. One got a glimpse of her through the service hatch. But sometimes after supper, in the cool of the evening, she would come out and sit in one of the chairs on the small quay, from which she had a view of the wide Giudecca, the shipping channel, and the pretty stone bridge that almost seemed to fly over the narrow *rio*, whose green water ran along the east side of the *pensione* and into the Giudecca.

The cooking at the *Seguso* was deservedly famous. The recommendation given me was fulfilled. Although the Signorina Seguso knew no English, one endeavoured to pay her a compliment on the evening meal. Poor soul, she was so very fat and always looked so very hot that she merited a compliment. An important part of the establishment was a large cat, Moses, adored by the sisters. To notice Moses, to enquire into the state of his health and to show admiration of his intelligence was to win the sisters' hearts.

I had a delightful room on the first floor. Its windows overlooked the broad canal on which the passing liners and merchant ships glided on their voyages to and from the Mediterranean and the Orient. Eastwards over the *rio*, I looked into a high-walled garden with oleanders, orange trees, and two dramatically dark cypresses. The corners of the wall surrounding the villa were decorated with white stone figures of cherubs. And just below I could see the marble parapet of the arched bridge over the *rio*. My room was exceptionally well furnished, the sisters having made a feature of their furnishing. There were some excellent antique pieces. All augured well for my visit.

The first evening when I went down to dinner, I was given a single corner table. The room was small and crowded with guests. There were a few Italians but the greater part were unmistakably English. The room was lit by a large central Murano glass chandelier and small table lamps. Next to me there was a single table, set, with no one there. The occupant was late. On it were a napkin in a painted wooden ring, a bottle of Chianti in a metal swing holder, and a bottle of San Pellegrino water, also a small bottle of white pills.

The soup had been served when a woman threaded the tables towards the unoccupied one near me. Her progress required care for she was a tall stout person and the tables were very close. She confidently made her way, saying loudly to the left and right, with an all-embracing smile—"*Scusi! Scusi! Buona sera! Buona sera!*" It seemed she knew everybody, or was determined everybody should know her.

She wedged herself down, undid her napkin, and then fluently talked with the maid who came up, whether about food or events I could not tell. Then she looked at me and I knew at once she was going to speak to me.

"It is very warm this evening," she said.

"Yes," I replied, not too affably. This was a woman to be avoided, certainly a spinster, a *pensione* harpy. She was between fifty and sixty and would prey on the male young in that "I'm old enough to be your mother, so don't be afraid" manner.

"You are a new face. *Benvenuto* to the *Pensione Seguso!*" she said.

"Thank you," I replied, and returned to my fish.

"But it is not your first visit to *la bella Venezia?*"

"Yes, it is," I replied, reluctantly.

Her eyes opened wide, expressing glad astonishment.

"My! *Non è possibile! Che meraviglia!*" she cried, as if she had found a ruby in her soup.

It was not going to be so marvellous if I was going to be stabled at meal-times with this old bore. I made no comment. My silence did not in any way disturb her.

"*Allora!*" she exclaimed, "Since we are neighbours and I am an old Venetian,"—here she gave a little chuckle through her uneven teeth—"let me introduce myself. I am Signorina Saunders—Jane Grant Saunders. American by birth. Italian by absorption!"

She gave a gurgling little laugh, and pulled out the Chianti cork with a pop.

"Thank you," I replied, withholding my name.

Unconscious of any snub, being exceedingly good-natured, she continued—"Of course, now you've come once you'll come again. Venice is so beautiful. *Evvero!* I came here sixteen years ago—I've been here every summer since. And," she added, roguishly—"you know it is the *Città d'Amore!*" Byron, La Guiccioli, Alfred de Musset, George Sand, D'Annunzio, Duse!"

I nodded. Not one of the pairs was respectable. They had all had notorious affairs. Fortunately at that moment her veal arrived. She ate it vigorously and I was spared further comment. I examined her covertly. She was utterly un-American in appearance. She had no white grizzled hair, no rimless glasses. Her voice was not strident, her dress was in no way smart. Indeed she was dowdy, with straggling grey-streaked

hair. Her nose was very long, her chin pointed, with two under-
folds, her eyes baggy. No, this was no typical American club-
woman, such as I had encountered in clusters visiting Rome,
voluble, in ecstasy, suspicious of being cheated. I was just
finishing my fruit when she spoke again.

"Do you know Florence—*Città dei fiori*?" she asked. It seemed
no sentence of hers could go unembellished by Italian.

"Fairly well."

"*Ah, come è bella!*"

I agreed that it was beautiful.

"I live there, high up, in a little *palazzino*—tiny!"

She put two fingers up to demonstrate how tiny it was. Then
she adjusted two bright silk scarves round her corrugated neck.

The fruit finished, I rose, bowed to her, and left the dining-
room. I would ask to be moved. My table was too near Signorina Jane Grant Saunders, a triple name like that so often
adopted by lady novelists. Her type was not unique. She had
many English sisters here in Italy, their speech dripping with
Italian phrases.

I walked out on to the Zattere, a long wide quay by which a
number of ships were berthed. Across the water glowed the
lights of the long low Giudecca. The flagged pavement had a
number of cafés at which clients chatted in the warm night.
Next door to the *Seguso* there was another pension. On its front
it bore a plaque recording that John Ruskin had once lived
there. It had a pontoon opposite, on which coffee was served
under gay parasols. Then came the noble façade of a church,
tall, with a classical pediment, and, further along, after passing
over a delightful little bridge spanning another canal, there was
a palace with a stone balcony and lovely Byzantine Gothic
windows, which I learned later was the Palazzo Rondanelli.
I took a seat at the café, happy in the warm night. Tomorrow I
would begin my exploration of Venice. I thought about Signorina Saunders. What an extraordinary woman! She radiated
affability. Perhaps I had been rather churlish. Perhaps not.
She might easily become a nuisance.

II

Within a week I had somewhat changed my opinion of Miss Saunders. She was full of fun and gaiety, almost skittish despite her years. She was a mine of information and supplied me with books and booklets about Venice. I owed to her visits to Venetian houses. She knew a number of artists and writers of various nationalities, and introduced me. They all seemed to be having a struggle but had found delightful little nests for themselves up a hidden *calle*, in a remote leafy *corte*, or on a floor of some ruinous old palace with faded shutters, vast dark stair-case and a water-rotted gondola entrance.

She persuaded me to make an excursion down the lagoon to an isolated old fortress, a massive brick affair, on an island low in the water. It was windowless, octagonal in shape. Its walls were penetrated by antique embrasures for cannon. I learned that it had been a Venetian fort to guard an entrance into the lagoon in the days when the Genoese beseiged Venice. An American had bought it and lived there. A sailing-boat col-lected us from the steamer and took us across to the fort. We entered by an iron doorway to find ourselves in a bowl that contained a house hidden below the round parapet. There was a garden full of flowers. The family lived in the old powder-rooms, with heavy barrelled ceilings, whose windows looked inwards to the garden. There was a delightful guard-walk around the inside of the parapet, with magnificent vistas of the lagoon, across to the faint blue Euganean Hills on the mainland, and down the lagoon to old Chioggia, home of the fishing fleet, beloved of artists. It was a little nest of hospitable Americans, one of whom had married an Italian countess, our hostess.

I was amused to see that on the steamer Aunt Jane, as our hostess called her, chatted to everybody. She bought lollipops for the Italian children of some peasants coming back with empty fruit baskets from Venice, and soon had all their names by heart. There was a great waving and shouting when they left the boat. Aunt Jane went on to the bridge of the steamer and learned the state of health of the captain's wife, in hospital for an operation. The servant at the fortress almost embraced her. The boatboy who took us across beamed with delight when she spoke to him by name. She complimented him on the colour of his shirt.

I learned from one of the *Seguso* sisters some astonishing facts concerning the *molto simpatica signorina*. When Italy entered the war in May, 1915, she joined an Italian nursing unit. She was in the disastrous Caporetto defeat, staunchly commanded her field hospital unit, and was decorated by the Italian government. I could almost see her waving a flag and crying *"Avanti, ragazzi!"*

It soon became obvious to me that she had no sense of values. All Italians were angels. Every author or painter she knew was a genius. The most frightful scribblings and daubs that they brought to her were hailed as masterpieces. Her dress was unique and startling. She wore enormous broad-brimmed straw hats of vivid colours, round the crowns of which she draped a scarf of lace that trailed down behind. It looked as if she were going on a kind of *shikari*. Her skirts were of voluminous muslin that fell down over her ankles. She had large feet shod in heel-less sandals. Around her neck she hung three ropes of highly coloured beads, large and of no value, to which were added odd amulets. Her voice wobbled with emotion. She was seldom without a big cloth hold-all whose contents were almost in-describable—pieces of string and tape, a bunch of grapes wrapped in tissue paper, a bar of chocolate, various ointments for mosquito bites and stings, a bundle of pencils bound by a rubber band, packets of sweets for darling *bambini*, a white woollen pullover in case of a chill, a pair of pearl opera glasses for use as field-glasses to read what boat was coming up the Giudecca, and, most singular of all, a bundle of small American flags on sticks that, with a candy, she bestowed on odd children. Frequently I met mothers nursing dark-eyed babies holding little flags in their fists and knew that Signorina Saunders had been that way.

Fascism had just begun to show its ugly head, and that strutting egoist, Mussolini, with the pushed-out jaw and the glaring eyes, had begun trying to persuade the happy-go-lucky Italians that they were born lions. The era of slogans and officious little upstarts in black shirts had begun. Aunt Jane thought Mussolini was a saintly leader whom God had sent to lead Italy back to its old Renaissance glory. She wore a fascist pin. It would not have surprised me had she appeared in a black blouse.

Another hero was the mountebank, D'Annunzio. She was pained when I said I thought his poems and plays were mostly fustian. "But dear boy, he is one of the glories of Italian literature. He is immortal!" I remarked that he had annexed a German artist's villa on Lake Garda, with contents which he had sold, and would not get out for the widow of the owner. In the course of my banking business I had heard the inside story. She opened wide her eyes. "But darling boy, he is a great and noble patriot!"

It was no use my wincing at some of her beliefs. By the end of a fortnight I was being addressed as "Darling boy". I saw it would be useless to protest. She seemed to have hundreds of "darling boys" and "sweet darling girls" among her acquaintances. She had a considerable correspondence with "darling boys", Italian, English and American, whom she had mothered during the war. Faithful, they all came to see her when they visited Italy. I was to discover, thirty years later, that her brood of darling boys had become quite disintinguished in many walks of life—a famous novelist, the president of a great American business, a director of the National Gallery in London, a Monsignor, the Provost of an Oxford College, a conductor at the Scala, all these were held in equal affection with little clerks, half-mad poets and an assortment of tiresome cranks. We were all "famous" or exalted. *All' Illustrissimo Signor Desmond Wellington* she wrote on a letter to me. She was quite positive that owing to my name I was somehow related to the Duke of Wellington. In Venice, on my second visit, I heard her referred to as "that crazy creature," but the term, I noticed, was one of amused affection.

Toward the end of my visit I had become aware of a daily performance enacted under my window. After lunch many of the *Seguso* visitors retired to their rooms for a siesta, or to rest their feet before a second spell of sightseeing. The *Seguso* fell silent. Moses, the cat, slept in the sun by the parasol-coffee table. A fisherman dozed by the balustrade of the bridge. I used the quiet interval for writing letters.

Around four o'clock I was conscious of voices and some excitement below my window. I got up from my writing and looked out. There was Aunt Jane with an open yellow parasol, carrying a guitar across her bosom. She stood above half-a-dozen stone steps, by the side of which was a small rowing boat no larger than a tub. It floated on the side canal. In it sat a stout, white-haired elderly man holding a pair of oars. At the coffee-tables visitors were observing the drama being enacted. There was the *Seguso* house-boy with the plank that he used to make a bridge from the gondola to the steps. With him, joining him in excited vocal gesticulation, was the younger Seguso sister. They were striving to induce Aunt Jane to walk the plank into the dinghy. Aunt Jane stood there hesitant, bleating *"Subito! Subito,"* but not moving, while the Signorina Seguso cried *"È sicuro, signorina, è sicuro!"* It was not secure, the plank shifted with the tilting of the boat as she put a foot forward. It was like expecting an elephant to embark.

With the encouragement of Signorina Seguso, Luigi the house-boy in a pink-and-white striped jacket, and the handsome old gentleman in the boat, the perilous passage was made. Aunt Jane sank, all smiles, on the cushioned seat, with an involuntary twang of the guitar. The yellow sunshade had been kept aloft with the skill of a tightrope walker. The spectators cheered. I clapped from the window above. We were given a gracious bow. The boat had sunk ominously. I noticed, as it pulled away that there were only two inches between the water and the top of the gunwale. The overloaded dinghy went under the bridge towards the wide Giudecca. It seemed to me utterly foolhardy. The wake of any passing steamer would swamp it. Presently, as the dinghy came into sight on the great silver flood, I heard soft music and a voice. It was Aunt Jane singing a Mammy song to the accompaniment of her guitar as her escort rowed her gently. Slowly, to music, the dinghy disappeared in the afternoon glow.

I came to watch for this daily performance. The plank-walking, its difficulties varying with the height of the tide, the

slow progress of the overladen dinghy, the guitar music, and the
singing that slowly faded out on the wide Giudecca, all took on
the nature of an idyll. The *signorina* was coy, the *signore* quietly
gallant.

One morning, coming back to the *Seguso*, I met them, and
was introduced to her companion. He was a very handsome old
boy, tall, with beautiful white hair and good features. His eyes
were remarkable, grey and ringed like a bird's. He had a very
gentle voice which matched his manners. He spoke English
with an attractive foreign accent. He was, to use an old and now
discredited definition, aristocratic. His name was Edoardo
Donati. He was descended from an ancient Florentine family.
I was not surprised to learn that he was an artist; his eyes were
quietly observant and he had the air of tranquillity that I have
noticed as characteristic of artists who work patiently in
silence.

Little by little in the next few days I learned something of his
history. As a young man he had been an art connoisseur. In
that way he had come to meet Pierpont Morgan, then creating
his art gallery. Working on behalf of this magnate, he had spent
some years in New York. He had published a book on what he
called "The gentle art of faking," exposing some aspects of the
art racket. Later he had returned to Paris where he had
studied in an atelier, and, after that, to Florence, his home town,
where he had a studio and gave exhibitions. His mother, a
widow, had inherited a little house in Venice. An only son,
unmarried, he lived with her during the summer until his
fiftieth year, when she died. He had continued to reside in
Venice in the same house each summer. It was obvious that he
was a much respected figure locally. He was president of the
Venetian Artists' Guild. He was consulted by the curator of the
Accademia, Venice's public art gallery. He had a private
renown as a flautist. I discovered that he was exceptionally
well-read in four languages. His manners were always gentle. He
dressed as an artist, with a loose black bow tie, a broad-
brimmed soft felt hat, and loose clothes. He was always well-
groomed. It was obvious that Edoardo Donati and Jane Grant
Saunders enjoyed each other's company. His little house and

studio, which I had not seen, was not far from the *Seguso*, off the picturesque Rio San Trovaso, beloved of artists.

When I left Venice I took some flowers up to Aunt Jane's room, a tiny back one, decorated with portraits of Mussolini, Queen Margherita, signed by her in the War when she had visited Jane's field hospital, and President General Ulysses Grant, with whom she could claim kinship, which explained the Grant in her name.

I was sorry to leave Venice, captured by its beauty. I made a vow to return each year. As the train carried me over the long bridge spanning the lagoon I reflected on the singular fact of my friendship with Aunt Jane. I would not have believed any-one who had prophesied that I should become one of her "darling boys". I was reticent, reserved, and hated demon-strative people, particularly those with floppy minds, unable to differentiate between the first-rate and the second-rate. I marvelled how I had come to be collected by this blowsy old creature. A young man of twenty-six, anyone over fifty was old in my eyes. When I went to say Goodbye I evoked an emotional wave that almost drowned me. She flung her arms round me, kissed me on both cheeks and pressed me to her ample cushiony bosom. "Darling sweet boy, it is too sad. All Venice will weep, but let us think! You are going to great triumphs! I see you controlling a vast business, helping hundreds of people, a great Power for Good!"

It was useless to protest that I was one of four sub-managers in a Roman branch of a London bank, without even an office of my own. For her I ranked with Pierpont Morgan. She gave me an address in Florence and extracted a promise that I would call to see her when I went there on business. She hurried to a drawer and took out a small parcel tied up with coloured ribbon. "And here is a wee momento! Perhaps somewhere in this tiny notebook Aunt Jane will have a *ricordo*!"

I was to become familiar in the next thirty years with those little parcels. They were encased in sheets and sheets of white tissue paper, wrapping on wrapping, tied with red, white and green ribbons, the Italian colours. There was always a note enclosed with the present. This sheet of paper was decorated at the top and round the sides with vivid, coloured flowers clipped out and pasted on, a jocund floral riot. I think she must have spent her winters cutting out the coloured illustrations in florists' catalogues.

She had a fat Birthday Book and none of her "darling boys" was forgotten on this festival. At Christmas and on birthdays she had a special form of gift of her own devising. There was a bookbinder's shop in Venice to which she introduced me. It was a delightful place with bindings, boxes, blotters, waste-paper baskets and other objects made of that hand printed paper known as *Carta Varese*. There were all kinds of colours and designs, the Medici coat of arms in red, the fleur-de-lys in blue, and little *settecento* patterns of flowers and dolphins. There were shelves filled with sheets of these papers that one bought for lining drawers or using as end-papers or book covers. The little shop was full of bookbinding tools and presses. Young men bound books in a room that smelt of cardboard, glue and paste. For three hundred years Venetians had had their books bound there.

It was from this shop that Aunt Jane got her papers, and her ideas. The Christmas following my visit a parcel arrived from her. After stripping off layers of tissue paper and ribbons, so that a white sea billowed at my feet, the ultimate object was revealed; a two-fold portfolio tied together with a gay ribbon. It was a hold-all made out of Carta Varese, which had been carefully pasted over a cardboard base. Its inside edges were decorated with a border of flowers, carefully clipped out and applied. There was a note enclosed, also with floral heading and borders. "To Darling Desmond, with fondest greetings for Christmas. What secrets and loving letters this portfolio may hold!"

Sometimes it was not a portfolio, it was a satchel made out of the same paper, with a flap, a framed slit, and a little tongue that fastened it. The whole creation was perfectly executed. What hours she must have spent on these things!

So I departed from Venice with a little notebook bound in coloured Venetian paper. On the front page Aunt Jane had pasted a large red rose, clipped from somewhere. Underneath

was written "A perfumed and loving memory—Aunt Jane."
Dear, sloppy, warm-hearted and preposterous creature!

III

I did not return to Venice the following year but went the year
after, staying again at the *Seguso*. My welcome from the three
sisters was most cordial. Even Moses rubbed against my leg. I
was given the same pleasant room overlooking the bridge. I
arrived very late at night, having come from Vienna that
morning. Tired, I went straight to my room to find a great vase
of flowers "Welcome to *la bella Venezia*, beloved wandering
Boy." There were other things also, a large coloured blotting
pad, a small bottle of ink, three pencils, some rubber bands,
envelopes, writing-paper and an eraser. The Venetian paper
blotter told me the source.

The next morning I breakfasted in my room, flooded with
the brilliant light of the September day, and then attended to
my letters until about eleven when I went downstairs. I enquired after Signorina Saunders. She had been in the previous
evening with the flowers and writing things. She was very well
and would be down from her room at eleven-thirty.

I waited for her in the little salon through whose windows
came the noise of water as it suckered on the brick walls of the
rio, and the sound of footsteps on the bridge. A door suddenly
opened and there was Aunt Jane. I was ardently embraced and
hugged. "Wonder boy! It is a great day and you have come just
right! *Evviva! Meraviglioso!* It is darling Edoardo's birthday!
Che fortuna! caro ragazzo! He's coming at noon for us in a gondola. *È il suo compleanno!* We are having a great celebration—
lunch at his cousin's, Signora Lambrini's, in her *piccolo palazzo*
off the Grand Canal! You are as young, as handsome as ever,
darling boy!" she exclaimed, breathlessly. "You must tell me
all the wonderful important things you have been doing. My,
you look radiant!"

At noon, as grave, as courteous as ever, Edoardo arrived.
He was dressed in a white linen suit, wore a panama, and had a
red carnation in his buttonhole. He was a really handsome old

man and very quiet in contrast with Aunt Jane, bubbling with excitement. Nothing had really changed in the two years I had been absent. Her vivid enthusiasm for life had in no way abated. Every day was full of children to be patted and talked to, as well as old gondoliers, barge-boys, fruiterers, the keeper of the flower stall, the white-haired Reverendo in his black cotton soutane, and Emilia, shaking a rug out of an upper window. As she progressed she embraced the whole world. Everyone smilingly saluted the Signorina Saunders.

There was the same entertainment every afternoon when Edoardo arrived in his dinghy to take her with parasol and guitar for the outing on the canal, to the accompaniment of Mammy songs. I watched apprehensively those two large stout figures crammed into the dinghy that was scarcely two inches out of the water, but nothing happened. I saved my bombshell for the last day of my visit, knowing the tremendous acclaim it would evoke. I announced that I was to be married next month in England. I thought Aunt Jane would disintegrate with happiness, so violent were the emotional repercussions. At once she had transformed my fiancée into the most beautiful, the most gifted young woman in England. She cawed and clucked over her photograph. We were at once blessed with a bevy of *bellissimi bambini*.

Just before my departure in a gondola to the station she appeared on the *rio* steps with a small parcel. "Dear, darling boy, a little wedding present to you both with all my love. *Un regalo per i promessi sposi! Arrivederci! Buon' Viaggio. Buona fortuna!*" Her wishes followed my progress down the canal until I was out of hearing. Later, in the train, I opened the packet. Buried in tissue papers and ribbons I found a Venetian lace tea-table set, a cover and six napkins. It was of the most exquisite workmanship. The four corners had little bells, *campanelli*, and the design showed a mitred bishop coming out of San Marco. It was a specimen of the finest Venetian point lace.

CHAPTER 4

I

AT THE END of 1928 I was transferred back to London, following my marriage. The next year my bank sent me to Canada for two years. Aunt Jane was not a great letter writer, she was too busy with so many things to be a good correspondent. When she wrote the letters were typewritten, very badly, with clogged letters and an old ribbon, but always with her herbaceous border. In the course of time our letters ceased. On my return from Canada I was immersed in work that took me to various parts of France, Holland and Switzerland but never, alas, to Italy. Then, in the spring of 1935, I was sent to Milan and found that I could snatch a few days in Venice en route to Trieste. My wife was not with me. We were expecting our second child. I at once thought of Aunt Jane but it seemed probable that she would be in Florence, her Venice visit being usually in the late summer.

I found the *Pensione Seguso* unchanged except that it had added a sub-title, "The Anglo-American". The American professors and schoolmarms had discovered it. I was surprised to find it thronged in early May. The three sisters were flourishing, as also Moses the cat, fat and old. It was difficult to believe I had not been there for almost seven years. I was received like the prodigal son. At once I enquired for Signorina Saunders, how she was, when she was expected. What! Did I not know? The good sisters stared at me, then the whole three of them broke into smiles and ejaculations. Signorina Saunders was married! "Married?" I exclaimed, really shaken. "But when? To whom?" The three sisters told me, all speaking, ignoring a new arrival at the desk. She had been married last December to Signor Donati. "They are living in Florence?" "No, no, *signore*. They are here now in Signor Donati's *casa* in San Trovaso."

Later I heard the whole surprising story. In October last

year Signor Edoardo had been seriously ill with pneumonia, perilous for a man of seventy. Jane had nursed him assiduously through seven weeks but he began to fail. The end was in sight. He made his final dispositions. There was a problem troubling him. He would like to leave Jane his little Venetian house but there were two difficulties. His legacy might create a scandal for her. Also since she was in no way related, the estate tax would be so very heavy that it would be impossible for her to retain the property. There was one solution. If she would consent to marry him, then, as his widow, there would be no scandal and no tax. His Florentine apartment would go to her also, and then to his nephew.

With tremendous agitation Jane agreed to marry Edoardo. The priest was called in and the deathbed marriage took place, in the nick of time as it seemed. But Edoardo did not die, he recovered, nursed back to life by the devoted Jane. Later she moved in as his wife. Such was the marvellous history of the Signorina, now Signora Donati. They were wonderfully happy.

The next morning towards noon I made a visit to the newly-weds. I had never known just where Edoardo lived. I found his house on a small canal off the Rio San Trovaso, behind the Palazzo Rondanelli. It was a little red-brick house of three floors with an *altana*, a roof-platform built over Venetian houses for taking the air, sightseeing, or drying the washing. The red-brick house, with windows framed in white Istrian stone, had a green door. It faced the little canal and had a garden, with a water-gate, enclosed by a high brick wall. It was very old, a perfect nest for an artist. I called on a sunny May morning. Purple bougainvillaea covered the garden side of the house. The wall was topped by flowering creepers. A cypress and a fig tree were visible.

I knocked on the door, heard footsteps and then a woman in an apron opened it. I asked for Signora Donati. The maid came back after some inner consultation and showed me into a long low salon, whose end-window looked on to a leafy garden. Behind an orange tree there was a lion's stone head spouting water into an ornamental basin, a pleasant noise in the still morning. I now saw that the garden was completely walled in. There was a delightful glimpse of the open belfry of the church of San Trovaso. What a little paradise it was!

A voice called. I turned from the window and there was Aunt Jane She rushed forward uttering cries of *"Caro ragazzo! Ecco!* I said you would return one day. My! My!" she cried, embracing me. "Dear Edoardo will be down in a minute. Welcome to Venice! Welcome to Domus Amicorum!"

"Domus Amicorum?"

"We call it Domus Amicorum because it is the wee house where we welcome our friends. Isn't it *carina?* But you must see it. Come!"

She caught my hand and led me out into the garden. It was shady with trees, cypress, fig, orange, lemon and oleander. An old vine clambered up the garden side of the house and contested with a clematis in violet flower for possession of a small balcony built out from the upper storey.

"Romeo's balcony—but there ain't no Romeo—he'll appear in a minute. Edoardo! Edoardo *caro!"* she called. A figure slowly came into sight, festooned with clematis.

"Edoardo, we've a most distinguished visitor from England. Look, *caro!"*

Edoardo, in a white shirt, appeared. He peered down through the greenery, saw me and raised a hand in salute, smiling. "Ah, how delightful to see you! I will come down," he said.

"Isn't it lovely?" asked Aunt Jane. "Don't you like Domus Amicorum! It is so warm we can eat in the garden. Darling boy, you will stay to lunch! A very simple one. My, you have grown still more handsome! And your wife, we shall see her?"

I explained that my wife was in London expecting another baby.

"Another baby. Two babies! My! My! *Come fortunato!* And the first—*un maschio!* How old?"

"Yes, a boy—five years old."

"The darling little fellow, have you a photo?

I produced one. She cooed over it. He was handsome, a marvel, *molto intelligente* like his dear father!

Edoardo came into the garden and greeted me. Again I

thought what a handsome old boy he was. And what lovely manners framed his distinguished appearance.

I was taken into the salon for an *aperitivo*. While we were talking a bird began to sing in the garden. Birds are rare in Italy. They net and shoot them as enemies of the fruit. They are almost non-existent in Venice except for caged canaries. This bird sang lustily somewhere among the branches. It stopped and then it began again.

"So this is a house of friends and birds!" I said, listening. "How beautiful, what is it—a thrush?"

Edoardo looked at Jane, who smiled. "It is a bluebird," he said.

"The bluebird of happiness!" exclaimed Jane.

"I didn't know you had bluebirds in Italy, or that they sang like that," I said.

The singing stopped but the bird had not gone. It began again, fluting liquidly in the tree.

We went out to eat at a stone table set in an arbour looking down the garden. The table was laid with bright mats, napkins, a great wine flask, green Venetian glasses, a wicker basket of assorted fruit. The maid brought out the lunch to us. We chatted gaily, going back over the years. My host and his wife were so happy, like a pair of turtle-doves cooing at each other. We moved to a little table under an orange tree for coffee. As we sat there the bird began to sing again.

"That bluebird—where is it?" I asked, peering up into the branches, always a bird-lover.

Jane got up and pointed but I could not see it.

"Darling Desmond, we must tell you. It's our own special bluebird of happiness!" she said, and went over to the tree and came back carrying a small round gilt cage. She placed it on the table before me. Then I saw what it was, a mechanical bird. It stood on a little perch, a tiny bird, with blue feathers, that automatically sang, opening and closing its beak and turning its head. Under the base of the cage was a winding key, and a lever that made the bird pause between catches of song. I had been utterly deceived.

"Darling Edoardo bought it for me. He found it in a shop in

Florence. It travels with us. It is our mascot—our bluebird of happiness—*un'uccello di felicità*" said Aunt Jane.

II

I had to leave Venice after only five days. It had been a very happy visit except for a shadow over the scene. Political trouble was brewing between England and Italy. Mussolini was threatening to invade Abyssinia. There was talk of sanctions at the League of Nations. Mussolini made some bombastic speeches violently attacking Britain. A shadow grew over the age-long Anglo-Italian friendship. We carefully avoided talking politics. I noticed that both Jane and Edoardo wore Fascist pins. Perhaps he had to, the social pressure of Fascismo being so great. On the centre wall of the salon hung a signed portrait of Mussolini, with belligerent eyes and out-thrust jaw. I felt even then that he would come to a violent end, and said so to some of my pro-Mussolini English friends. True, he had made the trains run promptly but he had throttled freedom of speech and set a happy people marching with his rabid oratory.

I promised to return soon, with my wife. Our parting was affectionate. It was good to see that dear old couple so happy. Sometimes when Edoardo sat painting in the garden Jane would come out with his great straw hat and put it on his head to protect him from the sun. And while we were having our coffee she would take her guitar and sing her negro folk-songs. Her repertoire was extensive nor was it wholly of negro origin. She had a number of humorous folklore songs and I particularly loved a ridiculous one called *The Bluejay died with the Whooping Cough* which she sang with tremendous gusto.

When I left she gave me a little present, a small, tooled-leather studbox, wrapped up in sheets and sheets of tissue paper and tied up with the tricolour ribbon.

III

The next time that I saw the Donatis was in 1938 in Florence. This time my wife was with me. We visited them in their small apartment across the Arno. It had a terrace overlooking Florence towards Fiesole. We were rapturously welcomed. I noticed that they had grown slower in their movements, but they were as intensely alive as ever. Aunt Jane bubbled over with happiness. She showed me a photo album of her "dear boys", all marvellous, all children of genius in their various ways. I met the English novelist who had written a book in their Venetian garden and dedicated it to them. The little apartment was covered with Edoardo's paintings, mostly of Florence and Venice. They were honest pieces of work in the style of a past age. Obviously Jane thought them masterpieces, though Edoardo modestly demurred. Wearing a black velvet beret and bow tie, with his silver hair and noble features, he looked the *maestro*. Aunt Jane still called me "Dear darling boy", and my wife was a little startled to find herself called "Beautiful honeychile".

The day we had tea there the bluebird sang for us at the end of the terrace, hanging in a bower of blue wistaria, for it was springtime in Florence and there was blossom everywhere. When we left I did not know I was never to see Edoardo again or stand on that terrace. For although the international scene was troubled, and Mussolini had joined Hitler in threatening Europe, we all hoped somehow that the skies would clear.

CHAPTER 5

I

THE SECOND WORLD WAR drew a black line through our diaries for the next five years. The holocaust destroyed so much in our lives that one became nervous in enquiring what had happened to friends scattered about the world. My work having carried me to many places in Europe, I had an international group of friends, French, Spanish, Italian, Dutch, American and even German. A wall of silence grew up between us.

Just before Italy went into the war on the German side I had a letter from Aunt Jane. It was almost a farewell salute. It had no political allusions. They knew a strict censorship was at work. There followed a long silence. Late in 1944 I heard, through a Swiss friend that Edoardo had died in Florence. I wrote a letter via a bank in Switzerland but had no reply from Aunt Jane. I calculated that she must now be about seventy-six years of age. Edoardo's death must have been a great loss to her, but all over the world death was taking young and old remorselessly.

Then one day, at the close of the war, a young soldier called on me. He had been with the forces occupying Florence. It was there he encountered Aunt Jane, who had turned her little apartment into a sort of coffee-tea-reading-and-writing-room for "the dear boys". Apparently she was still vigorous, and known to the British Army.

He brought me a letter. It was decorated by a few clipped flowers—perhaps the supply was running out. "Dear Darling Desmond, *Tanti saluti*. I am safe and well. Come soon. The bluebird will sing for you. *Viva Italia! Viva Britannia! Viva America!* You have heard I lost my beloved Edoardo? *Sempre tua devota*, Aunt Jane."

I wrote at once, hoping my letter would get through. There was a long silence. Two years elapsed before I found it possible to visit Florence. I made a special trip there in May. When I

arrived I had a shock. The building in which her apartment
was situated was a ruin, one side open to the sky. The mining
of the Ponte Santa Trinita and its approaches had resulted in
landslides, and Aunt Jane's apartment house had partly collapsed.

I wondered if I should find her alive but finally I traced her.
She had found refuge in a pension just outside the gates of the
Boboli Gardens. It was a warren of stairs and corridors. It
had been a convent centuries ago. At last I reached the floor
on which the pension was situated. I rang. A young girl opened
the door suspiciously. She did not know the name Donati. She
would go and enquire.

I waited in a long ante-room looking into a court. The whole
place was massively built. The maid came back. Yes, Signora
Donati was No. 34. She ushered me into a long dark corridor
and said the door was the last on the right. The corridor was
gloomy and chill. It seemed like a penitentiary. I wondered at
the lives of the nuns who had walked in this corridor through
the centuries.

I came to No. 34 and tapped. I waited, there was no answer.
I tapped more loudly. There were slow footsteps and the door
opened cautiously. Aunt Jane stood there peering into the
corridor. She could not see me at first and when I said who I
was she did not seem to comprehend. Then, on my repeating
my name, she gave a loud cry of recognition. The next minute
her arms were round me. "You darling wonderful long-lost
boy! Come into the light. Let my old eyes look at you. My! My!
Mamma mia! Caro ragazzo!" she cried.

There were tears in her eyes. I was glad to see she had not
changed greatly, perhaps a little thinner. She was as ardent
and loquacious as ever. I was drawn into a small narrow room.
I now realized that I had traversed a row of nuns' cells converted into bedrooms. This was one of them. It was a bed-
sitting-room with a long French window, a low bed with a
flowered Indian counterpane by one wall, a writing bureau by
the window. There were a cane rocking chair and two small
ones, also a table with a green plush cover and a vase of flowers.
Apart from an old mirror in a heavy gilt frame, the high walls

were covered with unframed water-colours fastened by thumb tacks. I saw at once they were Edoardo's.

After she had hugged me and examined me from head to foot, she led me out through the French window. I was surprised to find a long wide balcony with an iron railing. It had once been a covered walk for the nuns, now it had been partitioned off so that each room had its own balcony. We looked down on to a garden, very large, walled in and full of trees, rose-bushes and ornamental beds. Obviously this had been the convent garden. Aunt Jane made me sit down in an easy chair. She went back into the room and returned with a tray on which were glasses and a bottle of wine. She was very agitated and her hand trembled as she poured out some wine. Then she settled in a chair opposite me and asked a hundred questions. I reckoned that she was now nearly eighty. She was very active, only the increased bagginess of her eyes and a sharpening of the chin betrayed her years. But somehow, despite her vivacity, I suspected that all had not gone too well for her. Edoardo had died suddenly, I learned.

"Darling sweet boy, you know what he meant to me—but we had had almost ten years of serene happiness," she said. "And now even after he has gone my darling Edoardo looks after me. He saved my life!"

I looked a little bewildered. She reached out and took my hand, pressing it between her own. "As you know the Germans, when they left, mined the bridges and the approaches. You remember, we lived near the Ponte Santa Trinita, which suffered badly. Then the allies began to clear the debris to open a way. They mined some of it and that weakened our old building. I had gone to visit darling Edoardo's grave and it was while I was there that the *palazzo* suddenly collapsed, all one side falling away. Eleven persons were killed. Had Edoardo not called me to his grave—I had heard him call me that morning, very strange, for it wasn't my morning to visit him—I should have been killed."

"Your apartment was in the part that collapsed? I have just seen the building."

"Yes, I lost everything, all my furniture, all my clothes,

except for things in two back rooms. And what do you think, darling boy—God has looked after me. They were the rooms in which I kept my darling Edoardo's paintings! *Un miracolo, davvero!*"

Little by little I learned the whole story. There had been a financial disaster, too. Edoardo's small fortune had almost disappeared in the devaluation. There were ten years of the apartment's lease to run, but now they were of no value. She had sold *Domus Amicorum* in Venice and had fared badly in the deal. The cost of living had gone up. She had had to borrow, as her dollar income had been blocked during the war. So, economizing, she had moved into this pension.

"I get my food and I am attended to and they are very kind, and so, dear darling Desmond, I thank God for His mercies. There! We have a glass of wine! We are united again! So many of the dear boys write to me! *Quanto è bella la primavera!* How beautiful is the spring! Do you know who wrote that—Lorenzo dei Medici, here in Florence, five hundred years ago. And do you know, an old nun walks in this garden! I've seen her in the dusk, and spoken to her—she died here three hundred years ago! Now, dear wonderful boy, we must celebrate. It is the month of May when flowers blossom and friends rejoice!"

She filled my glass again, went to a little cupboard on the balcony and produced a box of biscuits. She also brought something covered with a cloth.

"*Questo è un giorno di festa!*" she exclaimed, and from under the cloth cover took a bird-cage. I recognized it at once, it was the bluebird.

"So it was saved also?" I asked, as she wound it.

"It was safe in Venice, and now it is back in Florence. *Come è felice!* It only sings on Edoardo's birthday—but this is a special day and it will sing for us."

So once again I heard the song I had heard in the Venetian garden in the happy lost years.

II

I did not see Aunt Jane for another four years, but we kept in touch. Always on my birthday and at Christmas there arrived one of her astonishing parcels. My wife and I almost shrieked in mirth as we unwrapped them; first, the top wrapping in brown paper with two pasted labels, also two tied-on labels. All of these had a spray of flowers gummed on. After the top wrapper, tied up with yards of string and sealing-wax, came the successive layers of snow-white tissue paper, each layer fastened with Florentine paper seals. We once counted eight of these wrappings. Then came the last sealed wrapping, this in a special floral paper. I always felt that it was like getting at the tomb of Tutankhamen.

At last we came to the gift. It was always one of her stationery concoctions, a blotter, a portfolio, a collapsible file or a simple satchel with a silk ribbon fastener. The inside of the portfolio or box was gaily decorated with applied flowers culled from God knows what catalogues and magazines. There was also always a sacred card of a saint or madonna and child, and a greeting in the form of a spray of flowers carried by cherubs which proclaimed *Tanti Auguri* or *Buon Natale*. She must have spent months on these creations, and I am sure they went to many of her "dear boys" all over the world.

One day I received a letter that sounded a note of desperation. "I hope you will come soon, darling boy. I very much want to talk to you. You are a very great banker and I want to profit by your wisdom." I had an idea what the trouble was. She had told me at our last meeting that she had an income of only eight hundred dollars. "But I manage very well," she said. But did she? Under three hundred pounds a year, with the cost of living rising all the time, was very little. The days of the English residing in Florence on two hundred pounds a year had gone. Florence was emptied of its spinsters, bachelors and artists, such as it had known for centuries, endowed with sufficient to keep a maid and pay for a carriage ride. The Europe of foreign residents in choice little apartments had vanished. The era of the brash tourists in collective groups with money to spend, whirled in and out of historic towns, had begun. Soon the motor-charabancs and cars were to shatter the tranquillity of the ancient scene.

I answered her letter, saying I would be in Florence soon. I also informed her that her "dear darling boy" had just become a grandfather. In September I took a short Italian holiday with my wife and younger son. We stayed at the Excelsior Hotel and I went in a taxi to collect Aunt Jane and bring her back to dinner.

I found her all dressed up and excitedly waiting for me. I was rapturously received but I was shocked by the change in her appearance. She had grown very thin. Her skin hung loosely on her large frame. The poor dear looked like a deflated elephant. But she was nimble on her feet and had lost none of her *joie de vivre.*

She astonished us by her hearty appetite. She went through every course and left a cleared plate. Obviously she had enjoyed her dinner. "Do you think she is hungry?" asked my wife. "She ate as if she had never had a good meal." I said I thought perhaps the change of food, very well cooked, and in a luxurious atmosphere, had increased her appetite.

The next morning when I went to see Aunt Jane for a consultation I learned the truth. She was hungry. To economize she was living half-pension. It transpired that from necessary reinvestment and fallen rates her income was only six hundred and fifty dollars a year, some two hundred and thirty pounds, not five pounds a week. She had been using some of her capital and was getting frightened. "I did not expect to live so long," she said sadly. It was the first time she had expressed any fear of life.

I also discovered something else. She had begun a vigorous campaign to promote dear Edoardo's immortality as a great artist. This consisted of a wide correspondence with prominent people and the directors of galleries in Europe and the United States. Elatedly she produced a portfolio of letters from Sir Winston Churchill, General Eisenhower, Signor Einaudi, Bernard Berenson and the various curators of the National Gallery in Rome, of the Uffizi at Florence, of the National Galleries in London and Washington, of the Louvre, the Prado, the Rÿksmuseum, the Metropolitan, the Huntington. To all of these she had presented one of Edoardo's water-colours.

She had received from them letters of thanks signed either personally or by secretaries. There was a "wonderful" article by a critic in a Florentine magazine discussing Edoardo's art, with a portrait of the artist and of his Venetian studio. This she had reprinted in pamphlet form. Heaven knows what all this had cost in postage and wrapping. But she was exultant as she told me all this in the little room, lined with Edoardo's works. "The world will now know the genius of my darling husband!" she proclaimed proudly.

There were other charges on her meagre resources. She gave little sums here and there for ailing children. There was the cost of the tea-parties for the "dear boys" who called to see her from time to time. Her stamp bill, replying to the "dear boys", was considerable. Those birthday and Christmas packages cost money also.

She had an idea for the increase of her income. It was pathetic and utterly impractical—to publish a new edition of her Mammy songs which had been out of print fifty years. Its publisher was long dead, its sale had long ceased.

She produced some correspondence with her bank in Baltimore, where her investments were kept. I read this through and was appalled to find that her total capital was now only twelve thousand dollars, and little by little that would be diminished. She had now used up the money received from the sale of *Domus Amicorum*.

It was the kind of story I was only too familiar with in my banking experience, of helpless old maiden ladies or widows whom the post-war devaluation and the ever-rising cost of living brought to genteel poverty. Here was Aunt Jane, eighty-three and in good health. If she lived only six more years she could spend ten pounds a week of her capital. But I knew from experience that even if you set the span of life of a client at one hundred years he baulked at any definite term. Few persons are willing to contemplate finality although Death snatches their relations and friends. I recalled my own aunt. I had brought her back from Paris one of those "perpetual" calendars. She was seventy-eight and I pointed out that it lasted until 2010. "Oh, is that all?" she remarked, thanking me.

Nevertheless, I made a proposal to Aunt Jane. I suggested that instead of spending capital she could insure continuity of income by the purchase of an annuity. At her age she could have about four hundred pounds a year.

"Dear clever darling boy! What a wonderful idea!" she cried clapping her hands. "And I shall be able to provide for Elsa, she can have it after me!"

"Elsa?"

"Elsa Howarth, my darling friend living here. She is so kind, she reads to me and helps to write letters and runs errands. She's very young for eighty and I'm sure she'll outlive me! She's poor and I do want to do something for her."

"But, Aunt Jane—if you have an annuity there's no capital left, it is sunk in the purchase of the annuity, which ends at your death," I explained.

"But where does the capital go? Surely they are honest and would give it to darling Elsa!"

Very patiently I explained the principle of an annuity and as it became clear to her I saw the joy leave her face.

"Darling boy, I could not die happy knowing that poor Elsa would not be looked after."

I was defeated. Without being brutal I could not point out that if she went on as at present there would be no capital for either of them unless they died in time. She said she would think about it and let me know. I saw that the suggestion of an annuity was dead. She was spending seven pounds a week, I learned. If the cost of living did not rise, and I was sure it would, she could last for some ten years. Death might take her in time, mercifully.

Her gaiety quickly returned. She replenished my glass. "Dear darling sweet boy, thoughtful and kind always, we will put our trust in Him. He has always looked after me. And my darling Edoardo will look after me too."

I left her, not altogether easy in my mind. She walked the length of the corridor with me. At the door she hugged me almost fiercely. *"Arrivederci, caro ragazzo!"* she said, and waved as I went down the wide stone staircase. *Arrivederci*—till we meet again. I reflected that at eighty-three reunions are problematical.

III

I was wrong. I saw her twice again. I returned in four years and found her full of vivacity. And God, or Edoardo, or both, had looked after her as she had foretold. An American friend, hearing of her situation, wrote and promised her five hundred dollars a year. There was no more need for cheeseparing. I found her in a larger and brighter room. It had no balcony but it faced east, looking into the Boboli Gardens of the Pitti Palace. She was well, except for occasional headaches that bothered her. She produced letters from her "darling boys", mostly ex-soldiers to whom she had played aunt in Florence. Two more galleries had accepted dear Edoardo's paintings. Her room, though larger, was lined with them.

"I have only one worry, dear sweet boy."

"What is that?"

She hesitated for a few moments, and then looking at me very seriously, said, "Darling Desmond, I wonder if I was ever properly married!"

"What?" I exclaimed, startled.

She took my hand between hers, which were surprisingly unveined for a woman of eighty-seven.

"You see, dear darling boy, when I married Edoardo, I was a Protestant. I became a convert later. Perhaps I should have married Edoardo again, when I was a Catholic."

"But it was a Catholic marriage, performed by a Catholic priest?" I asked.

"Yes."

"Then I don't think you've anything to worry about. It seems to me a proper marriage, and you became a convert, anyhow."

"Yes," she said, hesitatingly. "Yes, in a way."

"In a way—what do you mean?"

"Darling boy, I hope you won't think me wicked," she said, pausing.

"You're as near to a saint as I'm ever likely to meet."

"Well, I feel I must tell someone—and you are my very dearest friend. You see, I became a convert because I wanted to be buried with dear Edoardo, in their family mausoleum here, and, dear boy, at heart I'm still a Baptist. I never go to confession, I just can't stomach it!"

I burst out laughing. She had turned *me* into a father confessor, with such a look on her face, half-contrite, half-impish.

I pressed her hand. "My dear Aunt Jane, I'm sure you've nothing to worry about. God and Edoardo between them will put it right. And I rather suspect the Pope will look the other way!"

She recovered her spirits at once and laughed with me. I had kept a taxi waiting to take her out to lunch. She powdered her nose, applied lipstick and put on a half-veil, with all the eagerness of a girl going to a party. I was delighted to find, also, that age had in no way diminished her appetite.

IV

When I received the command to be present at Aunt Jane's ninetieth birthday I felt it must be obeyed. My wife and I left for Florence. My welcome was as exuberant as ever. But this time I found her in a large chair. "Dear darling Desmond," she cried, "My old sticks won't function! I'm not *in gamba* these days!"

Her legs had failed but not her spirits. There were half-a-dozen people in the room, the faithful old friend Elsa, Edoardo's nephew Enrico and his wife, and the signora of the pension, who had supplied the champagne. It was a sunny September morning and someone had made the room a bower of flowers. When we had drunk her health Aunt Jane clapped her hands, took a cloth off the gilt bird-cage and cried, "Now darling Edoardo's bluebird is going to sing a few words!" She touched the lever and it started off merrily. When it had finished Enrico said—"*Cara zia*, won't you sing for us?"

Aunt Jane looked very surprised and coy but I sensed it was prearranged. Enrico produced the guitar.

"But dear darlings, I'm not in voice!" she said, to which we all demurred.

She began one of her Mammy songs. Her voice was shaky but

her fingers were firm on the strings. She sang *Swing low, sweet chariot* and *Momma's feet's bad but her heart's sho' sound*, and then, knowing it was my favourite, *the Bluejay died with the Whooping Cough*, and we were back in the garden at *Domus Amicorum* with Edoardo in his big brimmed hat and Aunt Jane on a stool under the orange tree.

v

Two years later, one morning in October, I received a letter from Italy in a strange hand. It was from Enrico Donati informing me that Aunt Jane had died peacefully, aged ninety-two, and had been buried in the family mausoleum. She had left me the little singing bird. Should he send it or would I collect it sometime? I wrote back expressing our sadness at the news and saying that next April I would come to Florence. I asked him to hold the bird for me.

On a bright April morning Enrico Donati took me to the Catholic cemetery, and in front of the marble plaque bearing Aunt Jane's name, I placed my flowers. Inwardly I smiled a little to think how a good Baptist had succeeded in lying beside her darling Edoardo. Her timing for the journey to him had been perfect. She left one thousand pounds, divided between Elsa and Enrico.

I brought back to England the little bluebird, now standing on my desk as I write these lines. It is a lovely reminder of a very simple sweet-souled woman. It is also the only legacy I have ever had. I treasure it.

BOOK 6

The Robin and The Wren

CHAPTER 1

When Jesus in the manger lay
The birds did sing, the lambs did play,
But more than any others then
Did sing the Robin and the Wren.
They sang from dawn to set of day
For Him, wherefore did shepherds say,
Hearing the Robin and the Wren,
That they were God's Two Holy Men.

I

AT THE CLOSE of the first World War Dr. Richard Wren and his family settled in the long low white house at the bottom of the lane in West Cleebury. The house overlooked a sea-water creek, sandy flats, and the great expanse of water towards Hayling Island. The site was bleak and cold. The winds blowing in from the sea had bent the branches of the trees so that they all grew landwards. West Cleebury in those days was a quiet Sussex hamlet. Six miles from Chichester, with no railway, it was an isolated spot. There were very few shops and the community, scattered in low whitewashed houses, prided itself on being select. It was a haven for those who loved quiet and sailing. Dr. Wren loved both. He was a radiologist at the hospital in Chichester and motored into that delightful old town every morning. The Wrens were a happily married young couple with two boys. Two years after the arrival of the younger son, a girl was born.

From the windows of *Longview* the Wrens looked across a rough grass field to the sandy creek where the slender masts of sailing-boats could be seen bobbing with the ebb and flow of the sea-tide through the shallows. The creek was busy at week-ends with men, women and children clad in the loose garments affected by nautical enthusiasts, thick pullovers, flannel trousers, scarves, seaboots, and in the summer months, singlets, shorts and no footwear. A score of years were to pass before the mob, as the residents disgustedly called them, discovered West Cleebury as a weekend paradise for sailing and camping.

It was in the last year of the First World War that young Dr. Wren, newly appointed radiologist, had discovered *Longview*. The village was then almost deserted with its youth away in the Services. The house stood empty, the garden had gone to seed behind the red brick walls that enclosed it. It was going cheap. Dr. Wren bought it and with his wife and the two children, Timothy aged three, and Christopher, aged six months, moved in. Then came Jenny.

They were a healthy, merry family. They scrambled in and out of boats, especially on Saturdays and Sundays when the doctor stayed at home from the hospital. The keen winds brought roses to the cheeks of the children, moulded their strong frames, impervious to cold. They bubbled over with vitality.

Everyone knew and liked the Wren family. The young doctor and his wife were hospitable. They danced well, played a good game of bridge, and could handle any boat along the creek. In the course of a few years the three children tended to run a little wild. Mrs. Wren was happy-go-lucky. "They'll have enough trouble in the next fifty years," she said, being acquainted with sadness. Two brothers to whom she was devoted had been killed in the war. The house was run with the assistance of a Nanny, a bustling white-haired woman of fifty, rather domineering, to whom the Wrens surrendered.

Nothing escaped the children. Whether it was from sailing, with its need of quick decisions, or from a gift of nature, they were swift as birds. It was some time after Timothy had gone to his preparatory school, while home from the summer holidays, that he burst in with the astonishing news.

"There's someone in the Barn!" he shouted, coming to the dining-table.

"Who's someone?" demanded Christopher, aged ten.

"It's a man!" said Timothy dramatically.

"Have you seen him?" asked Dr. Wren, a little incredulous. The barn at the top of the lane by the fishermen's cottages was almost a ruin. The weather had worked its will on the blackened

old shack. Tiles were off the roof, the panes of the window that
had been let into its side were all broken. The barn door was
blocked by wild tufts of grass. It seemed well on its way
to total collapse. It had been used for some years to store a
boat, but that was before the Wrens had come. The doctor
had heard it could be bought, with a quarter of an acre
of land, for fifty pounds. No one had made an offer. Once
Christopher and Jenny had broken in. Swifts had built nests in
its roof. Their curiosity was soon satisfied and they never went
there again. Every day the Wrens passed it, somewhat of an
eyesore in its tumbledown condition, as they turned to go down
the lane to their house. It had only one merit—a beautiful
great walnut tree overshadowed it. One day Dr. Wren thought
the barn might make someone a good garage, for cars were
coming more and more into use now the war was over, and
cottages were being snapped up and renovated. But as he did
not have fifty pounds loose he did not buy it.

"Did you saw him?" piped Jenny, aged eight.

"Did you see him, darling," said Mrs. Wren.

"See him?" repeated Jenny, corrected.

"I saw his back," said Timothy, pontifically.

"And what was his back like?" asked Dr. Wren.

"It was—it was—" began Timothy, reaching for the sugar
bowl and hesitating.

"You imagined him!" proclaimed Christopher, very scepti-
cal of everything.

"He was an old man," declared Timothy, annoyed.

"If you didn't see his face how do you know he is old?"
asked Mrs. Wren.

The boy shrugged his shoulders, disgusted with their doubts.

"Tomorrow we'll go there," said Christopher.

"We will go and look!" added Jenny.

"Then you go and look, and perhaps he'll gobble you up!"
declared Timothy, disgruntled.

The next morning they went to look. There was no doubt
about it. Someone was in the old barn. The door was open,
askew on its hinges. The three children stood on the far end of
the paddock.

"There! What did I tell you!" declared Timothy.

They watched, silent for a time. There were noises inside the barn. Suddenly there was a figure in the dark doorway, and an object was thrown out on the turf. It was a galvanized-iron feeding trough. There was more noise, and another object appeared hurtling through the air. It was a broken cartwheel. Obviously there was some clearing up being done inside by the mysterious occupant. The next object was a wooden barrel with broken staves. This time a man appeared in view. He was heavily built, an old man in the eyes of the three beholders. He did not look very clean. He was in his shirt sleeves, with a dirty brown scarf round his neck. He was unshaven and had a dark bristly growth on his face.

The Wren children did not move, fascinated by the signs of life that had come to the long deserted barn. They waited, silent, for new objects to be thrown out. Nothing came.

"Ask him his name," said Christopher to his brother.

Timothy did not respond to this suggestion. "Perhaps he's a tramp," he said, as the man disappeared inside again.

"He looks very poor," observed Jenny.

There was silence again while they stared at the barn, hoping something might happen. It did. The man appeared at the doorway, stared at them, and cried in a harsh voice, "Do you want anything?"

"No—no, thank you," replied Timothy, a little frightened by the man's aggressive tone.

"Then get along!" he said brusquely, and turned and went into the barn, banging the door behind him.

The children moved off down the lane.

"He's a nasty man," said Timothy. "I don't think we should speak to him."

"He doesn't seem to like us, does he?" asked Christopher.

"Perhaps he has a headache," said Jenny, always practical.

II

Despite the churlish nature of the new occupant of the barn, the Wren children were fascinated by what was taking place there. They never stood in front of it, remembering the ogre who had shooed them away. "You have no right to be so inquisitive," said Dr. Wren, when they related what had happened.

"Do you think he is a poor man, Daddy?" asked Jenny.

"I don't know but I can't imagine anyone who isn't poor living in such a hovel. I wonder the authorities allow it."

"Oh come, darling, you know how difficult the housing problem is! Perhaps he'll improve the place," said Mrs. Wren.

"He's more likely to make a slum there," replied Dr. Wren. "You children keep away!"

They tried to keep away, but strange and wonderful things began to happen. The old broken window now had new panes in it. Then the wooden barrel they had seen thrown out had been repaired. It stood on a layer of bricks at the corner of the barn where the rain had splashed down through a mouthless waterpipe. Now a pipe with a right-angle had been added and the rain fell into the barrel. A few days later the once grubby barrel shone with green paint.

Sometimes, passing quietly on their bicycles and pretending not to look, they saw the man working outside. He had repaired the door, put new hinges on it, and had made a path to the barn. An old lace curtain had been hung across the window. He appeared to be a man of about sixty, thick-set, with iron-grey hair. He took no notice whatever of the Wren children when they went by. One evening there was smoke coming out of the stove pipe that emerged from one side of the barn, and through the open door Timothy could see an oil lamp, lit, standing on a table. Little by little the place seemed to be becoming civilized. But no one was ever seen to call or to go in or out.

At the end of the summer holidays Timothy went back to his preparatory school. Christopher and Jenny attended the local school. They walked past the barn each day. It had been white-washed and part of the field in front had been dug over. It looked as if the occupant was going to make a lawn or a garden. Sometimes articles hung on a clothes-line, a man's shirt, underwear, socks and towels. Evidently the mysterious occupant did his own washing.

"I never see him in any of the shops. He never gets letters or goes to the Post Office, I'm told," said Mrs. Wren. "He's a thorough hermit."

One day Christopher and Jenny arrived home in a state of great excitement.

"Mummy, his name's up!" Christopher cried.

"On a board!" added Jenny.

"Whose name? What are you talking about?" asked Mrs. Wren, taking off their coats.

"The man in the barn! He's put a board up over the door with his name on it. Robin Redthorne," said Christopher breathlessly. "It's in white paint on a black board—ever so neat," said Christopher.

"And something underneath—'stolester' and 'Repairs' and 'Jobs done'," said Jenny.

"She means Upholsterer and Repairs and Jobs Done. Mummy, what is an upholsterer?" asked Christopher.

"A man who covers furniture and chairs," she explained.

Jenny had disappeared and came back with a dictionary. She was addicted to the dictionary. She put it on the table and began to look for the word but she could not find it.

"Let me, stupid! u's at the end—u.v.w.x.y.z," he said, proud of his superior knowledge. His finger ran down the page— "uphill, uphold, upholster!" he cried, and read aloud. " 'Upholster, *v.t.*, to fit out furniture with coverings, springs, padding, etc.' He's an upholsterer!"

"Upholsterer," repeated Jenny with difficulty.

"Mummy, can we take him something to cover, then we can have a good look at him?" asked Christopher. "That old chair?"

"I don't think he's a nasty man, Mummy. Everything's now very clean," commented Jenny.

"No, not just yet," replied Mrs. Wren. "We'll see about the chair later. We don't know how good he is."

Nanny came bustling in, frowning.

"How often have I told you children to wipe your feet before you come in! You've brought in a ton of mud!" she complained.

"Not a ton, Nanny, an ounce," corrected Christopher.

"Ounce! Pound! Ton! Whatever it is, you've made a mess of the hall floor which I'd just finished waxing," said Nanny, going out.

"Mummy, do let's give Mr. Redthorne something to do," pleaded Christopher. "The board says 'Jobs Done', that's everything, isn't it? Perhaps he could put the bottom back in my steam-engine?"

"We'll see later, darling. Now go and get your tea," said Mrs. Wren, pushing them towards the dining-room.

That weekend just as the Wren family were beaching their boat—they had spent a lovely October Sunday across the estuary—Christopher cried—"Look, there he is, Daddy!"

Dr. Wren looked. A solitary figure was walking along the high bank by the beach where the boats lay sideways, with the tide running out. He looked neither to the right nor left and appeared quite uninterested in the people on the shelving shingle who were making fast their boats for the night. He walked on, his head up, briskly, and passed them as if unaware of any other person in the world. He wore a thick brown sweater, flannel trousers and a cap. His hands were in his pockets. He had black eyebrows and a strong heavy-featured face.

"He's a queer fish," said Dr. Wren, as he walked away along the footpath. They watched him cross the rough field until he came to the barred gate that led to the lane at the side of *Longview*. To their surprise he did not climb over the gate but vaulted it.

"He seems pretty active for his age," said Dr. Wren.

"*You* couldn't do it, could you, Daddy?" asked Jenny.

"Well, I might with an effort," laughed the doctor.

"I'd rather you didn't try," said Mrs. Wren.

III

A week later it was Jenny who broke the ice, or rather, Jimmy the dachshund. Jenny had taken him with her that Saturday morning when she went to post some letters for her mother. On coming back she passed the barn. The man was digging in the garden. The dachshund darted off and began to bark violently at the stranger. The man stopped digging and looked at the little dog shaking with agitation.

"Jimmy! Jimmy! Stop, you naughty dog!" cried Jenny, running forward to pick him up. "I'm so sorry, Mr. Redthorne."

He stood looking down on her as she held the wriggling dog, still barking. Then he spoke, quietly.

"That's all right. Dogs are born to bark. How do you know my name's Redthorne?" he asked.

"It's on the board."

"Of course! You've sharp eyes. And what's your name?"

"Jenny Wren."

"Why, that's the name of a bird!" he said.

"You've the name of a bird—Robin!" replied Jenny.

"So I have!" he laughed, looking hard at her.

She put down Jimmy, quiet now, and pointed to the red cardigan the man wore. "Robin Redbreast!" she said.

He seemed very amused. He stuck his spade in the soil, and ran his hands down over his plump stomach.

"Robin Redbreast and Jenny Wren—I like that! Perhaps I'll change my name from Redthorne to Redbreast," he said. "But I don't eat worms and I can't sing."

"We have a bird that can sing—a canary," said Jenny solemnly. "Have you a bird?"

"Well, I have and I haven't. It certainly can't sing and I'm sure it never could. Would you like to see it?"

Jenny hesitated. It meant going into the house, but her curiosity overcame her. "Yes, please," she answered quietly.

"Come along," he said, and he went up the path to the door.

Jenny followed, her heart thumping, Jimmy at her feet.

The old barn was quite surprising inside. It was not dark. The walls had been whitewashed. Plenty of light came in through the window. There was a black iron stove with a pipe that went up towards the roof and then turned into the wall. It was lit and warmed the room. At one end a screen with a door had been erected. It was made of cardboard, nailed on to wooden laths. It shut off the end of the barn, The screen was covered with coloured pictures cut from magazines and was quite gay. Along by the window there was a heavy workbench with a screw vice, and on a board on the wall, with canvas pockets, hung an assortment of tools. There were two chairs, one an armchair with a cushion, the other a plain deal one standing by the stove. On a round mahogany table with a pedestal base and a tassel-fringed crimson tablecloth, stood an oil lamp with a white globe.

Jenny's eyes slowly examined the room. "You look very comfortable, Mr. Robin Redbreast," she said solemnly.

"I am comfortable, Miss Jenny Wren," said her host, "And I've done it all myself, with odd things I've picked up."

"We saw you were working very hard."

"Yes, I saw you watching me, you and your brothers."

"Yes, you shouted at us!" said Jenny.

"I'm sorry. You see, I was very busy then. And now here's my bird!" He turned to a side table and brought from it a large glass dome and put it on the table. Inside the dome there was a brownish stuffed bird with big eyes. Jenny studied it carefully.

"It's an owl," she said at last. "I've one in my bird book like that. Did you shoot it, Mr. Robin?"

"No, Miss Jenny. I don't hold with shooting birds. I found it here under a lot of rubbish in a corner. I've cleaned him up, his feathers were thick with dust."

Jenny examined the bird, impressed. Then she saw a chair with a broken cane bottom. There were long thin laths of yellow cane sticking out of it.

"What are you making there?" she asked, pointing.

"I'm mending the bottom, plaiting the cane. I do any odd jobs like that," answered Mr. Robin.

"Are you very clever?" asked Jenny.

He laughed and said, "Well, I don't know about that, young lady, but I'll say I'm handy. If your mother has any odd jobs I'll be glad to do them."

"My brother has a steam-engine with the bottom fallen out— it got too hot. He would like it mended."

"Then bring it along, Miss Jenny," he answered.

"I must go now. Jimmy, come along!" she said to the dachshund which was sniffing around. "Goodbye, Mr. Robin Redbreast."

"Goodbye, Miss Jenny Wren. Bring your brother along with the engine."

He watched her, then closed the door. He picked up the owl in its glass bell. "Well, if that isn't an astonishing kid! Mr. Robin Redbreast—I like that! And Jenny Wren—the old bird and the young bird," he said aloud to himself, replacing the bell.

CHAPTER 2

The fireside is for the cricket,
The wheatstack for the mouse,
When trembling nightwinds whistle
And moan around the house.
The frosty ways like iron,
The branches plumed with snow,
Alas, in winter dead and dark,
Where can poor Robin go?
Robin, Robin Redbreast,
O Robin dear!
And a crumb of bread for Robin,
His little breast to cheer.

William Allingham

I

JENNY WREN having blazed the trail, there was much visiting
between *Longview* and the barn. A few days after the owl
incident Jenny took along Christopher, with the loose bottom
of his engine.

"I'm Christopher Wren," said Christopher, when the door
opened on his tapping. Jenny stood at his side.

"He's my brother!" she proclaimed. "He doesn't believe
your name's Robin Redbreast, because over the door it says
Robin Redthorne."

"It isn't, but since you're Jenny Wren I don't see why I
can't be Robin Redbreast, I've only got to change a thorn
for a breast. It's a much nicer name, and after all, you called
me that!"

"Yes, but you had a red waistcoat!" said Jenny, looking at
his blue pullover.

"Ah, then I'll put it on! Come in!"

He went over to a recess with a curtain drawn over it and took out his red cardigan and put it on.

"I like you in that," said Jenny, approvingly.

"There was once a famous man who built St. Paul's in London. His name was Christopher—Sir Christopher Wren," said Mr. Robin Redbreast, looking at the boy holding the engine, who was about ten, sturdy and fair. It was plain that he was Jenny's brother.

"My daddy says that I am called after him, and Jenny's called after the bird," explained Christopher. "I've seen St. Paul's!"

"Have you really, and you've an older brother—what's his name?" asked Mr. Robin.

"He's Timothy. He's named after my grandpa."

"He's big," said Jenny, raising her hand over her head.

"So I've seen. How old is he?"

"Thirteen. He goes away to school," said Christopher. "He'll be home for Christmas. He plays cricket in the team!"

"Wonderful! Now what can I do for you, young man?" asked Mr. Robin, looking at the engine.

"If you please, first, he wants to see the owl," said Jenny.

"Very well. Put your engine on the bench."

He went over to the wall, picked up the dome of glass and brought it to the table.

The two children stared at the stuffed owl.

"Can you take the glass off?" asked Christopher.

"Yes," said Mr. Robin, obligingly removing the dome.

"You mustn't touch!" cried Jenny.

"You can both do it if you do it very gently," said Mr. Robin.

In turn the children ran a finger softly over a wing.

"Can it say To-whit! To-whoo?" asked Christopher.

"It's stuffed, silly!" cried Jenny, knowledgeable.

"I suppose once it did," said Mr. Robin, replacing the dome. "But it's been dead a long time, I think. Perhaps it's older than you. Now what about your engine?"

He went over to the bench and picked up the piston engine. The bottom of the boiler was loose.

"Daddy says it wants soldering, and it will have to go to London. Can you do it—you have a notice 'Jobs Done'?" asked Christopher, hopefully.

"Yes, I think I can do it," said Mr. Robin. He picked up the burner with the wick, smelt it and asked, "Have you been using paraffin?"

"Yes."

"Ah! You mustn't use paraffin. You must use methylated spirits. The paraffin makes soot, the soot gets red-hot, and then the solder runs," explained Mr. Robin.

"When will it be mended? And Mummy said I was to ask you how much," said Christopher.

"You must leave it two or three days. When it's mended I'll have to test it. As for the cost, I'll tell you what I'll do," said Mr. Robin, removing the spectacles he had put on. "You can bring me a geranium for my garden."

"We'll bring two geraniums, Mr. Robin," affirmed Jenny.

"Well, thank you, Miss Jenny—but only if I can make the engine go. Now a moment, I've something to show you."

He went to the shelf and took down a piece of wood, placing it on the table. It was a wooden mousetrap.

"It's a mouse! A live mouse!" exclaimed Jenny, seeing the bright-eyed little animal inside.

"I've heard him around for several days and so I set the trap and got him in the night," said Mr. Robin.

"Are you going to drown him—or cut his head off?" asked Christopher, excitedly.

Mr. Robin looked sternly at the boy.

"Young man, I wouldn't kill anything. Let him enjoy his life. He's not a house mouse—he's a field mouse. I'm going to put him back in the field."

"Can we see you do it?" asked Jenny, eagerly.

"Yes—we'll do it now," said Mr. Robin, picking up the mousetrap. For a while he watched the mouse. "I don't like to see any living creature penned up in a cage," he said.

"You are a kind man, Mr. Robin," said Jenny gravely, looking at him. "What a lucky mouse!"

"If you were a real wren would you like to be kept in a cage?" asked Mr. Robin, going to the door.

"Oh no!" said Jenny. "I should die."

"Bird or man, it's a wicked business," said Mr. Robin. "Now we'll go into the field at the back."

They went round the corner of the house, crept through a fence and found themselves in a rough stubble field. They walked some way across it.

"Well, now!" said Mr. Robin.

"Will he know where to go—has he a home?" asked Christopher.

"We don't have to worry about that! He knows these fields better than we do."

"Perhaps he'll find his family—I hope so," said Jenny.

"I imagine he took refuge in the house when they were cutting the hay. Well, here goes—and good luck to him!" cried Mr. Robin, stooping and opening the trap.

The mouse leapt out. At first it seemed bewildered. It stood perfectly still for a few moments, then, in a flash, it had gone.

"I'm sure he's happy now!" said Christopher.

"All creatures are happy when they get their freedom—it's natural," said Mr. Robin, putting the trap in his big coat-pocket. Jenny took his hand and they went back to the house.

II

Three days later the engine was mended and the geraniums were delivered.

"I think you should have paid him something," said Dr. Wren. "It seems to me he's having a struggle in that old hovel."

"It's really very nice, Daddy. I would like to live there," declared Jenny.

"He has an owl under a glass dome. It's dead. He says it is cruel to keep anything alive caged up," said Christopher. "He let a mouse go—we went to do it with him."

Their breakfast finished, the children ran out of the room. Mrs. Wren looked at her husband reading the morning paper.

"Richard, I suppose it's all right letting Jenny and Christopher go there?" she asked.

"Why not?" he said, turning the paper.

"Well, we really know nothing about him. It's very odd his turning up like this, settling in that awful barn, knowing nobody, having nobody with him. Mrs. Hodley at the Post Office says he's a very surly, unpleasant man. He never has a letter or posts one, and spends practically nothing in the shop."

"If he pays for what he gets, what's the complaint? Just because he won't gossip with Mrs. Hodley! I've not spoken to the fellow but I do notice how he's cleaned up that place—he's industrious and tidy and seems kind to the children. Still, my dear, if you're nervous, stop them going."

Dr. Wren folded his newspaper and stood up.

"One reads such dreadful things in the papers these days," said Mrs. Wren, collecting dishes.

"I must be off," said Dr. Wren. He crossed the room and kissed her. "I'll leave Robin Redbreast to you."

When her husband and the children had gone, in the quiet that settled on the house, Mrs. Wren thought about Robin Redbreast and the children. She did not wish to spoil their happiness, and the man had been very kind to them. Then an idea came to her. The children had told her about the cane chair he was repairing. He had a sign over the door "Upholsterer". There was a Bergère chair in the drawing-room, used now only by Jimmy to sleep in. The cane bottom had given way and the back also. She would call and ask him whether he could repair the chair. In that way she could have a good look at this stranger Jenny and Christopher had become so friendly with.

That morning, returning from some shopping, she turned up the path leading to the door of the old barn. There were some winter chrysanthemums flowering in the beds on each side of the path. The door had been painted a vivid green, the frame white. Overhead was the board with its lettering *Robin Red-thorne. Upholsterer. Repairs. Jobs Done.* Mrs. Wren hesitated a moment and then knocked on the door. A man between forty and fifty, heavily built, with iron-grey hair matted on his head,

P

and heavy black eyebrows, stood in the door. He wore a woollen black-and-white diced shirt open at the neck. He was clean-shaven and had a cleft chin. The mouth was heavy, the eyes very dark with thick lashes. He was a broad-shouldered, powerful man. He looked at her frankly and took the pipe out of his mouth. His hands were strong and rough.

"You are Mr. Redthorne? You know my children, Christopher and Jenny," she said.

"Yes, ma'am."

"I believe they call you 'Robin Redbreast'?" asked Mrs. Wren, with a smile.

"Yes, ma'am. Your little Miss Jenny called me that."

"I understand you do upholstering?"

"Yes, ma'am."

"I have a cane Bergère chair—the back and the bottom have gone. I wonder if you could repair it—it's rather fine canework."

"If you would let me look at it, ma'am, I could tell you."

"Oh yes, well, if you'll come I'll show it to you. I shall be in this afternoon—would around four o'clock suit you?"

"Very good, ma'am, at four."

There was a long pause. He seemed to be waiting for her to say something.

"You've made the place look very nice—it was such an eye-sore for so long," she said, breaking the silence.

"Thank you, ma'am," he answered gravely.

There was another silence.

"I hope you are comfortable here?" asked Mrs. Wren.

"Yes, ma'am, thank you."

"You are alone here?"

"Yes, ma'am."

"And you look after yourself—no family?"

"No, ma'am. No family."

"You are new here. What part do you come from?"

"Up country."

There was another silence. Curious to see what he had done inside she had hoped he would ask her in, but he made no move. He stood motionless in the doorway.

"Very well. I'll expect you at four," said Mrs. Wren. "Good-day."

"Good-day, ma'am."

He waited until she had gone down the path, then closed the door. She had learned very little, she thought. In fact, she had learned nothing she did not know, except that he came from up country, which could be anywhere. Obviously he did not want to enter into any conversation; a recluse, a very determined recluse who kept his mouth shut and his door shut. She was more than ever surprised by the way in which her children had got on visiting terms.

Back home Mrs. Wren told Nanny that the man up the lane, an upholsterer, was coming at four to look at the Bergère chair.

"I want you to stay in the room and tell me what you think of him," said Mrs. Wren.

"I can tell you now. I'm fed up with Mr. Robin Redbreast! He's much too familiar with the children. They've got him on the brain, what with his old barn, his owl, his mouse, and his red waistcoat. Robin Redbreast—what a name!"

"Jenny gave him it."

"A bit of nonsense—but to carry on with it!"

"I think it's rather sweet—Jenny Wren and Robin Redbreast," laughed Mrs. Wren.

"His name's Redthorne—if it's that!" exclaimed Nanny. "No one knows nothing about him. He's been here over four months and nobody in the village knows where he comes from or who he is. He never opens his mouth. He has nobody in. He gets no letters!"

"You've been talking to Mrs. Hodley."

"And others—they all have the same tale—he's mysterious!" said Nanny, emphatically.

"He was quite polite to me when I called."

"The more polite they are the more you'd better be on your guard. How do we know he hasn't deserted his wife and family—or the police aren't after him?" asked Nanny, drama in her voice.

"The police would have been here long ago if they wanted him. I think you're being ridiculous," said Mrs. Wren.

"Well, I'm just warning you, ma'am. He won't talk, they says, and folks as won't talk are hiding something!" declared Nanny, straightening her apron.

Redthorne came promptly at four.

"The upholsterer, ma'am," said Nanny, showing Redthorne in, her face a mask.

Mrs. Wren rose. She saw he had put on a tie. He examined the chair at the end of the drawing-room.

"Yes, I can do it, ma'am, but it'll take two or three weeks. I'll have to get some darker cane," he said.

"Oh, there's no hurry. The dog's been using it for over a year," said Mrs. Wren.

"I'll have to do a very good job to satisfy the superintendents," he said, standing up.

"The superintendents?"

"Mr. Christopher and Miss Jenny," he added, with a smile.

The smile, she noticed, changed his whole face. It lost all its gravity and heaviness, it was a warm, happy smile, like the sun coming out of a cloud. It showed his good level teeth. She was surprised to notice how tall he was. She had a vision of him as a powerful and possibly handsome young man.

He lifted up the chair easily and carried it to the door.

"Good-day, ma'am," he said, his face again grave.

Nanny closed the hall door on him and came back into the drawing-room.

"Well?" asked Mrs. Wren, smiling.

Nanny threw up both her hands. "My, he's a strange creature!" she said.

"In what way?"

"I just wish I could say—he gives you nothing to go on. But I'm certain he's got a past."

"At his age everybody's got a past," observed Mrs. Wren.

"Well, mebbe, ma'am. But I know mine's respectable!" she said, leaving the room.

Mrs. Wren smiled to herself. Nanny's trouble was a little jealousy over the children.

III

The chair was returned in two weeks. It was beautifully mended, as expected by Mrs. Wren, who had received progress reports from Christopher and Jenny.

Timothy returned from school. The Christmas festivities began. There were parties, and shopping to do. Robin Redbreast was neglected. They often went past but never saw him. It was winter and he did not work in his garden. The place seemed shut up, but a light in the evening told them he was there.

"I do feel you've neglected your friend. You were always in and out. You know what happens to Robins in winter?" said Dr. Wren.

> *The north wind doth blow*
> *And we shall have snow*
> *And what will poor Robin do then, poor thing?*
> *He will sit in his barn*
> *To keep himself warm*
> *And hide himself under his wing, poor thing!*

Dr. Wren quoted the words mournfully to the children.

"I hope he won't freeze," said Timothy.

"He's got a stove in the barn," said Mrs. Wren.

"And plenty of wood. I helped him to chop some," added Christopher.

"And he's a warm red waistcoat!" said Jenny.

"It's not a waistcoat, it's a cardigan!" insisted Christopher, "it's got woollen sleeves."

"Don't you think it would be nice if you gave Mr. Robin a Christmas present?" asked Mrs. Wren. "He must be very lonely."

The suggestion was loudly applauded. A noisy debate followed on what form the present should take. Agreement was reached at last. There was to be a plum pudding from Christopher, a pair of warm slippers from Jenny, and some tobacco from Timothy. They went into Chichester that same afternoon, bought the presents and posted them with cards.

On Christmas morning the Wrens had finished a late breakfast, with opened presents all around, when Nanny came in.

"The upholsterer's at the door," she said with an impassive face.

Mrs. Wren looked at her husband.

"Show him into the drawing-room," said Dr. Wren.

They all got up from the table and followed the doctor into the next room.

Robin Redbreast was standing by the far door, an old brown hat in his hand. He looked very neat in a white shirt with a blue tie, his greyish hair well brushed.

"Good morning, Redthorne," said Dr. Wren, going towards him and offering him his hand. "A merry Christmas to you!"

"Thank you, sir. The same to you!" replied the upholsterer, shaking his hand.

The family, in turn, expressed their wishes and shook hands.

"Have a drink?" asked Dr. Wren. "What'll you have?"

Redthorne hesitated for a few moments. "Well, sir, a Scotch and soda, thank you."

"Good. Do sit down."

"I've come to thank Master Timothy, Master Christopher and Miss Jenny for the presents and their cards. I'm boiling the pudding for tonight, and I shall wear the slippers and smoke the tobacco," he said, smiling at the donors in turn. "It's a long time since I've had a Christmas with presents." A smile hovered on his face and disappeared. He raised the glass Dr. Wren had given him. "Your good health, sir—and you, Mrs. Wren, and Mr. Timothy, Mr. Christopher and Miss Jenny!"

There was a silence. The children gathered their Christmas presents and displayed them to their guest. Dr. Wren studied the man's face, he had never seen him closely. In repose the face had a Dantesque sadness. This elderly man had not found life easy, he surmised.

"You've no family, I gather?" asked Dr. Wren.

"No, sir, no family."

"Ah, very sad! Never married, eh?"

Redthorne looked at the doctor and then said slowly "Yes—I was married."

"Your wife is dead?" asked Mrs. Wren, sympathetically.

"Yes, ma'am."

"I'm so sorry. It cannot be pleasant living so much alone."

"I'm used to it, ma'am," he replied. "You get used to everything."

"But you seem so fond of children," said Dr. Wren.

"I'm fond of your children," he said, quietly, looking at Timothy, Christopher and Jenny.

There was another pause in the conversation.

"What made you come to this part of the world—you couldn't find anything more remote!" observed the doctor, breaking the silence.

"Yes, sir. It's remote—I like it."

"I hope you're finding enough work. You made a very good job of the chair—and Christopher's engine," he added lightly.

"Thank you, sir."

Jenny went across to Redthorne and put a hand on his knee.

"Christopher says it's not a red waistcoat you wear—it's a cardigan," she said to him.

"That's right," he replied.

"Since they insist on calling you Mr. Robin Redbreast, I think they should have given you a bright red waistcoat," said Mrs. Wren.

A smile came to the grave face.

"Would you wear it, Mr. Robin?" asked Christopher.

"Why, yes. But you've been kind enough."

"Have you always been an upholsterer?" asked Dr. Wren. The moment he had asked the question he saw he had made an error. A look of caution came into the man's eyes. But he looked straight back at him.

"No, sir. Before that I was a soldier," he said slowly.

"A soldier! Did you ever fight?" asked Timothy, eagerly.

"Yes, I was in the Boer War."

"Did you ever kill anybody, Mr. Robin?" asked Christopher, excitedly.

"That's what soldiers are paid for, young man," replied Redthorne, a little grimly. He stood up, put down the glass and turned to Dr. Wren. "Thank you, sir, and thank you, ma'am. I'll be going. And a Happy New Year to you all!"

"Oh thank you, thank you!" said Dr. Wren, leading the way into the hall. The children followed to the door, chattering, and went down the drive with their visitor.

Dr. Wren came back into the drawing-room.

"Well?" asked Mrs. Wren. "I think he's rather a nice man. And do you know, I believe he's shy!"

"My dear girl—I'm sure of one thing, shy or not shy, there's quite a story there if we only knew it!" said the doctor.

CHAPTER 3

I

ALMOST IMPERCEPTIBLY but relentlessly Time brought changes to West Cleebury. The village grew larger and larger, the Wren children taller and taller. Timothy went to Marlborough. In turn, Christopher and Jenny left for their boarding schools. Unbelievably soon, Timothy was going to Cambridge, and Christopher to Rugby, a lanky boy and an excellent bowler in the School Eleven. Jenny, the vivacious, at fourteen, was a tomboy, untidy, restless, fearless, outspoken. "The doctor's brat," someone in the village called her. "That kid's a marvel!" said the yachtsmen in the bar at Bosham. "She can sail anything, and leave us flapping."

Robin Redbreast, as all West Cleebury now called him with a note of disapproval, was as great a mystery as on the first day when he moved into the old tumbledown barn. It was tumbledown no longer. The garden was such a sight that visitors going to the creek paused to look over the hedge. "He's got green fingers," said a native, sourly. "Disagreeable bastard!"

The barn had now a name. On the door the owner had painted in white Gothic letters *The Nest*. It was appropriate that Robin Redbreast should have a nest. He prospered also and had plenty of work. With electricity installed, he now had a power lathe. He was skilled in making a kind of Windsor chair. His renown as an upholsterer had grown for miles around. But he was a recluse, regarded with suspicion. There was a report that he was an atheist. Tom Grey, a very popular lad, whose boat capsized in a squall, had been drowned. Miss Brown, very devout, who had given Robin Redbreast a job repairing her divan, had commented on this tragedy. "The Lord giveth, and the Lord taketh away," she said, sententiously.

"Nonsense, miss!" he said, brusquely. "What's He want with a fine young lad like that! And if you give a thing you should give it and not snatch it back!"

Outraged, Miss Brown said she would never employ him again. Such blasphemy! Such impudence!

Then there was the affair of the hen-coop that gave him a reputation for violence. Robin Redbreast had made a kitchen garden behind the barn. He had also built a large hen-coop, with two shelves on which twenty hens roosted. He began to notice that the number of eggs grew less and less, reducing his income from their sale, the Wrens being his best customer. He began to watch from the back window. Early one morning he saw a man going into the hen-coop. It was an audacious robbery. The thief lived in one of the fishermen's cottages across the field. Robin Redbreast watched and saw him come a second time, a thin little man of about forty. With a quick movement, while the robber was busy, Robin Redbreast ran out, slammed the hen-coop door and snapped the padlock. The man was a prisoner among the clucking hens. Robin Redbreast waited a short way off, knowing what would happen. Presently there was a banging and kicking, and a great screeching of hens. Then the man inside, panicky, began to shout, "Let me out! Let me out!"

"I'll let you out, you bloody thief!" cried Robin Redbreast, unlocking the padlock and opening the door. As soon as the man emerged he seized and lifted him high up in the air. While the helpless man kicked and shouted, Robin Redbreast carried him calmly across the field. The man's strip of garden ran down to the hedge. At the bottom there was his small greenhouse. As if he had been a tennis ball the culprit was shot over the hedge and came down on the roof of his glasshouse. There was a resounding crash of splintering glass and breaking wood.

The story might never have got out, but a neighbour, digging in his garden, saw the amazing flight through the air. It was soon round the village, given point by the egg stealer's bandaged face and hand. There were rumours of prosecution but nothing happened. However, Robin Redbreast got a name for violence. "He's well-named," said a customer in *The Wheatsheaf*. "A robin'll kill any other bird that walks on his ground!"

Between Robin Redbreast and the Wrens the friendship

grew warmer with the passing years. Christopher and Jenny were not in and out of *The Nest* as much as they used to be, being away at school, and then taking holidays on the Continent, but when home they were always there. A puncture wanted mending, a spar for the boat was needed, something in the house wanted repairing. He also supplied eggs, potatoes and tomatoes. He put up some needed bookshelves in Jenny's bedroom, he made a sledge, he mended a car jack. When the ever increasing weekenders began to invade the field between *Longview* and the creek, making it an untidy car park and obscuring the view, it became necessary to gate the end of the lane. Robin Redbreast made the gate, five-barred, with a shot bolt and padlock. It was a beautiful job. "I believe the fellow could perform an appendectomy if he was put to it," said Dr. Wren.

Between Nanny and Robin Redbreast there was now a cold truce. Her last battle had been over the drawing-room carpet. It was very worn and the Wrens bought a new one. The matter of the disposal of the old one came up. *The Nest* had a rough brick floor with only a snippet rug in front of the combustion stove.

"Mummy, let's give it to Robin Redbreast—it would be wonderful for him," said Jenny.

"I hope you won't!" interspersed Nanny, growing more and more dictatorial with age. "It would be lost on that ruffian."

"He's not a ruffian!" protested seventeen-year-old Christopher. "Robin Redbreast's a very intelligent man. Do you know about the comet that wags its tail?"

He addressed the question to Nanny, who stared at him, bewildered.

"Well, *he* does! It's got a head one hundred and twenty-five thousand miles in diameter, and a tail one and a half million miles long. A solar wind wags its tail every four days over a fifteen degree arc. Robin Redbreast told me all about it last night. He's mad on stars," said Christopher.

"I'd say he's mad on everything. Did you ever hear such things—to stuff people's minds with!" cried Nanny indignantly.

"I think it would be nice to give him the rug. A brick floor's very cold," said Mrs. Wren.

Nanny glared and walked off into the kitchen.

"Mummy, she does get cheeky!" complained Jenny.

"Poor Nanny! She realizes she's losing you, and is a bit jealous of Robin Redbreast," commented Mrs. Wren.

II

It was now known that the Wrens were upholders of Robin Redbreast. There had been a crisis in the second year of the occupancy of the barn. Dr. Wren came to the rescue on being appealed to. Out of the blue someone from the County Surveyor's Office had descended upon Redthorne.

"This place is condemned for human occupation. It was condemned ten years ago. You've occupied and built on it without permission!" said the official.

"But it was a derelict barn!" protested Redthorne.

"You've turned it into a house and workshop without permission. There's no proper sanitation."

"Sanitation! I like that! There's twelve fishermen's cottages —with a gent in one of them who comes down from London for weekends—and they've all tub closets like mine!"

"I must report it. We take a grave view of your breaking the regulations," said the official, getting into his car.

Four days later there was a letter from the Surveyor's Office quoting various Bye-laws and Regulations. The list of offences was formidable. He was given a month in which to vacate the condemned premises. Redthorne, very perturbed, took the letter to Dr. Wren.

"I've been paying rates and water rate for nearly two years. And now they come down on me like this! And it's my own property!" cried Redthorne.

"Nothing's ever our own these days of a free democracy," commented Dr. Wren. "I suppose you should have gone to them in the first place, and the vendor should have told you."

"How was I to know it was condemned, sir? I bought it from that old Mrs. Brown—she's dead now—and somebody had lived in it once—there was a sink and a closet there."

"Leave the letter with me. I'll have a word with the Surveyor—he's a nice fellow."

"Thank you, sir, that's what I hoped you'd do. They take notice of someone influential." He seemed agitated and frightened. "I don't like anything to do with officials and the law," he said. "You never know what they're up to."

"Their bark's often worse than their bite. You've made a very nice place out of the barn, a credit to the village. Don't worry," said Dr. Wren.

All ended well. Robin Redbreast, after filling in forms, remained in the barn. He also remained a stranger in the community. He went about his work quietly, he kept his door shut, he never appeared in *The Wheatsheaf*, at the cricket field, at church, at social reunions. He went in and out of the shops, paying down for what he bought, exchanging no gossip. It was known that he never received a letter or had a visitor.

There had been also the Boy Scout incident. When he was thirteen Christopher had joined the local troop. One day he called at *The Nest* in his uniform.

"Ah, so you're a Boy Scout!" exclaimed Robin Redbreast, and made a scout salute. "I once knew Baden-Powell."

"You knew him!" cried Christopher, amazed.

"Yes. I was locked up with him in the siege of Mafeking—that was in the Boer War."

"Oh, how wonderful! He was a very great soldier, wasn't he? Do tell me all about Mafeking."

For half an hour Christopher sat spellbound. To think that Robin Redbreast had been with Baden-Powell!

"And that's how I came to be a bit of an astronomer. We had nothing to do but keep the Boers out, so I used to look at the stars through a field telescope. We had an officer who'd been at the Greenwich Royal Observatory, and he used to tell me about the stars. I've enjoyed looking at them ever since—they make you think very little of the human race!" he said.

A week later the local scoutmaster called at *The Nest*.

"Christopher Wren has told us you were in the siege of Mafeking with Baden-Powell. Naturally our boys are very excited about it. We wondered, Mr. Redthorne, whether you would come and give us a talk," said the scoutmaster, genially.

The owner of *The Nest* looked hard at the young man, from the half-open door.

"I don't give talks to anybody!" he said, and abruptly shut the door.

Only the Wrens got inside *The Nest*. Its owner worshipped Christopher and Jenny. On his mantelpiece, in a frame he had made, there was a photograph taken by Timothy one summer's day. It showed his brother and sister standing with Robin Redbreast in front of his home. Under the photograph, neatly printed, were the names—Sir Christopher Wren, Miss Jenny Wren, Mr. Robin Redbreast. That was the summer when the barn got its name.

One morning when Christopher and Jenny called, the owner made a surprising announcement.

"I've got a visitor—a sort of relation," he said.

"Oh, Mr. Robin, how exciting! You never have visitors, do you!" exclaimed Christopher.

"No, but this is a special sort of visitor."

"Can we meet him?" asked Jenny, excited.

"I think so, but you must tie up Jimmy. He doesn't like dogs." He picked up a spade. "Come along with me."

They fastened up Jimmy and followed their host, who walked down the garden to a flower-bed.

"Now watch," he said, "and don't talk. Perhaps he'll come and perhaps he won't."

He began to dig, turning over the soil. They watched for a few minutes in silence. All at once there was a quick movement before them and a bird alighted on a stone, alert, tail up.

"It's a robin redbreast!" cried Jenny, jumping in her excitement. The robin seemed quite unalarmed, watching the digging.

"He's come to live somewhere around here. He follows me about. I've had him around for a week," said Robin Redbreast. He picked out a worm and threw it to the bird. It was quickly gone.

"I think I did well to call this place *The Nest*, with one robin

redbreast inside and another outside," he said, with one of his
rare smiles.

III

How quickly the years raced on! In 1938 Timothy had left
Cambridge and gone to Guy's Hospital, studying to be a doctor.
Christopher was in his first year at Oxford. He was now six
feet tall, the giant of the family, already in his college boat.
Jenny was at a finishing school in France. Robin Redbreast
was disconsolate. No young voices sounded now in *The Nest* but
during the holidays all was well again. They had a dozen jobs
for him, things that wanted mending or altering.

This was the year of the crisis with old Nanny. Unwittingly
Robin Redbreast was the cause of it. The winter had been
severe. Great gales had driven the seagulls inland. They flew
low over *Longview* making their mournful cry. The winds beat
down the trees and howled over the house. Even the sturdy
old yew hedge shook under the winter's fury. It was quite dark
at four and the lane became waterlogged. Then three days of
snow blocked the roads so that Dr. Wren had great difficulty
in his daily journey to Chichester. At times they thought of giving
up the place, it was so bleak and exposed to the gales, but there
was the sailing in summer which the family loved so much.

Towards the end of February Mrs. Wren became conscious
of the fact that for quite a week there had been no sign of Robin
Redbreast. He was not visible in the garden or down the lane.
She noticed there was no smoke coming from his chimney.

"I wonder if he's gone away," said Mrs. Wren, at breakfast.

"Why don't you call and see?" asked the doctor.

"That wants some courage, he hates callers."

But about eleven o'clock Mrs. Wren put on her high rubber
boots and went down the lane to *The Nest*. No one answered
when she knocked. She tried the door and to her surprise it was
not fastened. She stepped inside. It was the first time that she
had been in *The Nest*. She noticed how high seemed the dark
beamed roof. The place was gloomy and cold. There was no
fire in the stove.

"Mr. Redthorne!" she called.

A voice answered. It came from the direction of the long narrow partition at one end of the room. She went forward, lifted the curtain over the doorway and peered in. There was a kitchen sink, and a table. At the other end, so dark that she could not see for a few moments, there was a bed. On it, under a red counterpane, lay Redthorne.

"Who is it?" he called, rearing himself up.

"It's me, Mrs. Wren. Are you ill?"

"I've had the 'flu'."

"Is no one looking after you?"

"I don't want anyone looking after me," he said, gruffly.

"But you should have a doctor and fire and food."

"There's no doctor coming in here, ma'am, thank you," he said. "I'm getting up tomorrow."

"You must have a fire, it's too cold here."

"There's no wood left."

Mrs. Wren went over to him and put a hand on his brow. It was hot and damp. "You've got a temperature. Now, Mr. Redthorne, there's going to be no nonsense. You'll die if you stay here."

"I'm going to no hospital, ma'am," he said, firmly.

"I'm not sending you to a hospital. Put on all the clothes you can. In half an hour I'm coming with the car and taking you home."

He looked at her in silence. She left him and went back to *Longview*. There she called Nanny and told her to prepare the guest room. "Redthorne's ill, with no one to look after him. We'll have him here for a few days."

"Here! You're not bringing that heathen here?" cried Nanny, amazed.

"Yes, he's no fire and no food and he's running a temperature. I'm collecting him with the car. Put on the electric stove and get the room warm. And tell Amy to make some hot soup."

Nanny did not move, her face dark with anger.

"I want to tell you, ma'am, if you bring that creature here you'll wait on him yourself. I won't!" she cried, her voice husky with defiance. "I mean every word of what I'm saying, Nursing that tramp, indeed!"

"Very well. I'll say no more now," said Mrs. Wren. She went into the kitchen and gave Amy, the daily help, an order to make some soup. Then she got out the car and drove to *The Nest*.

Robin Redbreast stayed at *Longview* six days. Then, well again, he went home. The problem of Nanny was solved. She had been with the Wrens too long. Jealous and domineering, she made it difficult to keep any daily help. She had been an excellent Nanny but her real function had come to an end. Fortunately she had a widowed sister with whom she could live. The Wrens gave her a small pension. The parting was amicable and sorrowful but it had become necessary. When she had gone Mrs. Wren realized how she had compromised to placate Nanny's whims and moods.

CHAPTER 4

I

On September 1st, 1939, the world known by the Wrens, Robin Redbreast and millions of others vanished. A madman marched into Poland and set it on fire. England, the once impregnable island, guarded by her Navy, now found herself vulnerable to aerial attack. There was a rush to buy cloth for blackout curtains. Chichester soon had not a yard of black material on its shelves. The air raid wardens prowled at night looking for offending chinks of light. There was a distribution of food coupons and petrol coupons. The towns and countryside were emptied of its youth. The retreat from Lille, the epic of the Dover Straits, the collapse of France, left England almost naked before the Nazi Goliath.

The Wren home was desolate, as almost every other. It gave up its young. For a time Timothy was held by his studies at Guy's. Christopher went immediately into the Royal Air Force. Jenny, home from France, nearly nineteen, volunteered for training as a nurse. She went to the hospital in Chichester where her father worked. She did not like the work and was restive. One day she knocked on the door of *The Nest*. Redthorne appeared.

"I've come to say Goodbye," she said.

"Goodbye? Where are you going, Miss Jenny?"

"I am a Wren, so I'm going to the Wrens—the Women's Royal Naval Service. Don't you think it's a bright idea?" she asked. "Nursing's too slow for me, and I spend all the time counting and carrying sheets."

"When do you go?"

"Tomorrow morning."

"Oh dear! Everybody's going. If I weren't over sixty and they'd have me, I'd go," he said. "I think the world's gone mad, so it's no use trying to stay sane," he added gloomily.

"Well, cheer up! And take care of yourself. You'll soon

see me back on leave. So, goodbye, dear Robin Redbreast."

She put out her hand, he held it, and then impulsively pulled her to him and kissed her cheek.

"Hope you don't mind, Miss Jenny," he said shyly. "Goodbye and God bless you!"

"Of course I don't mind, dear Robin Redbreast!"

She gave him a kiss, a smile, and then hurried down the path. He did not close the door until she had gone from sight.

II

Jenny came back several times, as did Christopher, handsome in his flying-officer's uniform. They were both kept in England, straining at the leash. Then the long bitter battle for survival began. The bombers came over, night after night. Mrs. Wren sitting in semi-darkness, heard the drone of engines overhead, and thought about Timothy in London, her husband in Chichester, about Christopher and Jenny.

One day Christopher divulged what he was doing. He was with a night-bombing squadron. Then Jenny had a last leave before going overseas. Excitedly she flew round, bidding everyone goodbye.

"Cheer up, Robin Redbreast, the war will soon be over and we'll all be home again!" she said as she left him, so gay in spirit that it sounded as if she believed it.

A month later the blow fell. Christopher did not return from one of the raids over Germany. For some time the Wrens clung to the hope that he might be a prisoner. No news came.

III

One dark March night Mrs. Wren was preparing for bed when she heard a soft knock on the door. She was alone in the house. The doctor was in London for several days. There was only a daily woman coming in for two hours each day. Had it been a louder knock she would have thought it was Redthorne. He often came now at night when there was raiding, and sat with her if the doctor was late. But this was not his knock. The softness of it was eerie and alarming. She waited. It came again.

She went towards the door. "Who is there?" she called.

"Please," said a voice.

She unbolted the door and opened it. It was dark but she could see it was a soldier.

"Please don't be afraid," he said, and as he spoke fell forward. She caught him, and her heart stood still. He was a youth with a face smeared with blood. He was in a German uniform. She hesitated and then pulled him inside. He had wings on his jacket, a lieutenant's star on the shoulder strap. He was hatless, the wet hair plastered on his head.

She closed the door with one hand, still supporting him with her free arm. His uniform was soaked. With difficulty she took him into the study and turned on a table-lamp. He slumped in a chair.

"What are you doing here?" asked Mrs. Wren.

"We caught fire and went out of control. Some of us jumped for it."

She noticed the blood had dried on his face. He had blond hair and seemed about twenty, a mere boy.

"Wait!" she said and ran into the kitchen. She found the brandy and poured some into a glass. Then she collected a basin, filling it with warm water, and also a sponge. She carried them to the study.

"Drink that," she said, giving the boy the brandy. She soaked the sponge and bathed his brow and face. There was no deep wound, he had bled from some cuts. He trembled as she sponged his face. A pool of water began to collect on the floor.

"You're wet to the skin. You must get out of your things. Rest here, I'll find a change for you."

"Thank you, *gnädige Frau*."

The German words gave her a shock. It came to her that they had been talking in English.

"You speak very good English," she said.

"My mother is English."

"Where do you live?"

"Innsbruck."

Innsbruck! Only two summers before the war they had spent a month motoring in Austria and had been in Innsbruck.

"Are you Austrian?" she asked.

"Yes. My father is Professor of Biology in the University."

She gave him a towel to dry his face and left him, going upstairs. She came back with some woollen pyjamas and a thick dressing-gown.

"You must strip and get into these," said Mrs. Wren. She began to help him out of his heavy boots and waterlogged uniform. He grimaced as she pulled off his shirt and vest. She looked at him.

"I have a pain here," he said, touching his side.

She could see nothing and felt nothing. "Perhaps a strain," she said.

Stripped, he had a boy's slim white body. He swayed as he dried himself on the towel. She helped him into the pyjama jacket and trousers, and then into the dressing-gown. With a pang she realized they had been Christopher's.

"Now lie down here," she said, leading him to the divan. She put two blankets over him and a cushion under his head. He was still shivering.

"You are very kind," he said, looking at her with his fair young face and blue eyes.

"You realize that you are an enemy and I shall have to give you up? You can rest here tonight but in the morning I must call the police. Will you promise me you will not escape? I should be in great trouble if you did," she said.

"I promise, *gnädige Frau*."

"You are suffering from shock. You must rest. I am going to give you some hot cocoa," she said.

In the kitchen, while she prepared the cocoa, she reflected on the strange working of Fate. Here she was, nursing a youth, an enemy, who had come on a murderous bombing raid. He was in this house which had been Christopher's home, resting on the very divan where he used to curl up reading, wearing his dressing-gown. Christopher had died, at about the same age, on a similar ghastly mission. The whole thing did not make sense, Christian nations praying to the same God to assist them in murdering each other. She wondered about that English mother in Germany. Well, *she* would not lose her boy.

When she came back into the study he lay with his eyes closed. She put down the cocoa and felt his brow. He was feverish. She went out of the study and found an aspirin. His eyes were open when she came in again.

"Now drink this. I'm going to give you an aspirin."

He drank the cocoa slowly. "Please where am I?" he asked.

"You are in a village in Sussex."

"Are you alone?"

"Yes. My husband is a radiologist in Chichester."

A slight smile came on his face. "It has a beautiful spire!"

"How do you know that?"

"Every Christmas my mother receives an English calendar— a picture one. One was of Chichester Cathedral," he said.

"How old are you?"

"Twenty-one and two months."

"What is your name?"

"Franz Ritter."

"Have you any brothers and sisters?"

"Yes, two brothers older, in the army, one sister fifteen."

She asked him what had happened. It was his second bombing raid. They had been caught in "flak", the navigator was killed, a fire started in the starboard engine and they went out of control. Two of them were able to jump. He had come down in water and had a desperate time cutting himself free of the parachute.

"I thought I was drowning. I struggled and then found my feet in mud. I clambered up a bank and lay there for some time. Then I walked and walked. It was very rough ground. I could see the sea on one side. Then I fainted. When I came round I walked again, and saw a roof, and found your door. I am sorry to frighten you."

"You have not frightened me," said Mrs. Wren.

"I think I am very lucky. You are so kind."

She put her hand on his brow, smoothing back his hair.

"You see, Franz, I had a son your age. He was killed in a bombing raid over Germany," she said.

"I am so sorry," he replied. He put out a hand and touched hers gently.

"Now you must not talk any more. You must try to sleep. Here is a handbell. If you want anything in the night, ring it. I am just over you—I'll leave the doors open."

She picked up his drenched clothing to take into the kitchen, and hang it over the boiler.

"Goodnight," she said at the switch before turning off the light.

"Goodnight. Thank you, *gnädige Frau.*"

It was some time before she could sleep. What a strange thing! Here she was alone in the house with, downstairs, an Austrian boy who had come down out of the darkness, thwarted in his deadly mission, nearly drowned, and now resting, wrapped up in Christopher's pyjamas and dressing-gown. Yet she felt no hatred. There must be thousands of mothers like her, and still this ghastly war went on.

She slept brokenly. Just after dawn she got up and went downstairs. She peered into the study. His pyjama jacket was open at the throat, his tumbled hair spread over the pillow. He looked fifteen. It might have been young Christopher.

When she came down again he was awake. His eyes were very bright.

"Good morning. How are you?" asked Mrs. Wren.

"Thank you—*gnädige Frau*—but I have much pain as I breathe."

He put a hand over his left lung. Mrs. Wren felt his brow. It was very hot.

"Lie there. I think you have fever. I will send for the doctor," she said.

"And the police?" he asked.

"Yes, I shall have to inform the police. Now I'm going to get you some breakfast."

The local doctor came very soon. He examined the boy.

"I think he has two broken ribs, and perhaps pleurisy in the left lung. We must get him to hospital. I'll call an ambulance. But what about the police? They must be informed, Mrs. Wren."

"I've already told them."

As she spoke there was the sound of a car in the drive. "Here they are!" she said.

IV

The war dragged on, getting grimmer and grimmer. England bombed, bloody but unbowed, hung on. Mrs. Wren's anxieties were now for Timothy, working day and night at Guy's Hospital, London, for Dr. Wren on his periodical visits to that inferno, and for Jenny, moved from one post to another overseas. In March, 1944, she came home for a short leave, very smart in her blue officer's uniform, grown into a most lovely young woman and even more vivacious and full of laughter. She visited Robin Redbreast and took tea with him in *The Nest*. He had proved a most faithful guardian of her mother and kept watch over *Longview* when the doctor was absent on various missions.

The house was now very silent and more isolated than ever with the petrol shortage. The Wrens had considered moving since they would never need so large a house again. Timothy had married. But the housing shortage and other difficulties made them postpone the change. There were no weekenders, no boats along the creek, much of the shore-line was out of bounds. The silence was broken only by planes of the naval air base across the estuary. West Cleebury was dead.

Jenny noticed how much Robin Redbreast had aged. His hair was quite white, he was slower on his feet. He was still a recluse, unpopular and much criticized because he refused to join any of the local bodies active in various war services. A new vicar came to the village and called on him. The visit was not a success. The vicar was not asked inside and went away shocked. "Very unpatriotic and not imbued with the Christian spirit," he reported. It transpired that when, alluding to the war, the vicar had piously observed that the Lord would uphold the hand of the righteous, Redthorne had retorted— "He seems pretty paralysed just now!"

Jenny found that he brooded over the death of Christopher.

His photograph in uniform stood on the mantelpiece beside an alarm clock that Christopher had given him one Christmas. When she took her farewell of him, he held both her hands in his for some time and seemed to be struggling for words. At last he spoke. "Now don't let anything happen to you, Miss Jenny. You're the only bright bird left in our nest."

She laughed, kissed his cheek and said, "Don't worry, the tide's turned. I'll be back next Spring with all the other birds!" She waved to him at the bottom of the path as he watched her go.

V

At last, at long last the war came to a victorious end. There was never such a summer. No bombs fell, no rescue squads dug for the dying and the dead in the brick rubble of houses. England, exhausted, took a deep breath. It seemed as if the birds, knowing the winter of death was over, sang louder. Then the boys and the girls began to come home. Here and there the general rejoicing mocked those who knew there would be no homecoming for some. Jenny wrote from Malta saying she would be staying in the Service but would have a long leave soon.

On a warm summer's afternoon, while the doctor and Mrs. Wren were having tea in the walled rose-garden at the height of its petalled glory, the boy from the Post Office arrived on his bicycle with a telegram. Dr. Wren opened it.

"Jenny's coming on leave?" cried Mrs. Wren.

The doctor looked at the telegram and made no answer. Then he sat down beside his wife on the oak bench, put an arm round her and read to her the message from the Admiralty.

VI

The details of Jenny's death came later. She had been killed on a road outside Naples, where she was stationed. She had gone with a young officer in a jeep on an excursion up into the hills. The jeep had struck a land-mine and they had both been killed.

When he learned the news, Robin Redbreast drew down his blind and sat in the gloom for a week. He stayed away from *Longview*, then, on a Saturday afternoon, knowing the doctor would be home, he called. They asked him in. He sat in the study, and when he spoke, stammeringly, the tears rolled down his cheeks. It was they who tried to comfort him, and he seemed so dazed and frail that the doctor walked home with him.

A month later Robin Redbreast was surprised to see the postman's van stop in front of *The Nest* and the man come up the path with a parcel. It was the first time in all those years that any parcel had been delivered there, except on that Christmas when the children had sent presents to him.

"Are you sure it's for me?" he asked, when the man requested him to sign for it.

"Yes," said the postman. "Your name's Redthorne isn't it?" There was hostility in the voice.

When the postman had gone he examined the cardboard box. It was covered with foreign stamps and bore a label "Opened by the Censor". He cut the string and removed the lid. The box was packed with cotton wool. At last he came to two small objects wrapped in tissue paper. He carefully removed the paper. In each package there was a small bird in coloured porcelain. Between the packages there was an envelope endorsed "For Robin Redbreast". He tore open the envelope and found a letter on a sheet of official paper. He read it slowly.

Naples, May 10th, 1945

Dear Robin Redbreast,

We came here from Malta a few days ago. (I am allowed to tell you now!) It's a beautiful city but has been well plastered by us. The shops seem almost pre-war. There is a long Galleria with shops, and our eyes just popped. Well, in a china shop what should I see, among all sorts of figures, but some birds! One was a Robin and one was a Wren! Fancy finding Us sitting safe and sound through all the bombing, not to speak of the Germans who skinned the place. I felt we must have them. So here they are. They say they are Capodimonte, quite a famous make. Aren't they beautiful?

I shall get a long leave soon and when I come I shall expect to find them sitting on the mantelpiece in an English Nest. I am flourishing. Ever my love to you, dear Robin Redbreast,

Jenny Wren

He read the letter twice. Then he picked up each bird. One was a robin, one was a wren. They were delicate and bright and beautifully coloured. He put them carefully on the mantelpiece, one on each side of Sir Christopher Wren's clock. Then, after looking at them for a time, he picked them up, wrapped them carefully in the tissue paper, and placed them back in the wool of the cardboard box. He put the letter in its envelope on top of the wool, then, fixing the lid, picked up the box and slowly walked out of the house, down the path to the lane. He was going to *Longview* to show them the letter and the birds. It was like a message from beyond the grave.

It was a bright summer morning but his heart was very heavy as he walked down the lane.

CHAPTER 5

"Who killed Cock Robin?
"I," said the Sparrow,
"With my bow and arrow
I killed Cock Robin,
For his breast is red
With the blood he shed,
And now we'll hang him
To be sure he's dead!"

I

DR. AND MRS. WREN were sitting in front of the fire. It was a cold December evening. Outside a gale of wind was buffeting the trees sending the heavy clouds scudding over the moon and rattling the windows and doors. They had finished dinner and the "daily" had departed into the wild night. Dr. Wren was reading *The Times*, Mrs. Wren sewing. She looked up, leaned over, and stirred the log fire in front of which Jimmy's successor was asleep.

"I'm very uneasy about Robin Redbreast," she said, after gazing at the fire.

"Why?" asked Dr. Wren, peering over his glasses.

"He's not at all well. He's gone very thin and a bad colour," said Mrs. Wren. "He complains of a pain in his chest, says it's from bronchitis, but I don't think it is—he hasn't a bronchial cough. I want him to see the doctor but he's very obstinate and refuses."

"He's obstinate, all right—and as obstreperous as ever. Lansdowne, at the hospital, was telling me about him this morning. It seems his wife had a chair that wanted upholstering and gave it to Redthorne. He brought it back and she didn't like the way he had done the arms. He looked surprised, said

252

nothing, and took the chair away with him. The next day when she came in from shopping she was astonished to find that the chair had come back, quite naked! In a parcel was the covering material. The maid said he dumped the chair in the hall, said, 'Tell your mistress she'd better get someone else to do it', and went off with his barrow!"

"And yet he was always so sweet with Christopher and Jenny," commented Mrs. Wren.

"They seemed to have tamed him. No one else has!" said the doctor.

"How old do you think he is?" asked Mrs. Wren.

"We can pretty well guess. He was in the Boer War. That ended in 1902. If he was twenty-four then, that makes him around seventy."

"He looks much older. I often wonder what happened to him before he came here. He has no relations, no friends. He won't talk about the past but he did tell me he'd been married and his wife died young. Nobody has ever been to visit him in all the years he's been here," said Mrs. Wren, putting away her sewing. "Richard, do you know what I'm going to do about Robin Redbreast?"

"What, my dear? Be careful with that old bird!"

"I'm going to ask Dr. Johnson to call and examine him."

"He won't let him in."

"I shall go with the doctor and I shall insist."

"Well, it's on your own head, my dear."

II

Mrs. Wren succeeded, but the result was alarming. Dr. Johnson insisted on Redthorne having an X-ray of his lungs. There was a battle to get him to Chichester, but Dr. Wren took him and made the X-ray.

"He'll have to go into hospital," said Dr. Wren that evening to his wife. "It's cancer of the left lung."

Four days before he was due to go in the milkman asked to see Mrs. Wren.

"Old Redthorne's not collected his milk for two days, mum.

I've hammered on the door and get no answer. I know you're sort of interested in him."

"Thank you, I'll go along."

They had to break in. The door was locked. By the stove, that was out, sat Redthorne, dead. He had been spared the surgeon's knife by heart-failure.

III

His papers were very few. There was the conveyance for *The Nest*. There was no birth certificate, no Will, but in a wooden box in which he kept his money and some keys there was an envelope. On it was printed—"In case of death, post the enclosed." The envelope was stamped and addressed to Mr. James Blackwood, living in Nottingham. The Wrens posted the letter, informing Mr. Blackwood of the circumstances in which they had found it. They arranged for the funeral.

It looked as if there would be no one at Robin Redbreast's funeral save the Wrens and the vicar he had offended, but on the day before there was a telegram from Mr. Blackwood, saying he would arrive that evening.

Having found a lodging, Blackwood called on the Wrens, who gave him the key of the cottage. In the letter, he said, there had been a short Will leaving him everything.

"You are a relation?" asked Dr. Wren.

"Yes, his nephew," replied Blackwood.

He was very surprised to learn about *The Nest*. He had no idea his uncle owned it. They had not heard from him for fifteen years.

The funeral took place on a cold winter's morning. Dr. Wren noticed that on the newly dug mound of soil a robin had perched, its breast bright red in the sunshine. Afterwards, they went back with Blackwood to *The Nest*. They had told him about his uncle and Christopher, Timothy and Jenny, and his devotion to them.

Blackwood was a middle-aged, thickset man, quiet in manner. He said he would sell the place and the contents. "I've a hardware business in Nottingham," he said. They told

him various things he wished to know, including the story of the porcelain birds on the mantelpiece. Blackwood picked them up and examined them.

"I would like you to have them as a memento," he said, and insisted on the Wrens' acceptance.

"We always felt he'd had a very tragic life," said Mrs. Wren.

Blackwood stood silent for a few moments, then he said gravely, "I appreciate your great kindness to him. You thought he had a tragic life. You don't know how tragic it was. I have not been honest with you. I am not his nephew. I am his son."

"But your name's Blackwood?" asked Dr. Wren, astonished.

"Yes, doctor. So was his. It is quite a story and not easy for me to tell you, but I'd like you to know what your kindness must have meant to him, and those children of yours. My father fought in the Boer War. When he came home he found his wife living with another man. He strangled her. He was tried and sentenced to be hanged. On the eve of the execution he was reprieved and given a life sentence. After fifteen years in prison he was released. I was a child of two at the time of the murder. He had never seen me, for I was born two months after he had volunteered and gone to South Africa. My grandmother took me and brought me up. I was sixteen when I learned what had happened—after my grandmother's death. I wrote to him in prison but he did not answer. Fifteen years ago I got a letter from him for the first time. He said he had taken another name. It was better for me that he should be completely forgotten. There was no address on the letter. It was signed simply 'Your Father'. So I never knew him."

He looked at the Wrens, holding the two birds. "I've told you this in confidence, in gratitude. No one will ever know the truth about him—please?"

Dr. Wren, moved, cleared his throat. "You may rest assured of that, Mr. Blackwood," he said, gravely, "No one."